LINN B. H

I live in a small village in Gloucestershire with the man I fell in love with, virtually at first sight. We were at a party and our eyes met across a crowded room! My days are spent with characters who become friends and Mr Tiggs, a feline with catitude. I always knew that one day I would write romantic novels, but I never dreamed they would have a psychic twist! I've experienced many 'unexplainable' things, but it took a long time for me to accept the reality of what that means. Love, life and beyond…but it's ALWAYS about the romance!

You can follow me on Twitter @LinnBHalton.

ANN R. HALTON

Falling

The Complete *Angels Among Us* Series

LINN B. HALTON

Harper*Impulse* an imprint of
HarperCollins*Publishers* Ltd
77–85 Fulham Palace Road
Hammersmith, London W6 8JB

www.harpercollins.co.uk

A Paperback Original 2014

First published in Great Britain in ebook format by Harper*Impulse* 2014

Copyright © Linn B. Halton 2014

Cover images © Shutterstock.com

Linn B. Halton asserts the moral right to
be identified as the author of this work

A catalogue record for this book
is available from the British Library

ISBN: 9780008114916

This novel is entirely a work of fiction.
The names, characters and incidents portrayed in it are
the work of the author's imagination. Any resemblance to
actual persons, living or dead, events or localities is
entirely coincidental.

Automatically produced by Atomik ePublisher from Easypress

FALLING

Ceri

CHAPTER ONE

Being Me

I have no idea exactly when I began seeing angels, but I can't seem to remember a time when I couldn't. It feels like it's always been a part of my life. It's as natural as breathing and, yes, there are times when I wish that wasn't the case. I seriously doubt anyone would choose to get drawn into something they don't really understand. Why would they?

I've read books of course, and talked to many people who think they know how it all works. When I say 'it' I mean life after death, or whatever exists beyond the here and now. What I have found is a very diverse range of opinions, often given out as if they are factual and with a belief so strong that it seems unshakeable. And that's true whether the person is an adamant sceptic, or a believer. The point is—how can anyone know for sure until it's their turn to follow the light into what lies beyond?

As I stir my cappuccino, the heart-shaped chocolate powder begins to melt into a swathe of pale brown trails. It strikes me that it's a good analogy—when something you see is not what it seems. One moment it appears to be something of substance and in a flash it's gone. It's the same with my angels: almost real but not quite. I may be able to see them at times, but it's always merely seconds before they disappear.

"Penny for your thoughts." Seb's voice breaks my reverie.

I look up at him. "I'm thinking about angels."

"Oh, I'd hoped it was something more…normal." He closes the conversation before it has even begun and I realise that my wonderful brother is simply out of his depth. It leaves me feeling guilty again. Why do I keep doing this to myself and to other people? Haven't I been slapped in the face often enough to know that people loathe the word 'angels'. It reminds them of death: of loved ones lost and another world that only exists in fantasy.

Except, of course, I know better.

"So," I try to keep my voice upbeat and pretend I'm not disappointed he's failed the test again, "why an autumn wedding?"

"Anna has found her perfect dress for the day and it's red. Her heart is set on it and she wants the guys to wear Scottish kilts," he smirks.

"But there's no Scottish blood in our family," I point out.

"No, true, although Anna says her great-grandfather's second cousin was a Laird." We burst out laughing at exactly the same moment and say in unison, "Mega!" Typical of the link we have as non-identical twins who are in tune on many levels, but so opposite in other ways. I've never felt that we struggle to assert our own identities though and I like to think Seb feels the same way.

"And based on that tenuous link you'll be seeking someone to pipe you in I suppose?" I can't resist teasing him, but I'm simply masking my concern. I hate myself for the sense of 'knowing' that I can't shake off. She's going to hurt him, more than anyone has ever done in the past and he's going to crumble.

"How did you guess?" he quips, and I chuckle at the thought of someone piping my brother up the aisle. He has hairy legs, knobbly knees, and thinks that all Scotland has to offer is some amazing mountains to climb.

"Well, at least tell me you're going to Scotland for your

honeymoon," I reply. He shakes his head.

"No, California. Anna wants to do the Hollywood walk of fame."

I study my brother's face. He's a happy man and that's all that matters in the grand scheme of things, but the 'Anna wants' phrase seems to keep cropping up in every conversation we have these days. Is that how she's going to fail him? Or is it Seb who is going to fail, adoring her too much and making the relationship one-sided: all give and no take because he's sadly, madly in love?

"Fabulous," is all I can find to say, holding back the words in my head that have to remain unspoken. In my heart I know she's a lovely lady, but my brother is an interesting guy and he's never fitted the mould. A bit like me, I suppose. Only Seb doesn't see angels and sometimes I wonder if he thinks I'm possessed, or mad. I know he won't entertain any ideas about an afterlife, but aside from that he's used to thinking outside the box. My greatest concern is that Anna is rather…well, predictable, trendy. Okay, what I want to say is shallow, but that makes me feel mean and it's not true. Then I realise that it's the vibe again, 'the knowing.' When exactly the hurt will come I have no idea, but my instincts tell me it's there, somewhere in the future. Without understanding what or how, all I can do is sit back and wait, then help to pick up the pieces.

"I'm fine," Seb says, placing his hand reassuringly on my arm. "I love Anna and if that's what makes her happy then I'm happy too."

His voice breaks my train of thought. "The angels," Seb shifts in his chair uncomfortably, "you do know it's all a figment of your imagination? You're an extremely sensitive person and you over-think things, Ceri. I inherited the practical skills and you inherited the creative ones. Don't get sucked in, and remember that you can't believe everything you read." He fingers a book lying on the table next to him. The title is *Never Alone*, and it's about a woman who sees spirits.

I nod, inwardly shaking my head, and a part of me is sad that he has no idea. It's not that I know all the answers: if I did I would be banging his head against a wall until he listened to me. I can't prove anything and I wonder if that's the whole point. To believe you have to rise above needing to be shown. You simply need to see with your eyes wide open. What I do know is that so far I have a journal that shows I've altered the course of events for over one hundred and thirty-one people.

What that means, I have no idea.

CHAPTER TWO

A Normal Day

The moment I awaken I can feel it; a sense of uneasy anticipation. I try to shut it out and concentrate on the mundane—getting dressed, brushing my hair, cleaning my teeth. It doesn't pass, but the intensity lessens. I step outside and have to force myself not to turn around. Instead I stand for a moment, take a deep breath, and begin walking.

The sky is that shade of cornflower blue that heralds the start of a really sunny day. There's hardly a cloud in the sky and the bird-song sounds like an orchestra tuning up before act one. Suddenly I feel much better; lighter and more optimistic. I'm worrying about nothing and I give myself a mental shake as I walk. I have to stop living my life expecting something untoward to happen; maybe it's true what they say about karma and sending out positive thoughts to the universe. If I'm constantly sending out worry and apprehension, then maybe I'm a magnet for all the stray negativity floating around in the ether.

I break into a smile and the old lady walking past me glances my way, frowning. It makes me chuckle and I can feel the tension leaving my neck and shoulders. It's a good day to be alive and instead of pondering about what might or might not happen, I concentrate on my surroundings. It takes about twenty minutes to walk to the office and that's the beauty of living in a green and leafy part of Gloucestershire. I walk past the park, and the colourful blossoms breaking out on the trees are such a wonderful contrast to the constant stream of traffic in the morning rush hour.

"Ceri," my name appears to float on the gentle morning breeze. I turn my head and see it's my boss, Mason Portingale, striding to catch up with me.

"Morning Mason." I'm pleased that my voice sounds cheerful and confident.

"Ready for our big brainstorming session?" He peers at me and his tone sounds accusatory, as if I might have forgotten about it. Mason can't help being somewhat curt, it's the way he is and I have to be careful when I'm around him. Portingale & Hughes Advertising is a prestigious firm and the moment I step over the threshold I become a slightly different Ceri: reliable, solid, an 'ideas' person and bubbly. A sort of robot really, divorcing myself from the things that make me different to most other people around me.

"Can't wait," I smile encouragingly. Actually, I've thought of nothing else this last week.

"I'm counting on some good ideas coming from your corner. It's a big contract and we need to impress the Court-Abel executives with some original concepts."

I think to myself that a 'Good morning Ceri' would have been nice. I was hoping for a relaxing walk into work, not a business meeting. "Of course. I've come up with something a little different from their usual style. However, it really does depend on what exactly they are looking for, Mason. The brief is pretty wide-ranging." I glance at him, not wanting to connect for any longer than I have to. My instincts have always told me to be wary of him, but I have no idea why.

"Okay, run it past me." His clipped tone infers that I don't have a choice and the breakfast meeting has begun.

"Well, I know they are keen to keep pushing the organic content of their fruit juices, but their entire brand is synonymous with that already. Perhaps we should centre their next campaign on lifestyle." I pause to see if I'm way off with this idea or if he's interested, but he gives nothing away.

"And?" We stop to cross the road and I step forward, level with him; Mason seems rather annoyed I can't match his walking pace and I keep lagging a step or two behind. He glances down at me and it's hard to ignore the feeling that I simply don't like this man.

"Essentially it would focus on the happiness that comes as a result of pursuing a healthy lifestyle. The headline would be 'The sun always shines on happy people' and I'm thinking *Good Day Sunshine* by The Beatles. Short, simple."

"Mmm." That's it. No reaction. Oh well, we'll have to wait and see what the rest of the team come up with.

We enter the building, sign in at the desk, and he walks off in the direction of his office without saying another word. With Mason you can never tell if you've upset him or he's simply being himself. Rude often springs to mind.

A little shiver travels down my back. Wow—where did that come from? As I enter the lift I assume it's because the sunshine outside was really warm and the lobby is quite chilly. All that expensive marble I suppose.

***

It's a day of pre-meetings and planning before the client comes in at three o'clock for the brainstorming session. My colleague, Alex Delano, and I spend most of the morning pulling together some visuals to go with the 'Good Day Sunshine' idea. We search through the modelling agency portfolios for a suitable candidate whose appearance screams health, vitality and happiness.

"Love the look of this one," Alex beams.

"Keep your mind on the work, not what's in the bikini," I

remind him and we both start laughing.

"Such a hard job, but someone has to do it!" He rolls his eyes and raises his coffee cup. "Another one?"

"Yep, although I suppose we should be drinking some healthy juice that's full of vitamins and antioxidants."

"Okay," he interrupts. "I admit, you've come up with a great idea and the others aren't going to be in with a chance because we've heard all that before. You have a creative mind, Ceri, there's no doubt about that."

Alex sashays away, it's his trademark. I've often wondered if he's gay. He never talks about girlfriends, although I know he has lots of friends of both sexes. He's great to be around and he gives out good vibes. We work well as a team and there are times when I think that I wouldn't still be here, working for Mason, if it wasn't for Alex. His positivity and good karma make up for the discomfort I feel whenever I'm in Mason's company. Fortunately that's kept to the minimum, as Mason Portingale rarely mixes with the entry-level management team.

"Your coffee madam," Alex reaches across to place the mug in front of me.

"Thanks. So you think this is a winner then?" I look at the sheets we've quickly pulled together for the ten minute presentation.

"Sure do. I think centring the campaign on that iconic Beatles song is inspired. The words are such an amazing fit. It's a winner Ceri." His arm brushes against mine as he sits down and I move slightly, not wanting him to feel uncomfortable. We exchange smiles and I can't help shrieking. "I think we're on it with this one!" I fight to keep the volume down and we do the sitting down, stamping-our-feet happy dance.

"High-five boss, you've done it again!"

***

I leave at five-thirty and take a leisurely stroll back to my apartment.

I'm on a high because the client was full of enthusiasm for the ideas Alex and I brought to the meeting this afternoon.

Then it happens.

The dappled sunshine reflecting on the pavement from the tall trees overhead suddenly pales. Everything becomes slightly opaque: it's like looking at an old photo where the colour is toned down. My footsteps seem to slow for no apparent reason at all. The air is heavier, it's harder to fill my lungs and the sounds around me seem to have been turned down a notch or two. Then I see a young man. He fits into the picture in front of me as if he's a part of it, yet I know he isn't real. We make eye contact for the briefest second and he turns to face the road, then he's gone. That's if he was ever really there.

Panic begins to overtake my thoughts. A dog runs past me and my eyes follow it, wondering why it isn't on a lead. There's no owner in sight, then the young man appears again from nowhere, standing about five or six feet away from me. He's merely a shadow, like the pale, dappled pools of sunlight on the pavement. The breeze moves the leaves around high overhead and the light flickers, making him blend in even more. Our eyes meet, lock, and in that instant I can see him more clearly. He wants me to stop the dog.

I break into a run, wondering how I can waylay the animal before he reaches the busy main road. I'm carrying my mobile phone and my bag is slung over my shoulder, but aside from that I have nothing with which to catch him. My pace quickens and I can see that he has slowed, a little spooked by the sound of the heavy traffic ahead.

My mind plays out the scene of the dog running into the road and a car having to swerve suddenly to avoid hitting him. The car slews into a cyclist who begins to overtake him, angry he's slowed down with no apparent reason and unable, himself, to see the dog. The sound of the collision is sickening.

I throw down my phone and bag then quickly slip my arms out of my linen jacket. The gap closes and I toss the jacket into the air, hoping it will land on my target. It covers the poor little guy's head and shoulders, draping down over his front legs, and brings him to a halt almost instantly. All I can see is a rear end that quickly disappears as he turns half-circle, trying to shake off the jacket. He's only a few feet away from the road. I look to the left and I see the cyclist, slipping into the space in front of the car that is less than ten feet away from me. He's totally unaware of course and continues weaving in and out of the traffic. I close my eyes and utter a silent prayer. The sound of yelping brings me back into the moment. The dog has managed to free himself.

"Charlie!"

The dog runs past me in the direction of his anxious owner.

"Thank you." His voice reflects the fact that he realises Charlie was lucky. "I'm so very grateful to you. I can't believe he ran off like that, I don't know how you managed to act so quickly. Really, that was amazing. I can't even begin to think what might have happened if he'd caused an accident." He bends to hug Charlie, who is jumping around like a live wire. "You're lucky Charlie, lucky to be here and lucky you didn't get someone else hurt." Both dog and owner look up at me. I take a few deep breaths, trying to regain my composure, and focus on dusting off my jacket.

"No problem," I say casually. "Right place, right time."

The guy continues to stare at me when I say a casual goodbye and walk away. I can feel his eyes on me and a sense of disbelief at what has just occurred. The scene that keeps playing over and over again in my head is like a trailer from a horror movie. I wince as the sound of metal crunching against bone assaults my ears. Tears fill my eyes. I can't stop them brimming over and running down my cheeks. Another episode for my log: number one hundred and thirty-two.

CHAPTER THREE

Who's Naughty & Who's Nice?

"Ceri?" It's Anna and she sounds excited. "Seb told you about the wedding plans? You don't think it's over the top, do you? I mean the Scottish link is rather more like wishful thinking." She stops to laugh and I can't help smiling. "It's only that I think the kilts and things are so romantic." It almost sounds like she's pleading with me to agree. Why does it matter what I think anyway? That familiar sensation of sadness unsettles my stomach and I wonder what causes it. Anna is open and honest, so why do I believe she's going to hurt Seb in a way that he'll never get over? I close my eyes and wish it would all go away.

"It's your wedding and the bride calls the shots. Seb seems happy enough to go along with it, and he's the one who has to wear the kilt. He's trying hard to make you happy Anna, whatever you want he'll do everything he can to make it happen." I realise my words sound a little like a dig and I wasn't conscious of wanting to upset her. There are a few seconds of silence.

"I don't want to turn into bridezilla."

I've embarrassed her and I feel ashamed of myself. "You won't. It doesn't matter what anyone else thinks, it's what makes you and

Seb happy that counts. It's your special day."

"Oh, thank you so much Ceri. I worry that Seb is simply agreeing with everything I put forward and I thought he might have confided in you if he was unhappy about any of the arrangements. I also have a favour to ask." She hesitates, and I hold my breath. "Would you be my chief bridesmaid?"

It isn't what I was expecting at all, and while it's really not my thing I know I have to agree and sound enthusiastic. "That would be lovely, thank you!" In my head I imagine a red bridesmaid's dress with a huge bow on the back that makes me look like a badly dressed doll.

"Oh, Seb is going to be so happy! Two of my best friends are also going to be bridesmaids and you are all about the same height, so it's going to be great for the photos." She should have stopped at 'happy'. Photos are only photos, is it necessary to consider the size and shape of the people who will appear in them? I shake my head, glad Anna can't see that the truth is we have very different priorities. I put down the phone, relieved that at least I haven't upset the bride.

Maybe I'm old before my time because of the things I've experienced. Who knows? Maybe I inherited the sensible gene and that's why Seb has always been so adventurous in his life—he's the risk-taker. He's finally ready to settle down after realising that having someone to share your life with becomes more important to you the older you become.

When I think back over the guys that have come and gone in my life, I can see that there never was anyone with whom I felt a serious connection. I've always been in love with the idea of being in love, but everyone I've dated has only ever seen the shell of me. None could see inside and every single one of them backed off whenever anything odd happened. I can't blame them, the fault lies with me, but if I had one wish it would be to find a guy who could understand. I long to be with someone and not have to hide or explain anything. To find a person who can simply accept me

19

without judgment and with whom I could relax, confident that he would support me no matter what happened on my life's path.

My mobile kicks into life and I see from the caller ID it's Alex.

"Hey girl," he drawls and his tone suggests this is going to be gossip. "Thought you'd like to know that rumours are rife and it's all about you. The word is out that you are next in line for Scott's job when he leaves. First management team, here she comes!"

I was right. He's worse than the women who hang around in the coffee room speculating about who's dating who.

"Well, don't you think someone would have mentioned something to me about it first?" I laugh.

"Maybe today clinched it. After all, there are probably two other candidates I can think of who would be in the running." He pauses and I can imagine him, wine glass in hand; a blush wine, of course.

"Gee, so glad to have you on my team!"

"What? I'm being honest. You know he'd prefer a male candidate, but I think you hit it out the ballpark today lady!"

"Well, keep me informed. I'd hate to be late on my first day in a new job," I chuckle. "Stop gossiping and leave me alone. I need to lie down. I've just agreed to be Anna's chief bridesmaid. She's wearing red and the guys are wearing kilts."

"Eeek," his voice is almost a squeak. "Poor you! Red is so draining, you'll have to do a fake tan or you'll look like a ghost with your pale skin and hair."

"Oh yes, and arrive looking like I've just stepped off of the beach in the middle of winter? I think not. Maybe I can convince her red for the bridesmaids isn't such a great idea. See you tomorrow."

"Night, night, don't let the bed bugs bite," he says soberly. There's a hint of something in his voice, I'm not sure what exactly. Maybe he's worried that if I am promoted he'll have a new boss to contend with.

Chatting with Alex has at least left me feeling a little happier and upbeat. He always cheers me up and I'm so grateful that aside from being work colleagues, we're really good friends.

Setting everything up for the 'Good Day Sunshine' campaign leaves Alex and I very little time to think about who is going to replace Scott. Mason keeps close tabs on progress and for the first time seems to be a little more approachable. July quickly passes and August is upon us before the workload eases up. I'm pleasantly surprised when I have my first fitting for 'the dress' to find that Anna has picked a pale silver-grey. She's right - when we all stand in a line at the dressmakers we do look very photogenic. Her excitement is infectious and it's clear she loves every little inch of Seb, even his annoying habit of being so unpredictable at times when you really need him to be there. He missed his own fitting, would you believe, and he was the only one of the guys who couldn't make it. Was Anna fazed or disappointed? No. She laughed and said they would sort him out on his return, because he had a mountain to climb: literally, of course. He sloped off on a week-long climb with a group he'd met while he was in Australia back-packing. I marvelled at the way Anna took it in her stride and understood he'd given up a lot this last year for her. With each meeting I'm warming to her more and more, but whenever we hug it's there: that cold little feeling in the pit of my stomach that won't go away. Even when, on the day of the dress fitting, she whispered in my ear "I'm so glad to be gaining a sister. I always longed to have one!"

Alex noticed something was up. I've never shared any of my thoughts or strange feelings with him. We've worked together for two years, and while we are the greatest of friends in a work situation, we've only ever skimmed the surface about things that happen outside of the office. There's always been this invisible line between us. He knows about the wedding and that I worry about Seb, that I don't get on well with my parents. But that's it. In return I know that he has a sister he can't stand and that he's mad about formula one racing—fanatical even. But he's never mentioned a partner and I never talk about my dates, which is why I am caught completely off guard when he starts talking about dating agencies.

"I'm thinking about joining one of these dating websites," he casually drops into the conversation one morning, as we pore over the magazine mock-ups for the new campaign.

"Really?" I sit back to study his face, in search of some explanation for this sudden need to impart information.

"Well, don't look at me like that! Millions join every day. Why not me? Oh God, there's something wrong with me isn't there. Do I have bad breath?" He looks mortified.

"No," I wish I'd simply let the statement wash over me. "It's a bit of a surprise, that's all. I thought you might have someone."

He looks at me as if to say 'why would you think that?' "Well I don't. A guy can't go on forever existing on meals for one," he says flippantly and throws his pencil across the table.

"Sorry, I wasn't trying to imply anything at all. I only said—"

"Nah, it's me. I suppose I feel life is passing me by and I'm not top of the list when it comes to being boyfriend material. Doesn't mean to say I'm not interested though."

There's an awkward few minutes. I fuss around with the prints in front of us, but I can feel Alex's eyes on me.

"Well," I add, rather diplomatically, "I'm always around if you need a shoulder and all that…"

"Thanks, I'll remember that. Coffee?"

"Fab, thought you'd never ask!"

"You could make it yourself, you know," he quips.

"But you make it so much better," I laugh and the moment has passed.

My curiosity has the better of me though: will he be seeking out the gals or the guys?

***

I look at my journal, glancing over the pages of the last year. It seems that the episodes are becoming more frequent. Twice this week I've received what I feel to be a warning sign, on both occasions it was a female but they were very different. One was an older lady, and one a girl of probably no more than twelve years of age. There and then gone: mere seconds that prompted a déjà vu moment and then an action I felt I was meant to take. Often it's a simple thing that might not have had any real impact, but how am I to know that? On Tuesday it was an incident at work when one of the guys was over-reaching to lift down an armful of files. I was walking by and this old lady appeared, I literally walked through her before I realised what was happening. The image seemed to dissolve around me. It was enough to make me turn around though and catch what was about to happen. I immediately ran to help Isaac, who had started to topple backwards. What I saw in that split-second was contact between his head and the desk, then lots of blood. I held out my arms to steady the files which began to slip, he instinctively grabbed onto me and with that one simple adjustment, regained his balance.

"Wow, close call! Thanks."

"No problem."

The other incident was another 'something in nothing' moment. This time I thought the young person was real at first, the form had colour rather than shadow. It was more about the feeling that passed through me that told me it was another premonition. I was queuing in the supermarket and in front of me there was a small child sitting in a supermarket trolley. Her mother was busy loading the contents onto the conveyor belt. The little girl was probably around two or three years of age. She was within arm's reach of a tempting display of sweets and kept saying "chocolate treat Mama." I glanced at the mother and she looked stressed, ignoring the little girl's pleas. The child reached over and grabbed one of the colourful bags. When I caught sight of the young person in the next aisle I heard "No!" then the shape disappeared. It was so forceful I was sure it had been spoken out loud, but looking around it was clear no one else had heard it. Then a feeling of choking coursed through my body, as if I had swallowed something and it was stuck in my throat.

Fearful that the little girl would scream if I tried to take them away from her, I grabbed a small packet of chocolate buttons from the display. I offered them to her. The mother didn't even notice her drop the round boiled sweets when she took the packet from my hand. The mother looked up a split-second later.

"Oh, you'll get me into trouble one day missy." She laughed. "We'll actually walk out of a shop with something we haven't paid for!"

I smiled good-naturedly along with everyone else, but I could still feel the choking sensation in the back of my throat. The apparition in the next aisle was gone, but the feeling was strong enough for me to record it in my journal. When I think back now, I can vividly recall that beautiful little girl's smile.

As I close the journal and pop it back, sandwiched in the bookcase between Pride & Prejudice and my latest book on life after death theories, the doorbell rings. I wonder who on earth it can be at this time of day. Seb rang earlier, so I know it's not him.

Before I open the door, I place both my hands on it. The bell rings for the third time, whoever it is seems impatient but still I take a brief moment. A tingling sensation courses through me: this isn't going to be bad news or trouble. Swinging open the door, it's Sheena and my mouth falls open. I rush up to her and we hug. It seems the cosmos is sending me the help I need!

"Why didn't you say you were coming? But I'm so glad you're here," I almost find myself shouting with happiness and then I burst into tears.

"Hey, what's this all about? What have I missed? I've only been gone three weeks and you've been very quiet, girl. I was worried. Guess I was right! Put the kettle on and let's have a chat."

As the door closes I feel a sense of relief. Sheena and Kelly were my two best friends. They were both people who knew me: the side of me I keep hidden from everyone else. Kelly was diagnosed with leukaemia four years ago and died six months later. It was a blow from which I haven't yet recovered.

I'm still hugging Sheena tightly and marvelling at the fact that she has arrived precisely when I need her. "What's up?" Sheena asks. She heads straight into the kitchen. I sit myself down on a stool while she makes tea as if it's her own home. I love that: it's like I have a sister who comes back every now and again to rescue me from myself.

"Nothing and everything," I admit, miserably.

"Is it to do with Seb and Anna?"

"No, it's the usual. Things I can't explain. Déjà vu and the signs... people I don't know who tell me nothing, but appear for some reason. Why? Why me?"

Sheena stops and looks at me.

"We've had this conversation before Ceri. It's not helping you to keep thinking about the 'why.' You have to accept it - what's the point in fighting something when you have no idea what it really is? Heck, you should know from your research, you can't explain the unexplainable. So what's really bothering you?"

"Alex has joined a dating agency." I'm surprised at my own words. Where did that come from?

"You said you thought he was into guys, so what's the problem? Worried it will affect his work once he's on the emotional roller-coaster of the dating scene?"

"I'm not sure. I felt rather, well, disappointed. He has his first date this weekend but he hasn't given me any details."

"Oh." She hands me my tea and settles onto the stool opposite. "Hidden feelings? This isn't like you to begrudge someone a little fun. You're his boss, not his girlfriend."

I raise my eyebrows and shrug my shoulders. "I know. I'm being silly. With you travelling so much these days he's the closest thing I have to a best friend and his friendship means a lot to me. Except

25

he doesn't know of course…about…"

"Ah, you feel comfortable with him. Were you hoping he'd notice something unusual about you and ask the question? I mean, I know Seb gives you a hard time and you do need someone you can confide in when I'm not around."

We're both thinking of Kelly.

"Why do you think Kelly has never come through to give me a message?" It's a question I've had in the back of my mind for a long time. I suppose a little part of me is waiting, silently hoping for a sign, and now I've voiced it.

"You're the expert, what do I know? I have no idea how it all works, but I will tell you one thing, Ceri. I don't think it's going to go away and you have to find a way of reconciling yourself to that fact. I know I sound like a broken record, I've said this so many times before. How's the journal count?"

"One hundred and thirty-seven." I can't look her in the eye, I feel I'm declaring all the sins I've committed since the last time we were together.

"Worst one?"

"A young woman with a horrible cough, the message was clear. I saw this shape of an elderly man wrapping his arms around her. He looked up at me and the sadness was unforgettable. It was in a coffee shop and I was in the queue, she was sitting alone at a table for two. I asked if she minded sharing; luckily there were no other places available. We began chatting. I ended up telling her a story about my aunt having pneumonia and said she should have her cough checked out, it sounded similar." We exchange glances and Sheena can see it hasn't been easy. My story wasn't true, of course.

"Poor you, how did she take it?"

"She left shortly afterwards, but she did say 'thanks' when she stood up to go. She looked back at me, trying to judge whether I was a total nut or not. I gave her a smile and for a second we connected. I hope it was enough to convince her."

"But you will never know," Sheena said, sadly.

26

"No, I'll never know."

"So, back to Alex, you don't fancy him or anything daft like that, do you? I thought I'd ask the question in case it was an issue. " She reaches for the biscuit jar and takes out a handful.

"I don't know. He's like a BFF, I regard him as a girlfriend." I look at her and she's amused.

"Maybe he's a guy who is simply in touch with his feminine side. Perhaps he fancies you and wants to gain your trust first. He's trying to put you at ease by not making a play for you and you've misread the signals," she jokes. "Have you been on any dates lately?"

"One. It was a big mistake. Huge, actually. A friend of Seb's, and it was really awkward. We had absolutely nothing in common and he asked me out for a second time. Seb was a little upset when I said no. He was a nice guy, well most of them are if they're genuine, but no way was there any spark between us."

"Well, I'm still dating Mr Boss," she smirks, "and working under him gets better by the day." She gives me a sideways glance and raises her eyebrows.

"Sheena! Too much information - spare me the details. Anyway, I'm not sure sleeping with the boss is such a great idea."

"Ah, you're only jealous. I bet the truth is you fancy the pants off Mason Portingale and would jump into bed with him at the first sign of an offer."

"Now you're going to make me physically sick," I moan. "He's a creep. No, it's more than that. He's not a very nice person I think. I can only tolerate him in small doses. I sense a bad vibe."

"You know Ceri, you've spent your life rebelling against this and thinking of it as a burden. Have you ever stopped to think it might actually have been a blessing?"

She munches on her last biscuit. I can see she's serious.

"It's easy for you to say that. Try experiencing it first-hand."

"Okay, I accept that you've been through a lot and goodness knows I've seen how it's affected you over the years. But what if this sense of awareness prevents you from having dead-end relationships that would only end up breaking your heart? What if there's a special someone for you and, because you can read what's inside of people, all you have to do is wait for that first meeting. And bang, you've found your soul mate."

For Sheena, that's deep. She pretty much floats through life avoiding being tied down and never taking anything very seriously. That's why she's my right arm: without her I wouldn't function so well because she sees things in a different light. It helps to keep me sane.

"Well, if the cosmos is listening, I've had enough. I want a significant other. I don't want to be on my own anymore. But he has to be special. He mustn't judge or take flight when I have my…moments."

Sheena grimaces. "And of course, he has to be good-looking, talented, kind, and sexy too. Tall order! This isn't about Seb and Anna, is it?" She softens the last part, perhaps fearful she's hit upon the truth.

"No, not really. Well, maybe, I suppose, but I hadn't thought about it that way. I mean Seb and I might be twins, but we're very opposite in so many ways. He's never shown any signs of wanting to settle down until now, whereas I guess it's always been at the back of my mind."

"Ah, maybe the bond between you and Seb is causing your radar to malfunction. You're experiencing the strong pull of settling down that he's going through and assuming it's something coming from within you."

"Sheena, you never cease to amaze me. You really think I might be tapping into the emotional rollercoaster Seb's on at the moment? Well, perhaps there's something to that. What I could never understand though, is why I've always had these psychic episodes and Seb has never felt anything. In fact, he's so anti the idea of life after death that he gets angry if I dare try to talk about it."

"I'm only glad of one thing. That you aren't identical." Sheena laughs and sips her tea at the same time. It goes down the wrong way and turns into a fit of coughing, which makes me laugh.

"Hey, not funny. I could have choked to death."

"No, I'd know. I only wish I'd acted on the vibes I had about Kelly," I add, sadly.

"I know, honey."

"The hard bit was accepting that I wasn't meant to save her."

We hug like sisters would when mourning the loss of another sibling. One day she'll get in touch, that's one thing I know for sure.

CHAPTER FOUR

Bittersweet

Sheena stayed for a week and then headed home for a few days, before setting off for Germany. When I asked her how long she was going to be away, she said it depended on how protracted the contract negotiations became, but she thought it would be a while. Something told me she would miss the wedding, but I felt better for her visit. She always helps me to put things into perspective and I think she was right about Seb. He still has the occasional trip with some of his adrenalin junkie friends, but he's adjusting well to settling down and doing normal things with his chosen life partner. In fairness, I have to say that Anna is good for him because she's actually very relaxed and doesn't pressurise him. Maybe I'm simply being over-protective of my little brother. I am the eldest by a few minutes. We're on countdown to the big event: twenty-one days and Seb will have a wife.

At least I'm very happy with the bride's choice for our dresses and the silver grey, knee-length gown is sophisticated and flattering. It actually makes me feel a little taller, which isn't a bad thing, and slender. To be honest it's something I might easily have chosen myself and I hate that I still have this feeling when I'm around

Anna. She has done nothing at all to deserve it and each time I see her it's clear she is totally in love with my brother. What more could a sister want for her twin? But something is telling me not to let out a sigh of relief until after we get past those infamous words 'the groom may kiss the bride'. Will someone dash into the church at the last minute when the vicar asks whether 'any man can show just cause, why they may not lawfully be joined together?' A horrible thought pops into my head—what if Seb is the one who is going to upset things? I push it to the back of my mind. I'm not being given any vibe about this from the other side, so Sheena is right and it's probably a twin thing. It's kind of nice to think we're sharing his emotional journey and it makes me feel closer to him.

Work has calmed down and after over a dozen meetings and presentations, everything is ticking over nicely for the new campaign. However, Alex looks up the moment I step through the door.

"His Lordship wants you," he mutters, soberly.

I try to gauge whether I have any feelings associated with this sudden summons to the boss's office. "Do you think we have a problem?"

"Nothing I've heard about. His secretary literally stopped me on the way in, said it was important."

"I'd better get in there then." My reluctance is obvious and Alex gives me a wan smile.

"Good luck." He widens the smile into an encouraging grin.

"Before I go, how was the date last night?" I ask casually and then could cheerfully kick myself. It's none of my business and I don't know why I asked. All of his dates seem to end up the same way and this one didn't sound any more special than the rest.

"Good I suppose," Alex muses. "Maybe I'm just too fussy." The grin turns into a grimace. "Greasy hair. I really do think you should go," he says, waving his hand towards the door. I wonder if all men notice such small details. Or maybe only men like Alex, and I can't help but feel his heart isn't in trying to establish a relationship. I still don't know if it's guys he's dating or girls. Does he do that on purpose? Perhaps he thinks I won't approve.

"Oh, right. I'll be back." I exit after dumping my bag on the desk and head for Mason's office.

I knock twice and wait. No answer. His secretary isn't at her desk so I loiter, trying to look casual. She reappears a few minutes later with a stack of papers in her hand.

"Ceri, go straight in, Mason's waiting for you." I feel I'm being dismissed when she immediately turns her attention elsewhere. I knock once more before turning the handle.

"Ceri, come in and take a seat. I'll be one moment." He's on the phone and his voice is weird. Light, cheerful. Whoever he's talking to isn't one of his staff, but a peer. I try not to eavesdrop and my eyes wander around the office, trying to feign a casual and relaxed pose.

"Okay, will do. See you Saturday." I turn my head back after I hear the phone click into the holder. "Sorry about that. Thanks for coming straight in. I've been thinking about Scott's replacement: it's about time I made a decision. Are you ready for the step up? It would mean some out of hours work, accompanying me on client dinners from time to time. I try to keep it to a minimum."

I'm glued to my seat. First of all he's being nice, pleasant even. I've never heard that tone before. Secondly, I thought it was a rumour that he would consider me a serious candidate. This is the first time he's mentioned it.

"I'm flattered to be in the running but I've only recently started my third year with the company and I thought…"

"…that a minimum of three years with the company is required to step up to senior management level. Yes, this will upset a few people but I'm asking you to seriously consider the offer." He finished my sentence and then finishes with me. The conversation is closed and he has already picked up a file and begun reading the first page. I leave the room quietly; once the door is shut I lean against it to steady myself. When I look up his secretary is watching me. I stand up straight and walk steadily towards the exit.

"Alex, he's offered me the job!" I blurt out the moment I shut the door behind me. It's not exactly a shriek. I'm trying to keep my voice down, but Alex immediately jumps up. He throws his arms around me and draws me into him. It's the first time we've ever touched and it isn't until we pull away that we both realise this is an awkward first moment.

"Well done you!" Alex says. I move away from him, my body tingling slightly. Well, that was certainly a manly hug.

"I'm not sure what to do," I admit.

"Are you mad?"

I roll my eyes. "I enjoy what I do, but I'm not married to my work Alex. Mason said there would be functions I'd have to attend. Do I want work to spill over into my personal life?" Of course that's insane, I don't have a personal life at the moment—who am I kidding?

"Oh, he did, did he? Well Ceri, it's not for me to warn you off but I think he's a bit of a sleaze. Watch yourself there, I'd hate to think of him taking advantage of you because you're gorgeous and he thinks he can snap his fingers." Alex's words come out in a rush and he looks a little red in the face. Awkward moment number two and it isn't even nine o'clock yet. And Alex said I was gorgeous—he's definitely gay.

"Don't worry, I won't fall into any trap. I'm going to wander past Scott's office and see if I can have a word." I turn and walk away, thinking it's a terrible waste. Alex is such a lovely guy.

I have to hang around for a few minutes before I see Scott heading into his office and I follow him inside.

"Scott, hi, do you have a moment?" He turns around on hearing my voice and gives me a radiant smile.

"Sure, Ceri, anything for you." He's Mr Charisma and the sort of guy you'd expect Mason to pick for his senior management team, which makes it even more puzzling that he's offering the position to me.

"You're leaving us next week and Mason's looking for your replacement. We've had a chat this morning and I wondered if you could tell me a little bit about what the job entails?"

"Sure," he says, pulling out a chair for me. "Take a seat. It's an account manager role really. You are the first-line contact between the agency and the customer. I like to arrange a quarterly meeting for each account and more often than not they are happy to come here. Sometimes I take them out for lunch, or arrange for a buffet in the conference room. It's basically a review of where we are with the progress of each advertising campaign and flagging up their future requirements. It's all about making them feel their account matters and addressing any little issues that crop up. Of course, Mason requires a formal report after each meeting but there's a standard layout for that so it's not onerous. I think you'd do well, you project the right image." He dusts some invisible hairs off the arm of his jacket and then decides to slip it off. It's an expensive suit and the shirt looks handmade. Scott is a second Mason in the making.

"Right, I see. Thanks, useful." My words are stilted because he's not someone I feel comfortable chatting with. There's a question I have to ask, but I need it to sound casual. "I was wondering if there is any of out of hours work involved, attending functions and things."

He looks at me in surprise.

"Well, no actually. I did once attend an award ceremony on behalf of the agency because Mason was on holiday, but he usually covers all those things himself. He likes to be seen as the figurehead and he's a born networker."

"Great, that's reassuring. Do you mind if we keep this between ourselves? I have to think about this a bit before I decide."

"No problem, but if I were you I'd grab the opportunity. It's not simply the next step on the ladder: it's a substantial step up for you." I don't think he meant that in a disparaging way, at least

I hope not. I offer my hand and we shake.

"You will be missed," is all I can think of saying. In truth I seriously doubt he has much to do with the majority of the staff. In the two years I've been here I think I've spoken to him about three times.

He nods, accepting the compliment I'd intended it to be.

When I walk back into my office, Alex is on the phone. It's a long conversation and the moment he puts the receiver down it rings again. He looks stressed and I think the model we picked for the ad campaign isn't available, so he's trying to re-arrange the date of the shoot. I take myself off to the kitchen and make two cups of coffee. My mind is processing what Scott said and I think it's probably best I keep that information to myself for the time being. I can't figure out Mason's reason for offering me the promotion, other than he's looking for arm candy when he's out networking. The more I think about it, the angrier I become.

When I put Alex's coffee on the desk next to him, his head is in his hands. "Problems?"

"Well, the model is going on a big shoot to Greece for three weeks and our second choice isn't available because she's pregnant and has bouts of morning sickness. Apparently they won't let us book her because she's failed to turn up for several sessions. Her status is currently suspended. We have to start the search all over again." A part of me is thinking damn, I thought it was all wrapped up. Another part of me is grateful Alex hasn't grilled me about what Scott said.

It's going to be a long day.

CHAPTER FIVE

Crystals

I'd forgotten that I was supposed to meet Seb at lunchtime and had to dash out when I realised that I was already five minutes late. Luckily it was only a short distance away.

"So sorry, Seb." He can tell from the puffing and panting that I've run virtually the whole way. I flop into the chair opposite him.

"Busy morning?"

"Crazy, I've been offered a promotion. Oh thanks," the waitress sets down a tray with coffee and sandwiches. "Thanks, Seb, I'm starving."

"Congrats, sis. Was it out of the blue?"

"Yes, and I'm probably going to turn it down. But don't ask why, it's gut feeling stuff again." He looks at me and shrugs, then narrows his eyes.

"What's wrong?" Sometimes I feel he can read me like a book.

"Nothing I can put my finger on, so let's drop it. How did the fitting go? I bet you look splendid in your kilt." I can't help smirking at the thought. The attraction of a kilt has always been a mystery to me.

"Pretty damned good, even if I say so myself." I can tell the idea has grown on him and he seems genuinely relaxed. "And thanks, for being patient with Anna. I know you aren't into all this girly detail stuff. It's not you. But that's what I love about her, she needs protecting. She needs me."

I guess I never thought about it before. Seb needs to be needed. That's an unexpected surprise.

"She's lovely, I wouldn't want you to think I don't approve or anything…" I can't continue because I'm unable to explain my feelings. I know that Seb can sense my reservations and is probably misinterpreting them.

Then it happens again. This time it's a cold feeling, a sharp chill in the air. I look across at the young woman on the table next to us. She's seated opposite an older woman and I begin to pick up pieces of their conversation. I thought at first it was the waitress at their table, but whoever it was I saw out of the corner of my eye is no longer there. The presence was enough to attract my attention. It's difficult trying to chat to Seb about the wedding while trying to keep tabs on the conversation taking place three feet away.

Twice, when I turn away to look at Seb then turn back, I catch a glimpse of someone standing to the side of their table. Whoever it is wants me to listen. What do they expect me to do? It seems the younger lady is confiding in her friend that her boyfriend is becoming difficult to live with. Suddenly I'm filled with that familiar déjà vu feeling and what I see is the young lady being pushed down the stairs. She's lying on the floor but I have no idea if she's still breathing. Her skin looks grey and her eyes are open and unmoving. I shudder and have to look down so she can't see the look of shock on my face. Seb is talking to me and I ask him to repeat what he said.

"You haven't heard a word of it, have you? What's on your mind, you ought to share it you know. I can sense something's up. Is it work?"

I can't explain. Seb wouldn't understand so I tell him briefly about Mason and the promotion. At the same time I pick up my bag and begin searching through. I know I have a couple of crystals in a pouch and I try to discreetly open it and place one on the table underneath my napkin. Seb seems caught up in what I'm saying and doesn't appear to notice.

"I can't believe the man's making a move on you. Doesn't he know you'll scream sexual harassment?"

"It's not that bad, honestly. I'm probably making it sound worse than it is. Just because Scott didn't attend evening functions doesn't mean to say it won't come up in the future. I'm going to say no because I don't feel ready, therefore it won't be an issue." I feel awful about making conversation simply to distract Seb.

In between I'm keeping an eye on the person at the next table. She asks the waitress where the ladies cloakroom is and I turn to Seb, give him a weak smile, and grab the crystal from under the napkin. I follow a few feet behind her.

In the cloakroom we are alone. She disappears into a cubicle and I feel awkward hanging about. I walk over to a basin, pop the crystal into my pocket, and begin to slowly wash my hands. I look up and smile when she appears next to me. She turns on the tap and water splashes everywhere, spraying over the arm of my jacket.

"Oh, I'm so sorry! The water jet is rather fierce, I wasn't expecting such force." She grabs some paper towels and begins to mop up the trail of water. They say everything happens for a reason...

"No problem. It's better than a trickle, there's hardly anything flowing out of this tap." We exchange smiles. "Look, I don't usually approach people I don't know, but I'm psychic." She immediately stops what she's doing and looks at me, narrowing her eyes. She reacts to the word psychic: clearly it means something to her.

"Really?" she mumbles and I can see a hint of fear in her eyes. She's a believer.

"Someone in your life is upsetting you and it's going to get worse if you don't walk away. I'm talking physical abuse here. Not just a black eye, but broken bones. You need to put yourself first—you'll make the right decision although it won't be easy. Have courage." I thrust my hand into my pocket and pull out the crystal. "I can't tell you anymore, but the feeling is strong. Here, take this. Keep it with you. It will give you the strength to do what you have to do."

I hold out the clear rock on my open palm and she immediately picks it up. "Thanks," she mumbles and I almost run to the door. I've done what I can. Now it's up to her.

Seb looks up and can see I'm preparing to leave.

"A woman on a mission," he comments. Then he looks at me intently and I grab my things, hurrying to leave before the woman returns to her table. He follows me out a minute or two later, having taken care of the bill.

"What have you done now? Is it something to do with that woman you were watching? Ceri, you have to stop acting weird. One of these days it's going to go very badly wrong." Despite the severity of his words he throws his arms around me. "Poor girl," he whispers into my hair.

Walking back to the office I know that I probably deserve the telling-off Seb gave me. What was I thinking, approaching a total stranger that way? What if she leaves her partner and I'm wrong? What if the vibe I felt was for her friend and not her? I close my eyes for a few seconds and groan inwardly. When I open them it's like someone has lifted a veil and my thoughts are clear. The message was for her and if she chooses the right path then she will be safe. My instincts tell me she will.

Alex is much happier when I arrive back in the office.

"No rest for the wicked," I muse. It's obvious he's worked through lunch as the remains of a sandwich and a packet of crisps lay next to his keyboard. "I've made a decision. I'm not taking the promotion. I'll tell Mason first thing tomorrow. Are you out tonight?"

He looks up at me, surprised. "Why?"

"I wondered if you wanted to come around to my place for dinner."

"How odd, most people celebrate taking a promotion, rather than turning one down." His smile says yes and a warm feeling creeps over me.

"Eight o'clock then. Right, what's next on the hit list?"

CHAPTER SIX

Baring All

As Alex walks over the threshold, he hands me a beautifully hand-tied bunch of flowers. "Oh, thank you. It really wasn't necessary, my cooking isn't that good."

He grins at me and it's a good feeling.

"I can't believe I haven't invited you over before now."

"Well, I'd wondered if you were ever going to get around to it!" he retorts. A part of me hopes he's really thinking 'it's about time.'

Our pre-dinner chat is easy and we start on the wine. I'd never noticed before, but he has the sexiest wrists I've ever seen. He's wearing an expensive pair of jeans and a white linen shirt, with the sleeves folded back to his elbow. He has this thin, brown leather tie and the knot is pulled loosely so that it hangs mid-chest level. The top two buttons of his shirt are open and his neck looks inviting. I feel shocked at my reaction and I suppose it's because I'm used to seeing him in work clothes. His hair is immaculate, his skin is smooth. He's a man who pays attention to detail. I notice that he never comments on what I wear and he doesn't appear to have noticed the effort I've put in tonight on his behalf. But I haven't asked him here to try to seduce him because I see him as a challenge, although a part of me thinks it's such a waste of a perfect guy. I want him to know about the other side of me because our friendship is so strong. I trust him.

He picks at a bowl of olives as he sits on the stool by the butcher's block, watching me prepare the pasta.

"So why did you ask me around? Is this a date?" he muses, and it throws me. There's a hint of seriousness in his voice and I begin to feel a little embarrassed.

"We never talk much about out of work stuff. I thought it would be nice to share a few things." My voice is even but the nerves are starting to kick in. Maybe this isn't such a good idea after all. Why spoil the relationship we have?

"I thought you preferred it that way." He shrugs off my comment a little too easily. "Unless, of course, you are finally going to share your dark secret with me." I spin around in surprise at his words and our eyes meet.

"Only if you share yours," I retort. He looks down at his drink and then pops another olive into his mouth.

"That depends," his voice is quiet, gentle. I've touched a raw nerve.

"On what?"

"On how honest you are going to be with me."

Suddenly I feel that this is intense and it's not what I was expecting. I thought we'd laugh and chat like girlfriends. Maybe he'd admit to being gay and we could talk meaningfully about the dates he's been on since joining the website. Then I could bare my soul about my angels. For some inexplicable reason I think Alex would understand.

As if it was planned, we reach for our wine glasses in unison and raise them towards each other, toasting the evening ahead.

***

After a bottle and a half of California's finest rosé Grenache we're both feeling rather mellow. Dinner, thankfully, is much lighter and we talk about our respective childhoods. It feels cathartic, like starting our friendship anew, leaving behind everything connected to work. I wonder how wise it is to take the lid off the box—to look inside each other's lives with honesty. But in truth I'm in need of a friend I can trust who is around all the time and I feel Alex has a similar need. It strikes me he's a chameleon: different things to different people. Is that a coincidence? When he's with Mason he's more macho, even his tone becomes more assertive and clipped. With me he's... well, genderless is the way I would describe it. It's only recently I've allowed myself to think of him in any way other than a colleague, simply because I didn't think he was into women. I wonder if it's been the same for him because I've kept my distance.

"Sorry?" I don't catch his words; they are obscured by the clatter of plates while I clear the table. I turn around to look at him. I watch as he drops down onto the sofa and stretches out. I think it's the most relaxed I've ever seen him.

"I'm a lightweight when it comes to drinking and I've had far too much already," he repeats.

"Me too! My head is kind of spinning at the moment. Chill and I'll make two strong cups of coffee." I half expect him to vault up from the sofa and offer to make it, but he's content to relax and that makes me feel I'm being a good host. I smile to myself as I take the empty glasses out to the kitchen.

When I return Alex looks very comfortable, his body melting into the cushions. He takes a first sip of his coffee and grimaces. "You're right."

I slip off my shoes and sit down, swinging my legs up to chill out. "What's that?"

"I do make the best coffee." Positioned at either end of the long sofa and facing each other, we can't exactly avoid eye contact

"I'm being honest. I thought that was what you wanted." I'm beginning to see why he said he was a lightweight, alcohol lowers his inhibitions.

"Who's going to go first?" Our eyes meet and he breaks into that stupid grin of his. "Oh, so that would be me then," I remark, trying to sound a little put out. He laughs and settles back, wriggling to sink even further into the cushions.

"Where to start… Seb and I are very different. I know we're non-identical twins and that's obvious, but I have a gene that he hasn't inherited, or so it would seem." I look up at him, but he's looking away and appears to be listening intently. I take that as a sign he wants me to say my piece.

"He's the adrenalin junkie, the party animal and anything technical sparks his interest. I inherited the artistic gene and a sort of sensitivity." I pause, we exchange a quick glance and then he looks away. The silence is a little awkward if I'm honest and I wonder how far I should go. "I have these episodes of déjà vu, a sensation of premonition and I keep a journal of every single incident I experience."

It's my turn to stretch out and study him. A few minutes pass in total silence and this time it feels heavy. You could hear a pin drop.

"I see. How long has this been going on?" His voice suddenly sounds very sober and I'm relieved that he's taking me seriously.

"A long time, maybe forever. An incident is one of my earliest childhood memories."

"I'm no expert, but I have a mild interest in all things psychic. I've read a few books, I see you've read some of the same ones." He points to my groaning bookshelves. "Apparently we are all born with the ability to sense things but we bow to the general opinion that it's rather flaky."

I laugh at his choice of word.

"Flaky? I'd say unacceptable, unbelievable maybe—either way, things really do happen around me and it's not something over which I appear to have any control. And that's the problem. I simply want to be normal."

Now it's Alex's turn to laugh at me.

"Define normal." I sense a slightly bitter edge to his voice. Maybe Alex too feels different, only the reasons aren't the same.

"Well, not seeing angels would be a good start," my voice wavers slightly. I monitor the reaction on his face.

"Ah, I see. I didn't realise it was that heavy. I knew there was something and, if I'm honest, I suspected you had a perceptive nature."

I look at him rather shocked. "Does it show? I try very hard not to bring my personal life to work. Has anyone guessed?"

"Don't worry," he waves a hand. "It's more something I feel when I'm around you. That you're holding things back and that's why I've never pushed for more information. Besides, I love working with you." He moves his foot to touch mine. "You're the sister I never had," he jokes.

I kick his foot away, pretending to be insulted. Was I hoping for more?

"Okay, your turn. What's your little secret?"

Alex puts his empty coffee cup on the floor and sits forward, stretching.

"You think I'm not interested in women," he turns his head sideways to look at me before he continues. "I'm not. I'm only interested in one woman, and for some really obscure reason it's not meant to be."

He looks sad, no—more than that—beaten. It had never occurred to me that he was nursing a broken heart.

"I'm so sorry Alex. I never thought for one moment... and the dating agency?"

"It's lonely at times," he says, and it's almost a whisper. "Rather sad for a guy in his early thirties. However, I've realised that I'm not prepared to settle. Maybe some men are born to be single. I enjoy my own company, so I can't exactly complain."

I move around to sit up next to him. If you put a few books in between us we'd be a great set of bookends. Still, like statues, each consumed by our own thoughts. Sharing a sense of sadness for the things that life has given us to deal with.

"I think I need another drink," I say, heading off to grab what's left of the wine and two fresh glasses. It's going to be a long night.

***

I squint as the light filters in through the window. Closing one eye to avoid the brightness, I wonder why I forgot to close the curtains last night. My arm flops over the side of the bed and I stretch, my head beginning to clear a little. Oh, I'm never going to drink too much ever again. I haven't said that since I was a teen and had a drunken session with a couple of girlfriends. Hearing a groan, I roll over and my stomach does a queasy flip. Alex is next to me, thankfully facing the other way. I wriggle slightly and realise I'm naked.

I guess it was a night best forgotten, but a part of me would love to recall all of the details. It might just have been the best night of my life so far...

CHAPTER SEVEN

Letting Go

Mason doesn't take my rejection well. When I break the news to him, I realise there was definitely a little more to it than simply turning down a promotion and accompanying him to a few events. Fortunately I have a week's leave planned leading up to the wedding. I only have to get through today, however that also makes it rather awkward with regard to Alex and last night. By the time he stirred this morning, I was long gone I should imagine. I'd jumped into my jogging bottoms and t-shirt virtually the moment I opened my eyes and headed out for my usual run. When I arrived back home, the bed was stripped and the linen had been placed in the washing basket. He'd tidied up the kitchen and left a note.

A great evening, lovely company. Appreciated, Alex

I know that we have to address the elephant in the room before I leave work this afternoon. I couldn't bear spending the next week wondering if it meant anything. At lunchtime I suggest we go out to grab a takeaway sandwich, figuring it's easier to talk when we don't have to look each other in the face.

"I know this is awkward, but we can't ignore last night as if it never happened."

"Agreed, but I've been struggling as I'm not sure what to say. It wasn't exactly what I was expecting. There's one thing I do need to ask you," he turns to me, but I keep my eyes firmly fixed on the pavement ahead.

"Was it comfort sex? Please don't say it was pity sex."

Guess he's answered the awkward question whirling around in my head then, although I'm beginning to get a few flashbacks of some rather passionate clinches. It's all a bit vague still, but one thing I know for sure—it wouldn't have been either of those. I'm really attracted to Alex and even without total recollection, the bits I can remember were hot. We both let our barriers down and it's a long time since a man has held me like that. My heart performs a totally unexpected backflip and my cheeks begin to burn.

***

As often happens, the nervousness and sense of expectancy hovering around me while I dress for the wedding feels weighted by something else. It's a nagging worry that is growing by the minute, to the extent that I slink away unobserved and head up to the second floor of the hotel. The guys' rooms are two-one-five through to two-two-nine, but I have no idea which one is Seb's. I hang around until I see a face walking towards me that I recognise.

"Hi Ceri, are you looking for Seb?"

"Yes, I wasn't sure which room was his," I'm trying my best to remain calm and Tom doesn't seem to notice anything strange. He points to two-one-seven and I tap gently on the door, then more urgently when there's no reply.

"Seb, it's me," I whisper and he opens the door.

"Ceri, great timing. Can you sort this bow tie for me?" My brother looks amazing. A kilt suits him and I can't stop myself throwing my arms around him. Tears start leaking out of my eyes all over the place and he lifts me away from him to look at me.

"Hey, I'm getting married not getting the death sentence." He frowns when I don't laugh.

"Seb, I have a bad feeling. It's strong," I almost whimper.

Seb rolls his eyes and groans. "Not now, Ceri, not today. Please, for my sake and Anna's. I'll listen to whatever you have to say tomorrow at the family lunch, but for today let's keep it light."

I've upset him and the fact that he's offering to listen to me at all, shows how much I'm unsettling him. There's more than concern for simply upsetting Anna though, I can see a fleeting moment of hesitation. Does he feel just the tiniest little vibe too?

I'm left wondering, when Tom suddenly appears and the others begin to filter into the room. I hurriedly wipe my eyes, giving them all a watery smile.

"Best go touch up my make-up!" I say lightly. I know they all think I'm emotional because it's Seb's big day.

When I arrive back at the girls' main dressing room it's chaotic. No one seems to take any notice as I sit down and begin scrubbing off my make-up with a moisturising pad to begin all over again. It isn't until Anna's mum comes into the room looking rather fraught that I realise Anna went to the bathroom at the same time I went to find Seb. Looking around I can't see her and a chill hits my stomach. Several of the girls are still having their hair done and there's a sense of mild panic because the clock is ticking. That's not what I'm picking up. The feeling I have is overwhelming, as if it's the pre-cursor to a disaster. I overhear Anna's mum asking if someone can go down to reception.

"What's wrong?" I ask Anna's best friend, Eva.

"Wedding nerves, it will be fine. Anna's feeling sick and a bit faint. I'm sure all she needs is a valium to calm her down." Eva sounds confident, but something constricts my heart like a band has just been placed around it. I scan the room, looking for a spirit—anything out of the norm. But all I can see are bobbing heads, curling tongs being pulled high into the air while two hair-dressers work quickly to add finishing touches. Then everything is in slow motion. I raise my hand in front of my face and even that seems to take forever to move the few inches from my lap. I'm on my feet and running back up to the second floor before I have time to think about what I'm doing. I hear myself screaming Seb's name and when his door opens he runs towards me.

***

"No, no, no…" the tissues in my hand are soggy and the person sitting next to me grabs another handful, thrusting them at me. I have no idea who she is, but she's crying too. How can anyone accept what has happened today? Where is Seb?

One of the hotel staff enters the room carrying a tray of glasses of water, orange juice and tea. She does the rounds in silence, her face immobile. All around are little groups of people, huddled together. Some are still crying, others look ashen. Most of the family members are nowhere to be seen. How can this have happened? How can someone so radiant and happy suddenly let go of life as if it were a tenuous thread? Anna was healthy, this was the day about which she had dreamed all of her life. A part of me knows that I can't be with Seb at the moment and that he can't be with me, but I need to find out who's with him.

"Have you seen Seb?" I ask the woman who handed me the tissues.

"He's with Anna's mother and the doctor. Best leave them for a while." She chokes back a sob. "You're Seb's sister, aren't you? I'm Anna's aunt, Claire."

We acknowledge each other briefly with a nod, both trying to hold back the tears that keep filling our eyes. Looking around the room there are no words to deal with this moment, everyone is in a state of complete and utter shock. There is a low murmur hovering over people while they console each other.

"Do you know what happened? I think I fainted. I remember Tom helping me onto the sofa," I take a glass of water from the tray offered to me and Claire takes one too. We sip in silence.

"I didn't realise anything was wrong until I heard someone scream out. I think it was Anna's mother, then Seb ran past me and he began shouting for help. The doctor arrived a little while ago and shortly afterwards someone came in to say that Anna was dead. I can't believe it. She was fine this morning, a little nervous, but radiant." Another tear rolls down Claire's face and I can no longer stem my own tears. She places her hand over mine and squeezes. The unthinkable has happened. Anna has hurt Seb, but not in the way I had expected and my heart sends out a silent sorry. I knew it from the very start of their relationship, only I didn't understand how or why it would happen. In my heart I can feel that a little part of my brother died with Anna today and I know there is nothing I can do to ease his pain.

***

I extend my leave from work by another four days. It seems that every day is worse than the one before, while the reality of what has happened really begins to sink in. Seb can't talk to me yet about his feelings and I understand that. He has to keep going in the only way he knows how, and that's to hold his emotions in check while he helps Anna's family make the funeral arrangements. Alex offered to be my escort and he slept over for the first two nights after that fateful day. Nothing happened between us. We lay in bed, his arms around me and he let me cry. I slept fitfully, full of remorse and guilt. Another person I wasn't able to save. I had let my brother down. What good is a gift if you can't use it to help those you love, if you can't protect them from the pain of an unnecessary loss? Seb has been robbed of his chance of happiness and left with a scar that will probably never heal. It would have been better to find out your partner has cheated on you, at least then there is a focus for your anger. I'm worried Seb will focus his anger on me and my inability to recognise a warning. Anna had a rare heart condition. The doctor said it's something that often goes unnoticed if it doesn't present any symptoms early on. She was unlucky he'd said, as if life was a lottery and the ticket Anna had purchased wasn't a winner.

Everything happens for a reason and I keep saying that, except I can't think of any reason or logic behind Anna's death. The rest of Seb's life will be over-shadowed by the loss of her love, so where's the reasoning in that?

"Don't," Alex says, standing up and coming over to me. He throws his arms around me gently and squeezes lightly. "Don't keep going over and over it in your head. It is what it is, you can't change anything. It wasn't your fault Ceri, no one is blaming you."

I know his words are meant with kindness and I'm hearing them, but the pain I feel for Seb is real. The link between us means a part of me deep inside feels icy cold with the emotion he's battling to contain. Men feel they have to be strong when the going gets tough, but this is something totally different. No one is equipped with a coping mechanism for this sort of tragedy, we each have to vent our feelings or risk becoming damaged.

"Sleep," Alex whispers into my hair. "Tomorrow you have to go into work and begin functioning again. Life goes on Ceri, it's the sad truth and I can appreciate how awful that must sound to you at this moment in time. People suffer and some things don't make any sense, but life doesn't stop. You have to make yourself strong for the funeral, for Seb. That's something positive you can do. For the moment though, it's time to rest."

He backs me onto the bed, rolls me on my side with a tenderness that is heart-breaking and slips off my shoes. Sleep comes quickly, but the dreams are disturbing.

***

The funeral is the worst day imaginable. Seb is strong, but almost collapses towards the end of the ceremony celebrating Anna's life. Tom is there next to him and they sit throughout the last part of the service. He pulls himself together and stands next to Anna's parents while everyone filters out of the church.

It's a bright day, the wind is chilly but the sky is blue and the birds are singing as if this isn't one of the saddest days most of us here have ever experienced. It doesn't seem real, but one look at Seb's face reminds me that it is.

Within a week he's gone. A hastily scribbled letter drops onto my doormat.

I'm running away, I guess you knew that would happen. I can't be here Ceri, I can't pretend I want to get up each morning and think about pulling my life back together. I'm not sure what I'm going to do, but I'll be in touch when I can. I know you will understand, please apologise to those who don't. This isn't cowardice, this is survival. Take care of yourself.

And Ceri, you weren't to know.

Seb x

I was thankful knowing Seb didn't blame me for anything and a little relieved. Alex had Googled undiagnosed heart conditions and made me sit in front of the computer to read some of the stories. There was a bride of five months who died instantly when she stepped out of the Jacuzzi. Can you imagine that? Her husband was heart-broken and my heart cried out in sorrow, knowing the pain he was going through. But at least he'd had five months, five golden months with wonderful memories. I wanted that for Seb, but you can't turn back the hands of time.

About a month later, with no news from Seb, I received a small package in the post. There was a note inside from Anna's mother and something wrapped up in tissue paper.

I know that Seb needs distance to sort out his life, but I hope that someday he'll think about the time they did have together. About the happiness they shared. Our precious daughter is even more precious in death. We are clinging on to the good times and are determined to celebrate her life.

We wondered if you would look after the necklace that Seb bought for Anna to wear on her wedding day and the matching earrings, your lovely gift to her celebrating the friendship between the two of you. I think she would have wanted you to have them. Whether one day you pass them on to Seb, we are content to leave up to you. It seems too sad to leave them in a box with some of her other things and it felt the right thing to do. We think it's what she would have wanted; she spoke very highly of you.

Angela

It must have been so hard for her to write that note. I can't bring myself to open the package. I want to remember Anna wearing them and the sparkle in her eyes. I tuck them away in the corner of a drawer for safe-keeping. I have no idea when I will see Seb again, but I know it won't be any time soon.

CHAPTER EIGHT

The New Me

Alex's influence is calming. Since Anna's death I've stopped recording 'incidents'. They still happen on a frequent basis and I do what I can when each moment presents itself, but I no longer spend time analysing what has occurred. With the help of a new book I recently discovered which talks in depth about angels, I feel that I can at least justify what happens to me. It answers some of the very searching questions I've longed to ask, in a way that I can understand. For the first time ever I feel that maybe it is real and it feels I've jumped a big hurdle. Alex and I have discussed it at great length and he too is responsible for a major part of the change in me. He's open-minded, but prepared to challenge anything he feels isn't quite right. Maybe he's intuitive too, he's never admitted as much but he definitely has an understanding way beyond most other people's comprehension.

Mason has backed off and Scott's replacement was eventually announced. It's no big surprise that it's a guy and an external applicant. It recently came to light that he's the son of an old friend of Mason's. It's clear Mason took my answer as the rebuff it was intended to be, but in all honesty it's only a job to me. No more, no less. All I know for sure is that if Alex left tomorrow, then I would too.

Alex. Buff, sexy as hell, trustworthy, grounded…what more can I say? I'm in love with him and I know that's dangerous. It puts our friendship in jeopardy and alcohol can never come into the equation again when we are alone together. If it does, and we end up in bed again, then I will risk losing that precious friendship. He still hasn't told me the story of his broken heart and I don't feel I can ask him about it. On the bright side, he's in a happy place. Work keeps his mind busy. We spend a lot of time together outside of the office now and neither of us mentions dating. Yes, we are aware that love should be a part of our respective lives, but you can't control your fate. Maybe we are destined to be best buddies until one, or both of us, finds that perfect partner. If I'm truthful, I'd happily ask Alex to move in with me. He puts a skip in my walk and he understands me. But love has to be reciprocal, and I think I'm more of a sister to him—ignoring our one, drunken, night of passion. Maybe that was the point of that little episode, to show us that friendship is more valuable than the excitement of a one-night stand. But I can't help the attraction I feel for him and the way my heartbeat races whenever he's really close to me. It's tantalising and it adds a little spice to my life. I know that makes me sound like I'm a total flirt, which honestly isn't the case. I simply want to be with Alex. I feel renewed whenever he's around.

I am enjoying life though. I worry about Seb, of course, and the lack of contact. However, I understand his need to get away from everything that reminds him of Anna. Alex helps me to put everything into perspective and I know that I didn't destroy Seb's happiness; fate did. My brother is a strong person, he'll figure out what comes next.

Suddenly the sun seems to shine that little bit brighter and instead of viewing my life by seeing only a series of problems at every turn, I feel that I have real choices. I can always walk away from something and I don't have to feel guilty. How much of that is down to the healthy eating, exercise and supplement regime Alex has talked me into, I'm not sure. Working out alongside my best buddy means I can't slack off and I'm feeling in the best shape physically that I've been for a long time. I've declined a few offers from guys at the gym to go out for a drink, simply because I no longer feel there is anything missing from my life. I'm happy with things the way they are for the moment.

It sounds like every day is bright and breezy, but of course that isn't the case. But something has changed on the psychic front too. Before, each time I saw something it was a different person. More and more whenever that happens, it's the same man who appears. I never see a real close-up, it's too indistinct, but his shape is easily recognisable. This one change has made a big difference because instead of feeling freaked out, I feel a sense of being protected. There is a definite connection. I can't explain it in any other way. This guy isn't coming to scare me, but he's helping me deal with each situation. He even smiles sometimes, although it's the briefest of moments and it's as much about feeling that as it is seeing his expression. Maybe the cosmos has decided to give me a break, or maybe Alex's calming influence means I'm more relaxed about it all, I'm not sure. There's no point in trying to second guess the reason, when I'll probably never know what triggered the change.

I do have one theory that I haven't mentioned to Alex. I opened the package of jewellery that Anna's mother sent to me. I held Anna's necklace in my hands and asked her to forgive me for ever thinking she would knowingly hurt my brother. I talked to her and emptied my heart of the regrets I felt and the sadness for the loss of someone so young. Maybe those on the other side were listening and decided to take pity on me, sending me my own guardian angel.

As Christmas came around I missed Seb so much, but was very excited to receive an email from him. He was in Australia and working on some sort of scheme to help disabled children. He sounded fine, grateful he was able to do something that at least had some purpose to it. I didn't tell him about Anna's jewellery, it's still too soon.

New Year's Eve was strange when I found myself under the mistletoe and face to face with Alex, as if we were a couple. I wanted to kiss him so much and felt myself drawing nearer to his mouth. He turned at the crucial moment when someone called his name, seemingly unaware of my intention. I felt cheated, robbed of a precious moment that I would have remembered forever. He hugs me every day that we're together, but it ends there and it's clear that he doesn't want any romantic involvement. I'll be honest—it's tough. Not least because I'm beginning to think that Alex could be the special one I've been searching for all of my life. I can't risk losing him, so I have to accept that having his friendship is better than nothing at all.

Sheena came home for a spell after New Year's and it's great to have my best girlfriend to myself for a while. I introduce her to Alex and she confirms that I must have been insane to think he was gay.

"Tasty," she drools, when she gives me her initial reaction.

"He's not a cake Sheena," I reply, rather offended that she should refer to my Alex in such a base way. A part of me agrees though and I still experience flashbacks from our drunken night of passion. It's enough to give me a warm glow inside and make me shake my head with regret that he doesn't feel the same way about me.

Sheena insists I go with her on a double date with two guys she's recently met and I mention it to Alex. I wonder if I have an ulterior motive and what I really want is to make him feel jealous. Instead he tells me it will do me good and so, reluctantly, I make up the foursome for dinner. Carl and Luke are typical of the type of guy Sheena gravitates towards: smart, savvy, and high-income—very materialistic. I end up alone at the table with Luke, when Sheena and Carl stand up to dance. He's friendly enough, but the conversation is hard work.

"Who do you work for?" is his opener and my heart sinks. I talk briefly about my job and then ask him what he does for a living. He talks non-stop for the next hour, thinking he's impressing me by dropping some big names in the music industry. I feign interest, but really I'm clock watching and can't wait for the evening to be over.

**

The next day Alex is in a strange mood. He asks about the date but doesn't seem too interested in my answer, which is only to say that it was okay but nothing special. I decide he's having an off day and that I should give him some space. I'm getting ready to leave for the day when he suddenly looks up and asks if I want to grab something to eat at his place. I've never been invited back before, so obviously I'm intrigued. I accept gracefully and he scribbles down his address.

I change my mind several times over what I'm going to wear. I don't want to be too casual and I can't be too dressy. Alex's dress sense is perfect, but then he looks great in everything. I end up settling for black linen trousers, a crisp white cotton top, and a thin taupe-coloured knitted jacket. I decide to go by taxi in case I have a drink; a girl has to live in hope!

Sheena phones as I'm literally about to step out of the door. "I'm on my way to have dinner over at Alex's place." I hope she doesn't invite herself along, it's the sort of thing Sheena does without thinking. I'm relieved when she tells me she is meeting up with Carl a bit later.

"Well, have a fab time, Ceri. And remember, if you don't ask you don't get!" I put the phone down, thinking how typical that is of the way Sheena looks at life. However, I can only take things one step at a time with Alex for fear of scaring him away. There are no guarantees he'll ever see me in a different light.

Dinner is wonderful and a real surprise. That is, unless he bought it in pre-made and simply opened the boxes to heat it up. The kitchen is surprisingly tidy given that we had three courses, but there is enough evidence of chopping and slicing to convince me he knows what he's doing.

"Penny for your thoughts," he asks, leaning in to attract my attention.

"I was thinking that you are a much better cook than I am. I hope you cheated."

"I never cheat, it's not in my nature," he drawls.

"Of course, I know that. You're much too good." It was a simple remark, made off the top of my head. His reaction to my words is unexpected: the look on his face seems to indicate I've said something to really hurt him.

"If you think I don't have feelings, you would be wrong," he says in a clipped tone. Sitting back in his chair he twirls the stem of his wine glass in his fingers. He's obviously distracted and deep in thought—about what exactly, I have no idea. I change the subject and insist on clearing the table and stacking the dishwasher. Afterwards we head into the sitting room. I'm about to sit down when Alex unexpectedly takes one step nearer to me. I can feel his breath on the side of my face and I wonder if the wine is kicking in, but we've only drunk half a bottle between us during dinner.

"Ceri, I am attracted to you but that doesn't make it right," his words are slightly muffled and I'm not sure if it's emotion or he's upset.

"That's…um…I understand." Of course I do. He had a bad experience and someone broke his heart. He doesn't want to use me when his affections are elsewhere. Before I can think about what is happening, his arms are around me and this isn't a gentle hug. His body presses up hard against mine and he kisses me fiercely. I can feel the passion in him and he's holding me as if he never wants to let me go.

My mind whirls. What's going on? This isn't some alcohol induced embrace, it's something more. But he made it clear that he's not free to fall in love with someone else. My conscience tells me to pull away, that it's one of those crazy moments when someone lets down their guard. It's about a need, rather than needing a particular someone. But I can't pull away and before I know it we're heading for his bedroom. I'm not strong enough to fight what's in my heart, even though I know Alex will probably regret it in the morning.

The thing is—I won't.

CHAPTER NINE

The Argument

The morning after the night before is surprisingly relaxed considering the potential awkwardness of the situation. Because we were both sober, clearly it meant something. What exactly, I'm not sure either of us has yet been able to work out. Alex isn't regretful at all and certainly wasn't last night; in fact we spent most of it awake and wrapped up in each other's arms. The only thing he said that made me feel uneasy, was when he snuggled into my neck and let out a sigh.

"It's not right Ceri," he murmured in a low voice, and his breath on my skin made my heart miss a beat. "I'm using you and it's not fair."

"How can you use someone when you aren't hiding anything?" I retorted. Hey, I'm a big girl and I can make my own decisions. It all feels very right to me, but I can't say that in case it's too much, too soon. One day, maybe in the not too distant future. I begin to feel like I'm trying to trap him and that isn't the case. Or am I simply trying to fool myself?

We call into my place on the way to work so that I can put on some fresh clothes. Alex seems comfortable enough waiting for me, and when I finish changing and walk into the sitting room he's reading one of the books off the shelf.

"Can I borrow this one?" he asks, holding it up.

"*Living with Angels* by Ethan Morris. It's a good book." I nod, thinking that of all the books I have that's probably the one I would have recommended. Does it mean we're getting even closer and Alex is keen to understand a little more about the other side of my life?

It's an easy start to the day, but once we hit the office things start going wrong. Mason is in a really bad mood and everyone is on edge. The fact that Alex and I arrive together is unusual and doesn't go unnoticed. Mason hauls me into his office five minutes later.

He starts complaining that we're running behind on the schedule and implies that our minds aren't on the job.

"I don't encourage relationships between members of my staff," he sneers. I feel my face colouring. I have to bite my tongue not to bring up the out of hours socialising that went with the job he'd offered me. "And you're late." It isn't true of course, we were bang on time, but then we usually arrive early and never together. It would be today, when everything was kicking off, that we were the last to arrive. I walk back to the office and Alex looks up at me a little sheepishly.

"I've got you into trouble," he says.

"It's no big deal, Mason's in a mood because one of the clients isn't happy. It's not even anything to do with us. Let's keep our heads down until the panic is over."

***

At the end of the day Alex gives me a lift home.

"Why don't you stay?" I offer, keeping my fingers crossed he'll give in.

"I can't, it wouldn't be right."

My face falls and he looks cross.

"Ceri, I've been straight with you from the start. Last night was a big mistake, the first time it was the alcohol. Last night it was passion: a relationship is about more than that and I'm sorry it happened."

I'm stunned. He didn't look sorry last night or this morning. "I wish you'd be honest with me. You don't really regret last night, do you? It didn't feel that way and I thought—"

"You thought I was falling for you? I've told you the situation I'm in and there can never be anything long-term between us. I took advantage of you, what more can I say other than I'm sorry and it was wrong of me? I'm a man, we do that sort of thing. You are a beautiful young woman Ceri and any man would find it hard to say no to you."

His words sting. My head is all over the place while I struggle to understand what he's saying. Did he think I had come on to him? I cast my mind back, one minute we were talking and then the next he was pressing up against me. He kissed me. I'm sure of it.

"Does it matter whose fault it was? That doesn't make it wrong, not if it felt right at the time," I raise my voice, angry because I can't understand why we're arguing.

He crosses his arms, his body language telling me not to invade his space and risk stepping closer. "Perhaps you make it too easy," he throws at me, and that's the final straw.

"If that's what you think then you'd better leave," I say and he follows me to the door. I slam it behind him and lean against the wall, willing my racing heart to slow down.

I'm not exactly sure what happened. Is he saying I'm a tease, or that I'm trying to trap him because he's made it clear his heart belongs to someone else? Where are my angels when I need a little help for me? It seems they have gone rather quiet lately and I wonder why that might be.

***

I can't eat so I go to bed early, grabbing the first book on hand. I flip a few pages but my mind keeps going over and over the words that Alex flung at me. I can't understand what's going on with him. There's something more he isn't telling me but I have no way of finding out unless he opens up. And I doubt that's likely now.

Even worse, he doesn't turn up for work the next morning and Mason hauls me in to ask what's going on.

"This is precisely why I don't encourage staff to bring their personal lives into work." He gets up from his chair and comes to stand in front of me. "Lover's tiff was it?"

I turn, I've had enough and I don't have to take this, but he grabs my wrist roughly. His grip is tight and it hurts. I stop struggling as he spins me around.

"Don't think you can flaunt your little affair in front of me and get away with it." For a moment I wonder if he's going to lash out at me. What on earth does he mean? "I'm not the jealous type. I have more to offer you than Alex could ever hope to have."

"Please let me go." My voice is strong and I hold his gaze without fear. "Or I will scream." I don't think he realises he has me in a vice-like grip and when he lets go he too seems shocked by what just happened. I turn and run out of the office, down the corridor, grab my things and leave.

My heart is pounding and my eyes are filling with tears that threaten to obscure my vision as I leave the building. It's over, I'm done.

CHAPTER TEN

I Need to Get Away

"Sheena, its Ceri." The tears muffle my voice and it takes her a few moments to recognise who is calling.

"Ceri, what's going on?"

"I need to escape for a few days, are you at home?"

"No, I'm on the outskirts of Paris. I'm working on some legal documents at the moment," she answers with concern in her voice. "You aren't okay, are you?"

"My life is falling apart. I've walked out on my job and Alex has disappeared."

"What the heck… look, if you can hang on for twenty-four hours a colleague of mine is leaving the UK tomorrow for an evening tunnel crossing. He's taking over the case I'm working on while I'm on a week's leave. I'll contact him, I'm sure he won't mind having someone along for the journey. Don't switch your phone off and pack enough for at least a week." The line disconnects and I throw myself on the bed, absolutely distraught at how quickly things can go from bad to worse.

Alex doesn't answer his phone and I give myself a deadline. If I can't contact him before my lift arrives tomorrow afternoon, then

I will take that as a sign. I won't lay bare my heart for a man who believes I'm throwing myself at him. At least I can make common-sense out of Mason's outburst. He thought I'd do anything for a promotion and at least he has a reason to be bitter, even if it's totally unreasonable. But Alex knows I'm not a bad person and I don't throw myself at men. He's the only one night stand I've ever had and I've only slept with two men before him. Both were relationships that, at the time, I felt might go somewhere. But I was rather naïve and assumed anyone who cared enough to sleep with me would understand the sensitive side of my nature. That wasn't the case.

***

"I can't believe he said that to you," Sheena sounds angry on my behalf. "Who the hell does he think he is?"

I can't help but defend him, even though I'm hurt. "There's something not right Sheena. Alex is usually such a sensitive guy. Maybe he started to feel something for me and then felt guilty about this person he says he loves. It's painful when you offer your heart to someone and they reject you. I know that for a fact."

Sheena puts an arm around my shoulder and squeezes.

"Whatever, Ceri. You still don't deserve to be treated that way. Mason is another story of course and you can't get hung up on that. But Alex, well, I'm surprised and very sorry it should turn out this way."

I take a few deep breaths, determined that I'm not going to start crying again.

"What can I do? I have to work today and tomorrow, but after that we can head off to one of the small towns on the north coast. There are some lovely beaches and we can do some walking, blow away those cobwebs." Sheena pushes away the hair that's fallen over my cheek. "I am so sorry my darling girl, you don't deserve this and I won't let him make you feel you are a victim. If he has a problem then he has to deal with it. You've been through enough already."

I lean against the pillows on the bed, watching Sheena as she heads for the door. "I'll be back before you know it. Ring down for room service, the menu is on the table. Try to rest. There are a couple of books in my suitcase if you want to read."

As the door closes behind her I turn on my side and let the tears flow. I love you, Alex, and I know you are the one. Where are my angels? Why aren't you here when I need you?

It's the last thing in my head before I drift off into a deep and uneasy sleep.

ALEX

CHAPTER ELEVEN

Alone

I pop another pill, washing it down with a swig from the wine glass on the floor next to the bed. The room looks like a tornado has hit it; I roll over and sink into a deep sleep.

Ceri is there, slumped against a low wall, resting. Maybe she's observing one of her angels. The wind is playing with her hair, but she's oblivious to it whipping around in front of her face. She isn't moving and I realise her hands are almost blue with cold. My senses are screaming that something is wrong. She's dead. I cry out her name but then sleep claims me again, which doesn't make sense. I feel awake, if not alert, and I struggle to raise my level of consciousness to that place where I can make sense of what's happening.

"It's wrong, you know that. You shouldn't get involved and you need to back off." The voice is either above or behind me, I can't tell, and there is no physical presence attached to it. Is this all in my mind or is it a part of my dream? I'm trying to find Ceri, but I can't see her now. Is she alright? Is she alone? Why do I feel a terrible sense of emptiness? I need you Ceri, where are you?

Mason looks up, surprised to see me. "You're fired," he utters, barely able to look me in the face.

"I know; if I wasn't, I'd quit anyway. You're a piece of work, Mason, but I doubt anyone has the balls to tell you that to your face. Do you know where Ceri is?" It's not so much a question, more of a demand.

"I have no idea, she's fired too."

"Well that's good news then." I throw the words over my shoulder on my way out of the door.

No one in the office seems to know anything at all about where Ceri might be. I've been to her apartment a dozen times and there's no sign of anyone being there for the last few days. I've left a dozen messages on her mobile and put two letters through her door begging her to give me a call and let me explain. But what can I tell her? That for some reason I can't be with her and I don't know why? It doesn't make sense to me and it won't make sense to her.

The dreams are getting worse and every one is a warning. Something is telling me that I'm a danger to Ceri for some reason. That's why I have to keep away, but I can't. I've tried and it doesn't work, I keep getting drawn back because something here, deep inside of me, needs to be with her. I thought it was working, keeping my distance while being there for her, but look at the mess I made of things. Now she's run off, thinking I'm blaming her when really I'm blaming myself.

I decide to look up the author of the book Ceri lent me, *Living with Angels* by Ethan Morris. I put his name into the search engine and immediately the page fills up with articles. He's written over a dozen books on a wide range of subjects, but everything is related to angels or mediumship. There's a contact page on his website, so I type in a short message

My name is Alex Delano. I need to talk to someone about a friend. She sees angels. I've read your book, Living with Angels, and I have a few questions. I'm desperate to find some answers. You can reach me on this email address. If I can book a one-to-one session that would be great, but even to chat via email would really help. Thank you.

The next thing I need to do is look for another job. Heck, how did I manage to screw everything up so badly? What hurts the most is that I don't know where Ceri is or whether she's safe. She will be hurting and all I can do is wait for her to get in touch with me. I think of all the desperate voicemail messages on my phone the day she left, and where was I? Pathetically prostrate in bed, full of pills and out of it. No wonder she won't answer my calls now, she thinks I used her and then walked away.

***

"Thank you for agreeing to talk to me Mr Morris, I'll be brief." After speaking to his assistant and reassuring him that I wasn't a reporter or a stalker, he agreed to pass on my message. Within three hours I receive a personal email from Ethan Morris with his phone number and a message to call him at eight o'clock. Ceri has been gone for two whole weeks.

***

"Please, call me Ethan. I'm intrigued. You say you've read *Living with Angels* because you have a friend who has experienced seeing them. Tell me more."

He sounds ordinary, I can't tell what age, but from the bio photo on the back of the book I'd say he was in his early forties. I run a few of Ceri's experiences past him, trying to recall them in detail and careful not to add to what Ceri told me. I can hear her voice in my head, that night when we told each other everything.

Well, almost everything.

"Have you witnessed any of this?"

I concentrate, my mind replaying conversations full of emotion. I realise the answer is that I've never witnessed anything paranormal. I wonder if that will put Ethan off. "No, but her brother has seen some of the weird things that have happened. They are non-identical twins: Ceri was delivered a few minutes before her brother."

He listens and asks questions, some I can answer and some I can't. I can only repeat what I know.

"Well, it's not unusual, although you might find that hard to believe. The truly difficult part is getting your head around the fact that this life is only one small part of our existence."

I don't know what to say. I've read several different theories but he clearly has no doubts whatsoever. Was I expecting him to be a little less forceful, maybe?

"I'm way out of my depth here but I really need to understand a bit more about angels and why Ceri should have been singled out. Why do they present themselves to her and why is it someone different every time?"

"I doubt that what she sees is an actual angel, it's more likely to be a spirit helper or guide who has been sent to assist. Sometimes things go a little off course, shall we say. One tiny moment can send life spinning off in the wrong direction. For instance, near-death experiences caused by a genuine mistake or when it isn't someone's time to pass over but an unexpected turn of events means that they touch 'the path' of transition. The spirits on the other side will encourage them to turn back. Occasionally it can take a little persuasion because the experience can be uplifting. They glimpse a life that exists outside of this one, which is more peaceful and comforting. Much of what happens is forgotten, wiped from the memory. In theory we are supposed to have no recollection of what occurs when our energy slips outside of our body. You might have heard about astral travelling. Only higher evolved souls will remember their journeys. Few will repeat the details, unless they have been given permission to share something for the development of another soul. Someone sent here for a specific purpose."

"I think you need to point me in the direction of some more reading. When you talk about astral travelling, is it linked in any way to our dreams?"

"It can be. Someone with less experience might interpret an out of body experience as being merely a dream. We all visit the other side during our sleep, but it's rare to be able to recall what happens. There is a code and the whole point is that the planes are kept separate. There would be no point in having an earthly life if it wasn't necessary for the development of the astral plane. Does Ceri experience this type of dream?"

"I have no idea, but since I met Ceri I've had problems with some graphic dreams. They are always very similar and seem to be telling me that I'm endangering her in some way. What's crazy is that I only want her to be happy and safe."

"Look Alex, I think we should meet up. I'm back in the UK at the beginning of next week and I'm doing a talk in London. Would you be able to come along? I'll arrange for us to have a chat in private afterwards."

"I'd be delighted, that's very kind of you."

"I'll have my assistant email you the details of the venue. I must admit I'm rather intrigued by your story. It's unusual for one person to be affected by the sensitivity of another, when they exhibited no such traits beforehand. I doubt there's any danger, only lower entities cause mischief and they don't have enough power to do anything really menacing, despite popular theory. It's more down to the mind blowing a small thing out of proportion: people have a tendency to fear the unknown, even when there isn't really anything to fear at all."

"Well, I'll be interested to meet up with you and thanks for your time. I really appreciate it."

"I thrive on the unusual, so for me something that doesn't quite fit is a way of expanding my understanding. Gifts of insight are given for a reason. We're either here to learn or to help. It's been my pleasure. Before you go, can I ask you to begin making notes whenever you have a dream that you can remember afterwards. It might explain a few things."

***

I stare up at the ceiling, thinking of Ceri. My body relaxes into the bed, the tension beginning to ease. I wonder if she can feel my thoughts. What did Ethan say? We're either here to learn or to help. Am I here to help Ceri, or is Ceri here to teach me something? Is my path crossing hers or is it the other way around? I said that nothing strange had ever happened to me before I met Ceri, just over two years ago. Is that true? I let my mind wander. I have no recall whatsoever of having a bad dream prior to that time, of course that doesn't mean to say I hadn't had any, only that it wasn't a concern. Why is it that I can remember these dreams so clearly and they keep repeating the same message—protect Ceri but don't get too close? Watch her from a distance, but always stand back.

I pick up another of Ethan Morris's books from the bedside table. The title is *Worlds That Collide* and it's fascinating. He believes that there are multiple planes of existence and they all inter-relate. When we are here on the earthly plane, in our sleep we leave our bodies and go back to the ethereal plane to continue the work we do there. It isn't easy reading, but I'm halfway through the book now and trying to get my head around his ideas. I'm beginning to see what he's asking the reader to do, and that's to stop thinking about life here on earth as being the sole purpose of our existence. Instead he's suggesting we think of it merely as a place we come to learn lessons. We then return to the ethereal planes, where our energy will be advanced by our experiences in this life. Some 'energies' come back more than once. Well, I think that's what he's saying. It's not easy to take in, that's for sure.

CHAPTER TWELVE

Life Without Her

I've found myself another job. Fortunately not everyone gets on with the influential Mason Portingale and once the news was out that I was looking, well, wheels within wheels. Grey's Advertising is small and I guess in many ways we are a perfect fit. I'm flexible and live for my work—well, that goes without saying. What else do I have in my life? No Ceri, that's a fact. She hasn't been in touch and it's been over a month.

Ironically my dreams have virtually stopped. That might be because I'm hardly sleeping; I spend hours thinking about her and wondering what happens next. Sleep usually comes around four am and then it's only a few hours until the alarm clock wakes me for another day. Without the new job I have no idea what I would do. I know I can't sit around moping all the time, but that's my life pretty much outside of work now. I'm arriving early and staying late. At least the new boss is happy, although he must wonder why I don't want to go home at the end of the day like everyone else.

I had an email from Sheena and she made it clear Ceri didn't know she was getting in touch. It was brief. She told me that I'd broken Ceri's heart and that I was a rat. 'Stay away,' she said, and that was it. The thing is, when you are confronted with the truth about a situation, what can you say? There's no point in trying to deny what happened and there is no justification. The best thing I can do now for Ceri is to bow out of her life and hope that she finds someone who deserves to be with her and can keep her safe. She's bright, beautiful and a catch; she has no idea how truly amazing she is and that's because she hides herself away. At work she is outgoing, but the moment she lets down her armour, she's running scared. The other side of her life bewilders her and she's constantly seeking answers; that's the bit that other people don't understand, and there are moments when I've been with her where I too felt freaked out by something she told me.

I've decided I'll still meet up with Ethan next week. I'm going to take a day off work and visit a couple of interesting psychic bookstores while I'm there. I don't know if spending time with Ceri has awakened something in me. Ethan's idea that I write up all of the dreams I could still remember with some sort of clarity, has been useful. It has certainly made me wonder whether there's a message in there for me. What if meeting Ceri wasn't a coincidence? What if it was fate? I also told her a lie. At the time I felt I had no choice, but I'm not a guy to give in to fear. It doesn't sit well with me and my knee-jerk reaction ended up in my lashing out at her. I don't know how to undo the damage, because at the time I thought I was protecting her. Whether the warning was for real and the consequences could put her life in danger—I don't know, but that's not a risk I'm prepared to take.

CERI

CHAPTER THIRTEEN

Going to Pieces

It hurts. I have no heart, only little fragments floating around randomly inside me. How ironic that Seb and I seem to be mirror images, only the circumstances are different. When something shatters your life into pieces, you feel your reason for being no longer exists. Why am I here? What purpose does my life serve if I can't make anyone happy? Alex is no longer in my life and nothing else is working. I haven't had one single episode and it seems even the angels have deserted me. I failed them and I'm no longer useful. Was I so wrapped up in loving Alex that I missed a sign and failed to be the instrument of change? Did I miss the cue to put something right before it had a chance to go wrong?

Ironically I can see things more clearly now and maybe that's because my life is uncluttered. No Alex, no angels and no purpose. There are two sides to that coin. No job, no reason to get out of bed in the morning and no point to my existence. I count for nothing and the universe has recognised that. It no longer requires my input.

Long walks along the beach on the northern coast of France have kept me sane; kept me from doing something silly. I awaken each morning with a sense of dread at having to pretend to Sheena that I'm making plans to put my life back together again. The reality is very different. I don't know who I am anymore. My psychic side was a part of my identity. I can understand that with hindsight and, in a strange way, after meeting Alex things had begun to fall into place. I was coping with my incidents much better, my reactions were quicker and I was handling things in a seamless way. I was at last beginning to feel comfortable with the side of my life that I'd often regarded as a burden. People around me were hardly noticing my actions to alter the course of events.

A part of this clarity is down to a little old French lady named Voleta. I was curious whether it had a meaning: it wasn't a name I'd ever heard before and I discovered it means 'veiled'. I thought that was rather strange. She was certainly able to open my eyes to a few things.

It was the day Sheena and I left Paris and headed for the northern coast. We drove to a wonderful sea view hotel in a little place called Le Crotoy. It was an old manor house, sitting within a meandering garden that was surrounded by a beautiful old stone wall. All of the bedrooms on the first and second floors looked out over the sea, and our rooms had balconies. Sheena left me to wander around the shops while she went back to the hotel to make a phone call. It was a particularly charming part of Picardie, and the inhabitants are known as Crotellois.

There was a little shop tucked away in a side street and I found myself there only because I took a wrong turn, thinking it was a short cut back to the hotel. It was very small and outside there was a rack of tie-dyed t-shirts and skirts, plus a few baskets containing second-hand French books. The window was mostly taken up with incense sticks, candles, and crystals. That's what attracted me inside.

"Good day," the old woman behind the counter said, like she had been waiting for me to step inside. She spoke very good English, but with a thick French accent. I must have looked a little surprised, because she laughed.

"I married an Engleeshman," she offered. "It's the skin. So white."

I smiled and began browsing, but there wasn't really anything I wanted to buy. I was about to turn and thank her before leaving, when she began speaking to me again.

"J'ai lu les cartes de tarot." She spoke quickly and I only picked up the word 'tarot'. "Would you like I read for you?"

I didn't know what to say. I wasn't particularly interested but I felt I was a captive audience of one.

"Merci Madame, je m'appelle Ceri." "Voleta," she said, nodding her head to acknowledge the greeting. She came forward, changed the sign on the door to 'Fermé' and indicated that I should follow her.

The room behind the shop was cool and a little dismal. Heavy brocade curtains, an old sofa, and a few chairs gathered around a small, antique table. It must have been expensive when it was first purchased, because the legs were heavily carved. It was clean and tidy, but it felt like a place where time stood still. This was a way of living where the modern world was irrelevant. I couldn't see a TV or a radio and everything was useful, only small touches added that sense of homeliness.

"Alors mademoiselle, I think this will be interesting, non?" Her French seemed to mingle easily with her English and I felt slightly embarrassed that my own French was so poor. I can understand more than I can actually speak. She indicated for me to sit down at the table and took the seat opposite me. There was an old tin on the table, which Madame Voleta opened and carefully lifted from it a stack of yellowing cards. I watched her shuffle them and divide the cards into seven smaller piles on the table. She gestured for me to choose one, then gathered up the piles either side and gently placed them back inside the tin.

Her hands hovered over the table for a few moments in a meaningful way; her eyes were closed. Then she began laying out the cards in a line. They were beautiful cards, worn with time and unlike any tarot cards I had ever seen. The pictures were grand and ornate, faded so the colours were no longer crisp, but reminiscent of courtiers and palaces. Versailles sprang to mind, looking at the magnificent garden settings on some of the cards.

Madame appeared to be talking to herself and the only thing I caught was "Ahh, l'amour véritable!" Then she said, "mais pas." She searched my face, looking for something.

"Your man 'az a big 'art but now your 'art eez broken. Eez no fault. Eez fate. You must 'ave faith that life will change." She scooped the cards up, shuffled them and laid them out in a pyramid. She nodded. "Ah."

"Madame?" I enquired, anxious to know what she could see.

"You worry, but eet make no difference. What will be, will be. You save people you not know and that eez your gift." She muttered a few words then saw that I was struggling to translate. "You 'ave the gift to put somezing good." Her eyes shone with kindness and understanding. I felt comforted. "Lucky." She smiled.

"I don't feel lucky," I murmured and she frowned.

"C'est difficile, non?" she agreed, nodding her head. "Mais, what a life you 'ave. You make a difference, vous avez été choisis." I think that means that I have been chosen and she nods, as if reading my mind.

"Will I be alone?" I asked, and her face dropped a little.

"For a while, mais pas pour toujours." She reached across and placed her hand over mine. It was cold, despite the fact that outside it was a very warm day.

She surveyed the cards, "No worry," she explained, "spéciale, très spéciale. You cannot fight your destiny. Je suis honoré."

Why would she say 'I'm honoured?'

I picked up my bag to offer her some money, but she immediately said "non" and grasped hold of my hand. "Choisi," she repeated in her warm French accent.

"Merci Madame," I nodded my head and she smiled.

Walking out into the sunlight, my eyes took a few moments to adjust. Why are there never any answers, only little clues that often seem meaningless? But it made me realise that I've always felt different and maybe what I should have been feeling is 'special.'

Madame Voleta was right: I probably have changed people's lives for the better, but that doesn't help when you have a broken heart. If I had to choose between having this gift and having Alex in my life, I'd choose Alex without a moment's hesitation.

CHAPTER FOURTEEN

Realisation

I didn't mention Madame Voleta or the tarot reading to Sheena. I don't think she would approve and I don't want her to think I'm wallowing. Sheena is doing what she does best, trying to encourage me to leave my troubles behind and get on with it. At dinner last night she was firing ideas at me, things I could do now that I'm suddenly free as a bird. Well, Sheena calls it 'free as a bird' while I call it heart-broken and unemployed.

I know she has a point. Whatever I do next is important and maybe I'm at a crossroads. There doesn't appear to be anything or anyone around me to influence any decision I make. I have no constraints and no responsibilities. I could sell my apartment and settled down somewhere else. I could try living abroad even. I have some money saved and my needs are modest. However, too much freedom, too many choices, and nothing to really inspire me makes me feel that I have been set adrift. There's nothing comforting about it. Rather, it makes me feel sad and I'm often conscious of being alone, even when I'm surrounded by other people. Sheena is a great friend but she has a busy life; my parents and I don't understand each other and Seb was always the easy one, so their bond is strong. Being different has been a curse on so many different levels and people end up distancing themselves from you if they sense your feelings of isolation. I think Sheena has stuck by me because she knew me before things became so heavy, so she knows I have a perfectly normal side too. Alex, I realise, was the only one who hung around, didn't ask questions and accepted the 'me' I put out there. Even though he sensed my life was in two halves and I chose to show him only the side of me that was straightforward—that is, until we decided to share our secrets.

"You've gone off into your own little world again." Sheena waves a hand in front of my face.

"Sorry, I'm getting better though, aren't I?"

Sheena peers at me, her brow furrowed.

"Maybe. I was a bit worried at first that you wouldn't return from one of your long beach walks, but you're stronger than you think."

I laugh, then realise that she's serious.

"I feel lost," I admit. "I'm not used to being in a relationship… well, it was hardly a relationship. But you know what I mean. I felt a connection with Alex and I fell in love with him, maybe even the first time I saw him. That's why it was easy to be around him, and I didn't want to show him the secret side of my life because I knew it would change things. Perhaps he really wasn't different at all, only patient. He said I was gorgeous and I was disappointed in him, that he was yet another person who could only see the shell. It's what's inside that counts and what I had was special."

"Had?" Sheena's face registers surprise.

"Well, it's been a while. Nothing at all has happened since I've been in France."

Sheena shifts uncomfortably in her chair. "What?" Her face colours slightly.

"Well, I've seen at least three episodes. Maybe they are more discreet now, or maybe it's becoming such a part of you that it doesn't register."

We sit in silence. Can that be true? Instead of feeling shocked, I feel an over-whelming sense of relief. The cosmos hasn't set me free: it needs me to fulfil the destiny it has determined for me. Thank you! I will never, ever complain about my gift again.

**

We head for home and the black cloud that has been hanging over me has finally lifted. Having time to walk along the beach and think has done me the power of good. My life works best when I keep the psychic side of me separate from the normal side. So all I have to do is make sure I never bring the two together. I'm going to look for a day job that will keep me in the real world and keep my private life out of it.

I've also found myself a mentor of sorts, someone who has offered to help develop and channel whatever gift I have been given. His name is Mark Kessler and he's a celebrated local, being an acclaimed psychic medium and motivational speaker. He travels all over the UK and his events are always sold out. I've followed his blog for a while and read some of his books. I went to one of his talks and bought a few things afterwards from a display in the foyer. He came up and started casually chatting to the little group of people queuing to pay. I asked him a question about the programme he runs, which teaches people how to meditate and one thing led to another. We ended up going for a cup of coffee. I told him pretty much everything that worries me and he made me feel that there are things I can do to help myself. I decided to sign up for the meditation sessions and he also offered me a place on a Gayatri mantra workshop he was arranging. I thanked him, gave him my email address and went away thinking 'What on earth?'

I've never heard the term before and had no idea what it was, but when I Googled it millions of pages came up. Apparently it's one of the oldest and most powerful of the Sanskrit mantras. It is believed that by chanting the mantra and connecting with it, it will help you carry out the work that fate has determined for you. Your life will be full of happiness as you fulfil your true destiny. The way everything was happening, I wondered if this was a sign that the cosmos was giving me the information I needed to finally make some sense of my life.

The word "Gayatri" itself explains the reason for the existence of this mantra. It has its origin in the Sanskrit phrase *Gayantam Triyate iti* and refers to that mantra which rescues the chanter from all adverse situations that may lead to mortality. It sounded amazing, but then I saw a video of a group actually chanting. Was I out of my depth? How could I sit in a circle and chant with a group of total strangers? What if it didn't do anything for me or this wasn't something I was supposed to be involved with?

However, it was too late to change my mind and although I believe everything happens for a reason, I was really beginning to feel way out of my comfort zone.

***

Today I might have saved someone from committing suicide. I was on my way back from a job interview and found myself taking a short-cut through the park. There was a young guy slumped on a bench and I thought at first he was drunk. I started to veer away from the path and walk in a wide circle, rather than passing by within reach of him. Something kept trying to pull me back on course and then the ankle strap on my left shoe snapped without warning. I had no choice but to sit down and forage through my bag for a temporary fix, or risk tripping myself up.

I said nothing, simply sat down at the far end of the bench and plunged my hand into my bag. I was hoping to find something I could tie around my foot to keep my shoe on. I pulled out a handful of loose items, including some ribbon that wasn't long enough and then found a rather sturdy, stretchy hair band.

Fortunately it was a black one and wouldn't look too bad. Two minutes and I was done, able to walk again with the confidence that at least I would be able to make it home. I was about to get up and leave, when my eyes were drawn to the young man and I realised something was very wrong.

"Are you okay?" I asked, tentatively. He remained slumped. I reached out and touched his arm, but there was no reaction at all. I dropped my bag and walked over to him, his chin was resting on his chest and his arms were folded. Then I saw the needle on the ground next to the bench. I grabbed my mobile out of my bag and dialled with shaking hands.

"Can you send an ambulance immediately? A young man has collapsed on a bench and there's a needle on the ground next to him. I think he might have overdosed. Please hurry!" I described where we were and I kept checking my watch, counting the minutes that seemed to pass so slowly. Then, finally I could hear the ambulance siren. A convoy of two vehicles headed across the grass and I jumped up, waving my arms in the air to attract attention. The paramedic car, being lighter, was first to arrive while the ambulance struggled over the grassy bank that sloped down to the path.

The young man's pulse was weak. They worked on him for twenty minutes before he was stable enough to be lifted onto the stretcher and moved to the ambulance.

I thanked them and picked up my bag to leave. "You saved his life, Miss," the paramedic said.

"I hope so," I replied and walked away, willing him to hold onto his life. Everyone deserves a second chance and maybe sometimes you have to fly very close to the edge to realise how precious life is.

As I walked home a fleeting thought passed through my mind. Could I have taken my own life when I was at my lowest point? Or would the universe have stopped me in time because that wasn't my fate? I knew nothing at all about the young man, but for whatever reason someone out there was watching over him today.

CHAPTER FIFTEEN

The Circle

I suppose I was expecting a smart venue for Mark Kessler's Gayatri mantra session. I walk past the building twice before thinking about going inside. The hall is rather neglected and unprepossessing, with paint peeling off the window frames. Moving closer I notice there is a hand-written sign on the door 'Workshop attendees – use this entrance'. It seems superfluous as I can't see another way of gaining entry.

Inside it's much larger and brighter than I expect. There's a low buzz of voices coming from the far end of the room. Everyone is standing around an island, helping themselves to tea and coffee. People are introducing themselves and it seems most have come on their own, which makes me feel a bit better. I refuse the offer of a hot or cold drink and stand there feeling slightly self-conscious. I smile, listening in on the edge of conversations that are little more than pleasantries. I do a headcount and there are eighteen of us in total. There is a mixture of all ages, from a young woman who looks like she's in her early twenties, to a guy in his sixties. Now I'm wishing I had said no. The group is too small and I'm going to find it difficult, if not impossible, to relax and be myself. Every single person is going to be visible in what they do. There's no hiding away in the crowd.

"Hi everyone," Mark's voice travels towards us as he walks through the door. Someone else follows him in and they are both carrying boxes. "Welcome! This is Steven, he's going to keep the refreshments coming throughout the workshop and generally make himself useful."

Steven puts down the box he's carrying on the counter top and smiles. "I'm the general dogsbody really," he says, good-naturedly.

"Okay, if everyone can grab a chair and bring it into the centre of the hall, I'll explain what we're hoping to achieve today."

It's a fairly large circle, but it still feels like we are merely a blemish in the middle of the space. I realise that the ceiling height of the room is what makes the proportions even more pronounced. The high, vaulted ceiling probably has the effect of doubling the size of the room and every little sound seems to reverberate. Steven is at the far end of the room clearing away the cups and he drops something, shattering the silence. "Sorry guys! I'll be finished shortly."

Mark gives the person next to him a pile of A4 sheets and tells him to take one and pass them on. Everyone stops fidgeting and talking, all heads bowed while we read the information on the sheet.

The mantra is short but the words seem difficult to remember. My stomach begins to feel a little queasy. This is too weird for me. I look nervously at the door. Would it be such a long walk if I made a plausible excuse and left quickly? It's probably fifty paces. I continue reading.

The Mantra:

> *Aum*
> *Bhuh Bhuvah Svah*
> *Tat Savitur Varenyam*
> *Bhargo Devasya Dheemahi*
> *Dhiyo Yo nah Prachodayat*

Santhi (repeat three times = peace to your mind, body and soul)

The Purpose:

The Gayatri mantra is one of the oldest and most powerful of Sanskrit mantras. It is believed that by chanting the Gayatri mantra and firmly establishing it in the mind, if you carry on your life and do the work that is ordained for you, your life will be full of happiness. Gayatri is a treasure you must guard throughout your lives and the mantra unifies the mind, body and soul.

There are three deities - Gayatri, Saraswathi and Savitri. The first one is master of the sense, the second is master of speech and the third one is the teacher of truth. It is, therefore, a Trinity of the senses. The words unify the mind, body and soul and ask the Divine to remove the veil of darkness and open our minds to knowledge. The Gayatri is considered to be the essence of the Vedas. Veda means knowledge and the mantra is a gift to help us all, like a third eye revealing the inner vision. It protects us from harm wherever we are and followers will recite the Gayatri mantra at least three times each day. The purpose is to try to counteract the wrong doings that happen throughout the day and the belief is that it atones for each day's actions. Chanting will light your path and those who find themselves here today are here for a reason. It is a part of your onward spiritual journey.

When you pronounce AUM:
A - emerges from the throat, originating in the region of the navel
U - rolls over the tongue
M - ends on the lips
A - waking, U - dreaming, M - sleeping

"Okay. This is simply a session to demonstrate the power of the mantra. For those of you who are already meditating, that is also going to be a part of the workshop today. We are going to try to build our voices into one and in doing so, open ourselves up to what the universe has to offer. I have several hand-outs for you to take away, but I suggest we make a start. This is something that has to be experienced rather than taught," Mark enforces his words by clenching his fist and tapping his chest, "in here."

He can obviously see a few of us are uncomfortable and there is an exchange of nervous eye contact.

"Right." Mark's voice is reassuring and no one moves. I feel glued to my seat and while my legs want to walk, I know that I won't be going anywhere. "We will practice repeating the words. I will use my voice to speak the mantra three times, on my own, so that you can all hear the tone and intonation. If you haven't done this before you might feel a little uncomfortable at first. The acoustics in the hall will amplify the sound, but that's the whole point of using this venue. If you are happy to trust me, people, then I'll begin."

He closes his eyes, adjusting his body position. Both feet are firmly on the floor, his posture is relaxed. His arms lie loosely on his lap, palms facing upwards with the thumb and little finger on each hand touching. All eyes are on him as he visibly relaxes his shoulders and takes three deep breaths. The sound of 'aum' is startling. It shatters the silence and he draws out the syllables, increasing the volume and sending a resonating echo around the hall. It is, quite simply, beautiful. There isn't any other way of describing it. Each delivery of the mantra is slow and purposeful, his voice gaining strength with each repetition. He ends with the word 'santhi,' saying it three times in succession. He remains still with his eyes closed for a few minutes and then opens them, smiling.

"Easy," he states. It's probably one of the strangest things many here will ever witness and yet Mark manages to make it feel quite natural. "Now we'll all repeat the same process together."

He explains everything in detail before we start. The importance of our posture, feeling relaxed and closing our eyes so we are not distracted. He tells us we will very quickly forget our own voices and the sound will come from within. The first run through is awkward, I find myself trying to suppress nervous laughter. Some of the group are struggling to find the right key and it sounds a little flat. It's rather uncoordinated at first, but by the end of the third repetition it begins to flow more easily. Most of us have to keep our eyes open and glued to the printed words, but Mark explains that as we gather pace we'll be able to repeat it from memory.

We are going to do thirty repetitions and then he will lead us through a meditation. We will remain sitting in our circle and be invited to share our thoughts. The process will then be repeated all over again. The first meditation will take us into a forest; the second will be a beach scene. He asks if anyone has any questions. Only one voice breaks the silence.

"I've only recently begun meditating at home. I'm following your tutorial and with each meditation something different happens. It's very personal and I'm nervous about sharing. I don't want people to think I'm being negative. I also don't want to spoil it for everyone else." The woman speaking is middle-aged; she's smartly dressed and conservative. Out of all of the people in the group, she's the one I least expected to express her feelings. She has a guarded look about her. Then I wonder if that's a haunted look. I guess we are all seeking something and there is a reason why each of us is here today.

"Celia, only share your feelings if you are comfortable to do so. Some people have no-one else with whom they can meaningfully talk through what happens here. The Gayatri mantra is powerful and often the meditations that follow are quite intense. The process will allow you to relax in a way that you might not have been able to achieve so far. No one need feel uncomfortable, but if you are moved to share an experience you can do so knowing you are amongst like-minded friends. I think we are ready to begin."

As I hurry out into the warm sunshine, the light breeze is cool on my face. I feel at peace. A dull ache begins at the back of my head, causing me to wince with the movement of each step I take. The intensity of the experience has left me feeling curiously invigorated, yet drained. I lean forward to open the latch on the gate, when I hear a voice behind me.

"Ceri, Ceri—wait a second," Mark runs towards me.

"Sorry, I'm running late," I say, feeling bad that I left the moment the session ended.

"You felt it, didn't you?" He looks at me expectantly.

"What?"

"That sense of being at one with the universe. Your journey has begun Ceri, everything happens for a reason. There's no turning back now, it's an awakening that few experience." He reaches out and squeezes my shoulder. He emanates a sense of achievement and positivity that is infectious.

"Yes," I admit, "I felt it."

"Then we'll meet again," his eyes lock with mine for a brief moment and I smile in acknowledgement.

He was right; the experience had touched a part of me that was buried away, deep inside. Like a key turning in a lock and suddenly revealing something unexpected. There was no sense of recognition or familiarity, and no link to the physical me. I soared above my body, carried on the vibration that filled the room, as if it truly were a pathway opening up. It took me back to where that hidden part of me longed to be. I had come home spiritually.

I make my way slowly back to the car. That last meditation is still with me. A hand took mine, leading me on along a path from the beach, up a steep incline that levelled out into a meadow. Someone lifted me in their arms, twirling me around in a pleasant and joyful way. Suddenly I could see everything with a clarity that didn't exist before. I can't explain what I saw. It was more a series of moments flashing by, but it was the range of emotions that accompanied the experience that stays with me—happiness, love, compassion. I'm not sure what happened today, but what began as a faltering group of voices, to my astonishment ended up being one voice in unison. I was a part of something positive that went out to the universe. A sense of fulfilment flooded back through me when a connection was made. For a short time I was no longer the Ceri I knew, but the one I wasn't meant to see.

CHAPTER SIXTEEN

Reconnecting

The knock on the door is insistent, urgent even. I turn off the TV and my heart starts to beat faster. Then I hear Alex's voice and the banging turns into frantic hammering. I'm not afraid, but I'm fearful of what he's going to say. The door swings open and he stands there, running his hand through his hair.

"Thank you. Thank you for opening the door and I'm sorry for nearly bashing it down. Can I come in?"

I stand back. Seeing him is a shock and my heart performs a somersault. He looks tired and his hair needs cutting, which is unusual for Alex. Normally his appearance is perfect.

"Are you in trouble?" I ask and my voice is hesitant. "Come in. Do you need a drink? Coffee or something stronger?"

"Do you have any whiskey?"

"I'll see what I can find." I walk into the kitchen and find a bottle of Southern Comfort. I set up two glasses with ice and pour a slug into each. I turn, surprised to find Alex is standing very close behind me. Close enough for my hair to touch his face with the movement.

"Cheers," I hold a glass up to him and then we toast in silence.

I'm still in shock that it's him and he's really here. A part of me doubted I would ever see him again. I'm not expecting a string of apologetic words to tumble out of his mouth, but I'm worried he's agitated because he's angry with me for running away. Has he come to vent that anger? I suppose he would be justified, but what would be the point?

We walk into the living room and I sit down, expecting him to do the same, but he remains standing. He begins pacing back and forward in front of me, then knocks back his drink in three large gulps. The ice hasn't even had a chance to melt. I offer him mine and he takes it, gladly.

"Alex, you need to sit down and try to calm yourself. I'm going back into the kitchen to make some strong coffee. I'll be gone just a couple of minutes. Okay?"

He nods and as I stand up, he sits down.

It takes ten minutes of awkward silence before he settles. The coffee seems to work and the caffeine kicks in, relaxing him.

"I'm sorry Ceri. I don't mean to scare you, really. This isn't about what happened between us, this is something else. Well, no actually, it's probably all linked but I can't talk about what went on right now. I'll only say that it wasn't what you thought it was and I can only hope you'll accept that for the moment and listen to what I have to say.

"I don't care how this looks and I can't listen to—or argue—with you. This is too important. There's someone you have to meet. Don't do it for me, do it for you. He can help you make some sense of everything that has happened and that will happen in the future. It will blow your mind, but you have to hear it first-hand. You would never believe me if I simply repeated it to you. Grab your coat now, because I'm not prepared to take 'no' for an answer."

I'm beginning to wish that I downed the alcohol and wonder whether Alex is having some sort of mental breakdown. He is calmer now, but he's very anxious and he's watching me, no doubt wondering if I'll simply throw him out.

"Look Alex, can this wait? I'm not sure I feel comfortable—"

"Ceri, I've never asked you to do anything for me in the two-plus years we've known each other. I don't ask for favours. I'm asking for one now."

"Okay, I'll grab my coat."

***

"Ceri, this is Ethan Morris. He's a... umm, medium and he advises people on spiritual stuff, amongst other things. Sorry Ethan, it's a lot to remember," Alex looks embarrassed as Ethan steps forward to shake hands.

"Hi Ethan, nice to meet you." His hand is warm, his handshake firm.

"He writes books too, forgot to say that," Alex adds.

"I know, I've read one of them," I admit.

"And what did you think?" Ethan asks, pointedly.

"Do you want the truth?"

Alex looks nervously between the two of us.

Ethan smiles and steers us towards the sofas in the corner. "Of course, listening to feedback from readers is invaluable."

Alex flashes me a look. I think he wants me to take it easy on Ethan.

"Well, controversial is the word I would use. There were some rather unexpected statements. I think I can remember turning down the corner of a few pages."

"And that's a bad thing?" His eyebrows arch and I wonder if I should just gloss over this. It was a few years ago when I read *The Ultimate Journey*.

"No, it simply means there were things I didn't understand. But that often happens. Some books I haven't even been able to finish."

"Why was that?" He seems genuinely interested. "Please, take a seat."

"Thank you. Well, I'm not impressed by over-use of jargon for one thing or books that spend more time talking about ethics or religion. I suppose I'm searching for real answers that are explained in layman's terms."

"That's a very valid point. Has it ever occurred to you that some things are not meant to be understood by the masses, only by those who are ready? That if we knew everything about the universe and the ethereal planes, then the whole purpose of this existence would be negated?"

"Ah, a bit like God visiting the earth and then non-believers would suddenly have the proof they are looking for to allow them to believe."

He laughs. "Exactly! The whole point of religion is that the belief comes first, the proof comes later." There's a twinkle in his eye and even though I've seen his author photo, which is on the back of his books, he's younger than I first thought. He looks academic, studious, whereas I would have expected a smartly dressed, slick talker. I may have watched too many psychic programmes on TV I suppose.

"Ceri, do you mind if Ethan explains why I've brought you here?"

Alex reaches out and touches my arm. He's anxious, and a wave of guilt washes over me. I was wrong to take advantage of his friendship and burden him with the other half of my life; what did I expect?

I nod in agreement.

"Alex initially came to me seeking answers to a long list of questions he had. I have to start by saying that we aren't talking about something that is black and white here. There are many different theories and you've already found out that my own views are perhaps a little different to the mainstream. I'm excluding those who are writing on a totally different page, of course, and whose beliefs do not come from the heart." He pauses and looks briefly at Alex for approval, before continuing. Alex says nothing.

"Alex fears that you will not believe the explanation he has to give you for what has happened. Ceri, have you ever wondered why many of the genuine 'do-gooders' in life are often described as selfless? They don't have relationships, are often distant from their families, some are orphans. And yet they usually have charismatic personalities that allow strangers to draw close to them and accept the help they offer. How odd then, that their kind acts and generous nature should be rewarded with what could be perceived to be strangely solitary personal lives. It doesn't make sense. It conflicts with the very nature of karma and reaping what you sow. The reward is the happiness they bring to other people, but we generally accept that is merely one aspect of what is necessary to enjoy a fulfilled life here on earth.

"Have you ever stopped to consider that maybe you and your twin brother Seb are different because you weren't created in the same way? When the two eggs fertilised, one was chosen to carry your energy. You were created with a special gift, but Seb's creation was more in line with the mix of genes inherited from your parents."

"That's crazy! You can't expect me to believe it was some sort of divine intervention."

"It's not that simple Ceri. But the fact is, your energy—which I believe is a higher energy and more evolved—was thrown into the mix. From what Alex has told me I truly believe that you are here to correct the anomalies that happen on this earthly plane: things that would upset the general order of existence. Accidents happen, often due to the fact that people have free choice and don't always stay on the path that fate lays out for them, for all sorts of reasons. There is a little flexibility, of course, no path is meant to be straight. But to keep divine order, sometimes small corrections are required."

He sits back, reaches for a jug of water on the side table next to him and offers a glass to Alex and myself. We both nod.

"But the things that happen to me are mostly small things, insignificant really. Maybe one or two more serious ones, but hardly worthy of thinking of it as divine intervention! Maybe Alex made it sound more important than it is."

Alex downs his water in one. He looks dazed. I take a few sips and put the glass down. "Compared to mediumship for instance, my little episodes are nothing."

"Alex's dreams began when he first met you. It was no coincidence Ceri. Alex is a part of your destiny. I genuinely believe that he is here to help you and that's why the two of you met. There is a life mapped out for each of you, but not as a couple, and the dreams simply remind him of that. But first your paths have to cross until the purpose is played out and it is time to move on."

"Alex, do you believe this?"

"Ceri, when I told you that I was in love with someone and that they had broken my heart, that someone was you. In my dreams I receive warnings, the implication is that I'm hurting you by putting my emotions before my duty to keep you safe."

Alex's words astound me even more than Ethan's. This is Alex, marketing executive and ad-copy genius. Not a guy with superhuman powers, emerging like Superman to sort out my problems when I'm in too deep.

"I think we need a reality check," I say, letting out a huge breath.

"Ceri, you know my theory about dreams and I'm not alone in my thinking. It's all in the book. When we fall into deep sleep our energy revisits another plane to continue the work we do there. Our consciousness is not allowed the memory of what happens on those visits unless we are either highly evolved already, or a memory is left for a reason. Alex has been allowed to remember parts of his astral travels to correct the path he's on. It has been made very clear to him.

"You don't see angels, Ceri, you *are* an angel. Most angels never visit this plane. In the normal course of events there is no need for them to experience life itself. Alex is simply a spirit helper who is here to guide you and keep you safe during a difficult time when your abilities really begin to develop. Then he will move on to fulfil his own destiny. He's broken one of the cardinal rules. You were not meant to fall in love with each other."

CHAPTER SEVENTEEN

Fear

"I won't believe it. I can't believe it." I'm stunned by what I've heard. Alex holds my hand gently on the walk back to my apartment. I pull a tissue out of my pocket and wipe my nose.

"I love you, Alex, and I won't accept that someone 'up there' won't allow us to be together. It's crazy. Ethan's theory is just that—his personal interpretation. I can find another book, ten books, all of which will say something slightly different. You can't walk away from me if you really do love me."

Alex squeezes my hand.

"A part of me wants to believe that Ceri, but you need to understand something. As much as the things you've witnessed and been involved in are real, the memories I have after I dream or travel, or whatever, are real to me too. Have you any idea how scared I've been? Similar to a premonition, and I know you understand what that's like. If I stay with you, then you will fail because I will be your distraction. Think about it. Ignore the angel bit, just concentrate on what you know to be true. I'm convinced some of your actions have saved people's lives. If you knowingly try to change the course of your path who knows what might happen?

What if one of the people you are meant to save in the future is Seb, or Sheena? How would you feel knowing that you chose your own happiness over the chance to give them a future?"

"I'm not a saint Alex. I want to love someone and I want to be loved in return. I can't help the fact that I fell in love with you. It just happened, so who's to say it's wrong?"

Alex stops and pulls me close, nestling his face into my hair.

"I don't know, Ceri, I don't know. Ethan seemed to be able to explain everything and it fitted. In some ways it was a comfort to know what the dreams meant, because for a while there I thought I might be losing it. I don't want it to be true."

"What if he's totally wrong? What if we were meant to find each other and work as a team? Maybe together we will be stronger. If we live our lives in a way that's positive and help other people whenever it's clear we have something to give, then surely that's good karma? The universe sends back to you what you give out. We'll only send out positive thoughts and actions. Please Alex, if this wasn't a good idea, I'd feel that wouldn't I? My sensitivity would be screaming at me loud and clear. I'm right and Ethan's wrong. He's the one reading from the wrong page."

"Okay, I'm so out of my depth on this there is nothing more I can say. If it weren't for my dreams, I would tell you that it feels very right to me. The moment I met you I knew, but something told me not to rush things. At least that part turned out okay. What happened, happened when the time was right for both of us, so perhaps what you say has some truth to it. Maybe we can make this work." He rubs his hands nervously on his jeans. His mind is trying to make sense of our situation.

"I'm not saying I don't believe what Ethan was saying, but what if we can take control of our own destiny? Maybe we have a real chance to move forward together. The saying goes 'Life is what you make it,' and I always believed that."

"Ethan made me stop and think, Ceri. I don't want to put you in any danger; I love you too much for that. Even if I have to walk away in order not to hurt you any more than I have already."

His kiss is gentle and warm on my lips. He wipes away a stray tear that runs down my cheek. "Don't cry Ceri, we'll get through this. The more I think about it, the more I'm beginning to see that perhaps all of this has happened for a reason. Working for Mason wasn't doing either of us a favour and suddenly I have another job. You'll find something soon too. Things are meant to go wrong because sometimes we reach the point of needing to move on."

"I feel the same way. I've found someone who will mentor me and he feels strongly that I have what it takes to become a medium. After what we've been through I'll understand if you don't think that's a good idea, but I have to feel that what I do matters. If I can help people and pass on messages from loved ones then that seems a positive move to me. I'll keep the two halves of my life separate and we'll make a normal life together, I promise. If that's what you want too."

He holds me close, I melt into him. Letting go has never been easy for me; I've never really trusted anyone. Why does it feel so right when I'm with Alex? This can't be wrong and his response is telling me that he wants this too, for both of us.

***

Something disturbs me and I stretch lazily, then immediately snuggle back down under the duvet, not wanting to wake up yet. Another five minutes I tell myself. After all, the alarm hasn't gone off yet and it's cosily dark behind my eyeshades. An arm suddenly wraps itself around my shoulder and a little thrill passes through me. Knowing Alex is lying next to me makes everything in my little world feel so perfect.

It's a lazy feeling listening to the sounds of the world waking up. A car passes by, some birds start chirping, squabbling over a perch perhaps and fly off noisily. A light breeze blows in through the open window and goose bumps run up and down my arm.

105

I pull it back beneath the cover and Alex moves closer. He's still sleepy and content to enjoy a sense of knowing that we are together and nothing can pull us apart.

One moment I'm languid and the next I'm sitting bolt upright in bed.

"Ceri, what is it?" The concern in Alex's voice is clear. He immediately struggles to throw off the listlessness of sleep.

"Something is wrong, very wrong, but I don't know what."

"Calm down," he says, his hand brushes again my hair. He tries to shush me, as you might calm a child.

"You don't understand Alex, this is different. I think we were wrong."

"What do you mean?"

"Alex, when I opened my eyes I wasn't here, I was somewhere else."

"That's crazy. You've been next to me all night long. You probably drifted back into sleep for a few seconds and it disorientated you. No big deal." He smoothes my arm and then holds my hand, squeezing it to reassure me.

"Alex, I'm scared. I think it might be possible to be in two different places at the same time. A part of me is somewhere else, even while we're talking. I don't understand what's happening…"

FORBIDDEN

CERI

PROLOGUE

The Ethereal Pathway

I'm in a tunnel. It's dark and yet little rays, like pinpricks of sunshine breaking through foliage, seep towards me from every angle. Too minute to light my path, I wonder if they are really threads drawing me along in case I lose my way. My body is cold and I feel disconnected, as if I'm no longer whole. Alex is calling my name, his voice distant. I want to find my way back to him but I'm being coaxed away, carried on a wave of light within a dark place. Am I dreaming? Will this moment pass and then I'll simply wake up next to Alex, content in the knowledge that the future stretches out ahead of us?

Fear takes control of my mind. I want to go back. I'm frightened and I don't want to be in this place. It seems I am incapable of doing anything and the fact that I don't have a choice is terrifying.

Ceri's journey continues…

CHAPTER ONE

Transition

Something instinctive tells me that I have to make some sense of this quickly. The memory I have of the past is draining away, like sand running through a sieve into a black hole. Fragments of thoughts that are clear one moment, then hazy before my mind can play each one through to a conclusion. Is someone trying to erase my past, one memory at a time? Why have I been pulled into this vortex where time doesn't seem to be relative to anything?

I try to concentrate. What's the last thing I can remember? The sunshine was streaming in through the window and I turned over to find Alex lying next to me. My world felt complete and I was happier than I had been in a long while. I knew beyond a shadow of a doubt that Alex would love me forever, no matter what the future held. Someone told me I was an angel, but I can only recall the voice and not the face of the person speaking to me. Was it Alex? There was a warning… yes! The voice told me that Alex and I were not destined to be together and we had broken one of the cardinal rules: angels don't fall in love with their spirit helpers.

I feel as if I'm being pulled in two directions at the same time. Which way should I turn? I realise that I'm no longer attached to my earthly shell. The next part of my journey has begun.

My heart cries out for Alex, for his love. I won't let go, I won't let go…

CHAPTER TWO

The Healing

As my confusion lifts it's like peeling back layers of old paint. Each layer reveals something new and the deeper I delve, the closer I'm getting to the truth. I never believed Ethan Morris's words when he put forward his theory that I was an angel. Wouldn't I *know* if that were the case? Now I'm here – wherever it is – I'm not so sure, because this is such a weird experience. Have I died? Or maybe I'm in a coma. All I know for sure is I've never experienced anything like this before.

There is a strange feeling of familiarity I can't explain, though, a sense of knowing this place. I'm no longer scared, merely waiting for what comes next. I don't think this is the first time I've been in this situation. Have I come home to the place where I truly belong?

It isn't an unpleasant feeling, this sense of disconnection. It's rather restful. Time and space don't seem relevant anymore but I feel protected, as if someone is watching over me and guiding me along. Maybe I've been in an accident and I'm unconscious. That might be the reason why I can't feel anything in relation to my body. I try to reach out with my thoughts, hoping someone is listening and will engage with me. I can't seem to…

It hits me as hard as running into a brick wall. My head is suddenly full of a million thoughts. Memories whizz through my mind so fast and yet each one is familiar and meaningful.

Ethan was right.

I want to cry out in anguish as Alex's face appears before me. I find myself trying to reach out into the darkness, then realise none of this is physical. I'm in a void where there is nothing except my thoughts and memories. This is where our spirit returns when we are in transition: that place of nothingness where we rest.

All mental blocks are lifted. I remember that as an angel sent to administer on the earth plane, my vibration is restricted for a reason. All knowledge falls away and only a sense of knowing allows me to fulfil my allotted tasks. I remember little on my return here each night, when my earthly energy is in deep sleep, because that is the rule. My place and purpose in the universe is all-consuming. I now understand that a small part of me is bound to the earth until that part of my destiny is played out. It is only here that I can see the true nature of everything.

Then there is a presence. It's one I know and love dearly: someone who has been with me since my earliest memory. Each energy has its own unique identity, like an aura, but crossing the divide between the planes changes things. Here, everything is constant and our minds link with ease.

"You have a purity that means you are special. Few angels are chosen to touch the earth and carry out their work on that plane. We trust in you to rise above the burdens that weigh down souls in their mortal life. We know there are no guarantees and so many things can go wrong. All you can do is to be receptive and hold on to the knowledge that you are different."

"But what if I fail?" I ask, fearful of the unknown. Of all of the tasks I have been given, this seems the hardest. I'd heard so many tales about the coldness of human life, of the hardship and stark reality… which I now understood with heart-breaking consequences. I knew there was beauty too, of course, even before

I set foot there. Few angels ever talked about an earthly life, our vibration being on a different level to those energies who work tirelessly there.

There is so much more to the state of being than touching earth, no matter how many times some souls make the journey. Here, we gravitate towards like-minded energies. The level at which we work is irrelevant as there is no status, only purpose. I've enjoyed so many sectors of being: the nearer I draw to the core, the more I become a part of the whole and a little more of 'me' is lost. I wonder if I am destined for the highest honour, whether I am a splinter of the Source.

Of course, no one knows for sure that splinters really exist. Wider knowledge can only be given when it's appropriate. I believe that splinters will only gain that understanding when there is a call-back: a time when the Source of all being chooses to reunite all of the elements to its core. That would effect a critical change upon the universe, which I'm led to believe has only happened a few times. The Source of us all is benevolent.

On some planes, like earth, the decision was made that energy has to learn from making bad choices as well as good. Core change ripples outwards and whilst it will bring great joy to some, to others it will bring misery. Humans have affected the planet around which their lives revolve and there are serious consequences. It has upset the balance of things and it seems to be a pattern that is repeated, like a never ending circle. The only way to ensure earth continues is for change to be implemented at the highest level, to help redress the imbalance.

The next core change will be to bring back something that has been lost: closeness to the inner-self and the intuitive nature within all humans. On the ethereal plane we have all sensed this with growing concern. I feel I am destined to be a part of implementing that wider change. How exactly, I have no idea. There are times when I know things I can't possibly have learnt, things that come naturally to me.

I struggle to recall my memories, but transitioning back to my higher level energy now is draining and I have to be patient. It's a time of healing and when I'm recovered all will be revealed to me. A human's face appears in my consciousness for one brief moment and I feel a sharp stab of pain.

Do I know this man?

***

Healing is a time of rest, a time to wander with no agenda and I'm not totally comfortable with the sense of freedom and disconnection. It's often interesting, of course, merely watching other energies and souls as they go about their work. It too can be a beneficial part of the learning process, but I worry as there is still so much work to be done.

On my vibration level there are many I do not know and it's always a blessing to find myself travelling through space filled with new and interesting energies. There is so much to learn! But the best experience of all is when I'm with my own group. Energies that have been around me since time began. Souls with whom I will ways be linked forever, because in essence we are the same: we are family. Where our future journey will take us, I do not know, only that we will be together. Are we splinters? Will our energy levels become fulfilled to the point where we will have the power to change things? A time when the supreme energy, the centre of the cosmos, will call upon us to help renew the force that holds all the ethereal and life planes together? Are we perpetuity? I seriously doubt that splinters can simply acquire the knowledge. Some of it has to be learnt and developed, because that's how it works. The group might then come together to harness that power under direction. The idea both excites and frightens me.

Then I remember that I have now touched earth, a part of me is still there and the fact that I'm back in transition means something has gone wrong. I wish I could remember and can only assume that after my time in healing it will become clear.

I only know that I'm experiencing something new. I've never had a sensation quite like this, as if a part of me is missing. How can that be? Our essence and energy is one complete mass. Before my trip I didn't know any different, but now I have this sensation of having left something behind. How strange, or is that how it's supposed to be? I'm being impatient and I try to let the healing do its work. How I've missed the tranquillity of the universe; there is an incredibly harsh edge to life on the earth plane that grates on the soul. Such conflict—beauty and horror; happiness and sadness; love and hate. I wonder how the working energies cope with their many visits, and whether each of their mortal lives is different. With every mission being to help a soul on their life path, do they too return and feel a little part of their own energy has been left behind?

Healing claims me and I revel in the purity of feeling renewed. It blocks out everything else and a sense of peace begins to gather around me.

CHAPTER THREE

Trust

"Ceri?"

A voice floats into my mind, bringing me back into consciousness.

"You are still in transition. The part of you that remains on earth will restrict your consciousness. Your energy is split and will remain so until you are recalled permanently. I will always be with you, until you are fully back with us. The human element sometimes hampers our communication, but I'm by your side every step of the way."

I fleetingly remember the sensation of this presence, the energy who guides me. It is a feeling of wisdom and I have a desire to please him, to excel simply in order to bask in his approval.

"Have I done something wrong? It seems that way. I thought I'd forgotten, but now I remember. Is it to do with Alex?"

"Yes. We did not take the decision to let you touch the earth plane lightly. You are one of the splinters, and it is necessary for your development. You need to experience the emotions of the human plane if, when your time comes, your energy is going to be a part of renewing the force that controls everything. It isn't easy and things do go wrong. However, we are confused. Alex is the soul we have chosen to help you move onto the next part of your work on earth. You are destined to channel messages. It is your role to help many on their earthly path towards an understanding of the true nature of spirituality. Without the comfort of those personal messages from their kindred energies here, they will be hampered. Human life is a constant struggle for all believers and this is a vital element linking the two planes."

"I see. He was helping me, I think. I remember wavering, unsure what to believe. Is that normal for an angel's earth life?"

"There is no norm, few angels visit earth. It isn't necessary for their work. In your case, your experience will be enough to inform the kindred group when the time comes. There is only a need to feel those emotions that are peculiar to the earth plane and pass on that experience for understanding. That's the whole point of human life: extremes. Love here is pure, as are our energies, but to truly understand the whole of creation it is necessary to experience how life develops. Every single thing that happens on the earth plane is very real to the beings experiencing it, although there is no lasting relevance as such. It is simply about learning. Alex is a lesser energy, very young, and a part of his fate is to provide sympathy and comfort while you adjust to your next step on earth. He is merely a spirit helper and will go on to complete his own destiny to allow his energy to grow. You cannot be together Ceri. He never will be on your vibration level. He is not a splinter."

I feel elated, saddened, and chastised all at the same time. I want to make amends and prove that this was merely an aberration, a period of adjustment when I didn't know what I was supposed to be doing. Will I be forgiven?

"There is no need for forgiveness, Ceri," his words fill my head. "Simply follow the path laid out."

"What happens now?" I feel uncomfortable, unable to under-stand exactly how this works. A part of me wonders whether it will be as easy as following a path.

"Instead of only returning here when your earthly shell is in a resting state, we'll adjust the amount of your energy that stays on the earth plane. You will continue to carry out your duties here permanently, but simply be less productive. A part of you will continue to see out your earthly experience until that is due to come to an end."

"When will that be?"

"Another fifty-two earth years."

"How will this affect my earthly person? If I'm not there in full strength, will I still be able to fulfil what is required of me? Won't that hamper my ability to channel messages?" The concern I feel is unsettling.

"No, it will not lessen your psychic ability, as they refer to it on earth. But as you go about your work you will have an awareness of your ethereal existence. We regard this as a situation that isn't ideal. You might be tempted to share things that are not meant to be known earth-side. The two planes are very different. Human life is a training ground. No more, no less. But it is necessary and it has a purpose. So we're asking that you consider everything you do there from this point on with the benefit of your wider knowledge. Some of that will simply not make sense down there, Ceri, if you share it with a human." Hearing him use my earthly name is strange. It's out of place here.

"I'm not sure I'm strong enough..."

"No one can be sure of anything, until they try. We have ways of limiting damage, but this too is a part of your development. If you change things, then you will have to deal with the consequences. It's time for you to go back now."

As the voice floats out of my mind I remember Alex. Why didn't I ask the question?

How long will Alex be in my life and when will I have to let him go?

CHAPTER FOUR

Eyes Wide Open

"Hey, morning sleepy head." Alex adjusts the duvet, snuggling it around me as I bring myself back. I do a double-take as his head seems to shimmer, his aura clearly visible to me now with my heightened awareness. There is a sense of purity around him and I can't believe I couldn't see that before. How did I not recognise he was a helper, a young energy in training?

"Good," I try to sound calm.

Alex moves around the bedroom tidying things away before heading out the door. The energy radiating from his body resembles electric sparks.

"I'll make some coffee," he says over his shoulder as he disappears.

I pull myself up into a sitting position and slump back against the pillows. Oh my God! I really am still here, only it feels different.

The voice comes into my head. "Don't worry, you are adjusting and things will settle down. Give it time."

The silence in my head leaves a void which is quickly replaced by a stream of questions I can't seem to stem. How long will it take? Will Alex notice a difference in me? What should I say to him? I realise I'm in danger of hyperventilating, my hands grabbing onto the duvet and making two fists, the tension radiating up my arms. I lie back, taking a few slow, deep breaths. I close my eyes. Outside I can hear the birds and the faint sound of traffic. Is this the same morning that I was called back to transition, or has time passed here on earth? How will I explain what has happened to Alex?

Suddenly I feel as if someone has placed an arm around my shoulders and there is a sensation of great warmth. I wonder if it's going to lift me physically from the bed, it's so intense, but the moment passes. I'm not alone and understanding that helps a little.

Alex returns, humming a tune under his breath. The moment he walks back into the room, two steaming mugs of coffee in his hands, his face breaks out into a radiant smile.

"The first day of the rest of our lives." He sounds so happy, and I realise that to him there has been no disruption. I send a prayer of thanks out into the ether to my mentor. I need all the help I can get.

I take the coffee mug from him and return his smile. I try my best to match his air of unfettered optimism. "You sound cheerful."

His fingers brush against mine as he releases the mug. He lingers a moment before drawing away.

"I feel like celebrating," he muses, as if his mind is churning and he hasn't yet had time to process what's happening. He sounds like a kid, really excited and it's a big deal—he's about to open his Christmas presents or something. There's a liveliness about him and he can't seem to sit still. He walks to the window and looks out into the street.

"I wish I didn't have to go to work today," he mutters, more to himself than to me. "You know, I think last night was the first time I didn't have a bad dream. About us, I mean."

I'm fascinated by the glow that emanates around his upper body, pulsating gently, softening his outline. The clarity is breathtaking: Alex might not be an angel, but he's an energy that exudes healing and positivity. I long to get up and throw my arms around him, but I'm not sure my legs would carry me that few feet between the bed and the window. Even lying here, propped up against the pillows, I feel shaky and unsteady. I sip my coffee, hoping the caffeine will do the trick and begin to ground my thoughts.

"You stirred earlier and began talking to me, but you were still dreaming," he turns to face me, a little furrow on his brow. "Can you remember your dream? You thought something was wrong. I shushed you and you fell back to sleep. You aren't having dreams about us, are you?" he asks, tentatively, trying to hide his concern.

"No, I don't think so. I'm fine now, although I think I might be coming down with a sore throat," I offer, wanting...no, *needing* to reassure him and stop him dwelling on what happened.

"Good. You would tell me if you thought something was wrong, wouldn't you? You don't regret our decision to be together?"

His words are like a bolt of lightning. Now that I am consciously aware of the position we're in, and with an insight into both existences, how can I answer that question?

"Of course not." Fortunately my tone is even. I take a large gulp of my coffee to give me a few moments more to adjust.

Alex saunters over to sit down next to me on the bed.

"I want to explain." His eyes search my face, lovingly, like a gentle kiss. "I only sought out Ethan Morris because I was worried about what my dreams seemed to be telling me. After you asked me to leave I realised that I hadn't meant any of the words I had thrown at you. I was panicking because I couldn't figure out why loving you felt so wrong, so selfish. As if I wasn't putting your interests first, only thinking about what I wanted. When you disappeared I was frantic. All I could think about was whether you were safe and it hurt knowing that my outburst was a knee-jerk reaction to my fear. I know this must all sound a bit weird, Ceri, but I've loved you for so long. Since the first day we began working together. It was a long two years, being next to you five days a week and carrying this burden, this feeling that I must not let you know how madly in love I am with you. You kept it professional and I took that to mean you didn't feel the same way in return. I now understand that it's hard for you to show anyone the side of you that is different. It's a gift that makes living your life very hard at times. When you opened up to me and we ended up in bed, I was so happy and so scared. I'm sorry Ceri, you were right, we make our own future. You have a gift and maybe that was freaking me out a little. Ethan believes what he preaches, but who's to know how it all works? After all, we have free will—it says so in the Bible."

His words take me by surprise. I realise that when I ran away it must have been a real shock to Alex. I didn't want to believe what he'd told me about Ethan's theory either, but all of his concerns seem to have disappeared overnight. Has something changed in Alex that I can't see? His level of vibration is much lower than an angel's and he's not supposed to have conscious knowledge. Maybe his instinctive sensitivity is constantly picking up on what his subconscious is trying to tell him.

How can this work between us, with so much that can't be said or discussed? How far am I allowed to go before there is a consequence? As my mentor warned, I will then have to handle any changes that occur as a result of my actions. I've been talking Alex into believing that we can be together and make a future where we can become more than the sum total of two individuals. Am I now the one backing away? Does Alex sense that this morning? In fairness to us both, I need to think this through a little before I say anymore. I wonder, fleetingly, if the tables have turned. Am I in danger of altering Alex's future, robbing him of his true destiny in this life if I don't let him go? I wonder why we feel such a strong bond, which on one level feels so right yet on another so wrong.

"What? What are you thinking? Don't hide your feelings from me Ceri, that's all I ask. I'm sorry I panicked, that's all it was. You are right. Ethan's theory is only a theory."

"Let's take each day as it comes. Try not to worry too much about tomorrow for the moment. I'm feeling a little off-colour today…"

"Hey angel," I love the sense of warmth in his voice as he

says that word, "you *are* my angel, Ceri, beyond any shadow of a doubt. We've been through a lot and now it's our turn to grab some happiness. The thought of losing you completely scared me, even though it was due to my own stupidity." He places his hand on my cheek, his eyes gazing into mine as if he's searching for something. "Look, I'm going to be late if I don't leave for work. We'll talk about what happened when I get home tonight. Please try to have a relaxing day, you look really tired. I'll pick up something for that sore throat. See you later." He stoops to kiss me, lingering a moment to look at me before pulling away. "I never dared to dream this day would come. You'll still be here when I get back this evening, won't you?"

It's an attempt at humour that has a hollow ring to it: he's scared I'll change my mind.

"Of course, now go! You can't be late for work and I mustn't laze around all day. I need to start job hunting. I'll be here, promise!"

He turns to face me with the biggest smile on his face and a little thrill courses through my body. As I watch him walk away, I notice that what I always thought of as a sashay was really almost a dancer's glide. I believed Alex wasn't interested in women in general, but I'm beginning to see that it was his inherent sensitivity that helped reinforce my opinion. He's tall, slim and lean, his body isn't overly-developed but it's well defined. The way he walks lends an air of femininity and, because his face is so perfect, there's a sense of him not being quite real. Oh, listen to me! I can see inside him and I know the goodness and selflessness within his core, it's just unusual for the outside to match the inside. Before my trip back to the ethereal world, if anyone had asked me what a reincarnated angel looks like, I would have given Alex as an example. Thinking about myself, I feel I probably present as someone who is rather nervous and often prefers their own company.

A loud "Huh," escapes my lips. No one in their right mind would guess I was the angel. What I'm wondering is, how long would Alex have continued to live the life of a monk, hung up because he was in love with me but too scared by his dreams to say anything? His love has a depth that is way above his vibration level. It's an emotion that I invoke within him and I know beyond a shadow of a doubt that it exists within me too.

CHAPTER FIVE

A Friend In Need

I spend the morning phoning a few contacts, getting the word out that I'm looking for a job. Fortunately I know a lot of people in the business and losing my job with Portingale & Hughes Advertising isn't quite the disaster I thought it would be. No one asks why I left, and I draw the conclusion that most people in the business have heard about Mason Portingale's reputation. It's well known that he isn't an easy man to work for, although I wonder too if people sense he can be an outright bully at times.

Sheena arrived back in the UK yesterday and sent me a text suggesting we meet up. I'm longing to see her, but also worried that she'll notice a change in me. She knows me better than anyone else, aside from my brother Seb, and this is a big test. Seb is still travelling; it's his way of coming to terms with the sudden death of Anna on their wedding day. My instincts tell me he will eventually return, but not until he has worked through his grief in the only way that makes sense to him. He's flitting about from country to country, his adrenalin junkie days firmly behind him now. Instead he's using that energy to help people in need, as a volunteer. He's in Cambodia at the moment, helping to build a new water course. His emails are merely a line or two, he doesn't share much information and I know he's simply letting me know he's safe.

Not having him around makes Sheena's presence even more important. She's my family when Seb isn't here. I only wish my parents could live with the fact that I'm so very different to Seb. He was the easy child and I was the black sheep. I doubt that will ever change.

We meet up at Starbucks and I'm running late, so Sheena is already in the queue when I arrive. We grab our lattes and manage to find a small corner table.

"What's up?" She eyes me suspiciously, probably assuming I've had one of my psychic episodes.

"There's been a development." I feel a little awkward, not knowing where to start.

"Spill the beans." She slips off her coat and leans across to give me a big hug. The instant we touch it's like someone freezes the frame: that one moment appears to have stalled both time and movement. The seconds tick by and yet nothing moves. I break away, feeling as if someone has knocked the wind out of me.

Then I see her.

Kelly is here, as if she hadn't died four years ago and is joining us for coffee today. Sheena is busy folding her coat and trying to find space under the table to accommodate her over-sized bag. In that split second I understand. Kelly has always been around Sheena, I just couldn't see her before. She's one of Sheena's guardian angels. I shake my head, trying to clear my thoughts as Sheena peers across the table at me.

"What's up? You look like someone just walked over your grave." Her voice snaps me back. I have to pull myself together.

"I'm coming down with something. I have a really sore throat…" the words die in my mouth as it becomes dry with anxiety. Kelly is standing a mere two feet away and appears as real as any of the other people in the café. In fact, that isn't quite right. She appears

127

more real and they are simply a paler backdrop.

"Poor you, I hope it isn't so bad that you can't tell me all your latest news." Sheena adds sugar to her coffee, totally oblivious to the fact that Kelly is with us and for the first time in four years our little trio is reunited. I want to reach out and touch Kelly, to convince myself she's real and yet I know she's only here in spirit. Presenting to me, I swear, dressed as she was the last time I saw her. That was before the leukaemia had weakened her body and begun to claim her life. Tears gather in my eyes and Sheena is now staring at me.

"Ceri, what's wrong?"

Should I tell her about Kelly? Accepting my gift is one thing; understanding that everyone has a link with the other side is another. I don't want to frighten her.

"Alex is back in my life." I'd intended to tell her anyway and I only hope she thinks the tears are because I'm emotional.

"Well, I'm not surprised exactly, although the guy really hurt you. I've never known you to run away from any situation before, but the way he talked to you was unforgiveable. Is it going to be a permanent thing?" Her concern is tangible; she's looking out for my interests and thinks Alex might hurt me again. Kelly hasn't moved: her image isn't quite so sharp now but it's comforting to know she's there, listening.

"I think so. He stayed last night. He wants me to tell him about what happened while we were apart, hoping we can move on. I convinced him he has nothing to worry about and that we can be together."

"Then what's worrying you?" Sheena looks at life in a black and white way and I'm not sure she'll understand.

"What if I'm wrong?"

"Well, you've known him for a little over two years. Considering you were so convinced he wasn't into women at all, I think that says he isn't fickle. I doubt many men would stand by nursing a broken heart and sitting alongside the one they love at work day in, day out. I'd say he has commitment, although I'm puzzled by the things he said to you when he lashed out. It struck me as a little out of character at the time."

"I don't mean I'm concerned about his motives. What about mine?"

Sheena raises her eyebrows.

"What have I missed? When you joined me in France to get away from everything you never mentioned ulterior motives. I know you, Ceri, you don't play with people. You love him. Hook, line and sinker." She shrugs, obviously puzzled.

"But what if," I look around and lower my voice, conscious too that Kelly hasn't moved, "I'm using him. He's the first guy I've found that didn't back off the moment he found out that I see spirits. Quite the reverse, he's been a tower of strength. He had a mild interest in the subject, as many do, but after I left he read a book I gave him and then met up with the author."

"Really? Well, doesn't that prove he has your best interests at heart? That's a good thing, isn't it?"

"But the guy he saw said we shouldn't be together. He's a medium and spiritual teacher; I've read most of his books. Remember I told you that Alex was holding back because he kept having this dream about me? It seemed to be warning him to keep his distance, but also encouraging him to help me. Every time he drew close to me on an emotional level, his dream showed something bad happening to me. Ethan channelled a message and he told Alex we aren't meant to be together. I'm not Alex's life-partner."

I can't be any clearer and Sheena sits back, slightly open-mouthed.

"Rubbish, we make our own destiny." She looks a little annoyed. "Okay, I accept you see the other side but come on Ceri, a dream is just a dream. If it's repetitive then surely it's a hang up he has or some old memory about something unpleasant coming back to him. I doubt an hour goes by without you being in his thoughts, so they become tangled. Goodness, I dreamt about that guy from the latest James Bond movie last night, although that could be classed as more of a fantasy I suppose." Her gaze moves around the room and I wonder if she can see or sense that Kelly is here. She's never mentioned anything and I'm pretty sure I'd be the first one Sheena would consult.

"I feel like I'm trapping him. And what if we commit and then it falls apart?"

"Welcome to the real world. I live it each day," she mutters. "Look, I've spent my entire adult life looking for Mr Right and there have been a lot of Mr Wrongs. He's a dish, Ceri, he says he loves you and you believe him. I know how you feel about him, so for goodness sake lighten up. Stop looking for reasons not to commit, you'll make me think this is really about you being scared of having a real, meaningful relationship."

We move on to talk about Sheena's time in Germany and the next project on the horizon. She's been asked to accompany a business man on a buying trip to Italy. He's in the antiques trade and he's mega rich and, allegedly—her words, very handsome and dazzling company. I asked how she could possibly know that and she said she read all about him in one of the latest celebrity gossip magazines.

"Are you sure this is a translation job and not an escort service?" I can't help myself laughing and then I notice that Kelly has disappeared. I stop mid-laugh and stare at the empty space.

"I probably shouldn't ask, but are you having one of your psychic moments?" Sheena's voice breaks into my thoughts.

"No, I just realised something about myself, that's all," I hedge. I can feel that Kelly is happy to be around Sheena to help and there is no need for any explanation of the role she's playing in her life. I send her a virtual hug, knowing that she'll feel it and appreciate our ethereal link.

"Well, stop being a drag and looking for the down side of everything. It's a trend you seem to be following more and more these days. Let Alex brighten up your life and go for it, lady!"

It hit me that the moment Sheena and I hugged, I could see with a clarity I didn't have before. Kelly has obviously always been around her. But when I'm close to Alex I can't sense anything. I can see his aura, his energy and the goodness in him, but whatever links he has to the ethereal plane are hidden from me. Is that what mortal loves does? Invoke some invisible wall through which the future can't be glimpsed?

Sheena leans forward, placing her hand over my arm.

"Take a little bit of advice, Ceri, meant in the spirit of sisterhood love. You have always felt you were unloveable, mainly because you never fitted in when you were younger either with your parents or your peers. Let go of it, don't carry that scar around with you and let it influence the rest of your life. You are a catch and Alex is an extremely lucky man. Heck, if you don't want him, throw him my way."

CHAPTER SIX

Coming Clean

"Hi, my little angel." Alex wraps his arms around me and squeezes, then kisses the top of my head. He doesn't let me go, but rocks gently back and forth on the balls of his feet. "Oh, this feels so good, coming home to my woman."

I can't help myself as I burst out laughing. He sounds like the hunter-gatherer, home from a hard day's work. He sniffs the air and I look at him quizzically.

"I love a woman who can cook for her man and yet the house smells as fresh as if she hasn't lifted a wooden spoon or boiled a pan of water. Now that's what I call skill." He smirks.

"Could be because this woman has nothing planned for dinner and hasn't even given it a thought."

He feigns a sad face and, catching my hand, spins me around. "Then I'll take you out to dinner, or would you prefer takeaway?"

His happiness is infectious, but the last thing I feel like is getting ready to go out. "Takeaway?"

He nods. "Glad you said that. It wouldn't be so easy to talk in a public place. I don't want to force you though, if you'd rather not tell me where you went and what you did when we were apart."

He follows me into the sitting room, shedding his coat, tie, and shoes as we walk. In true Alex style he gathers them up in his arms and places them neatly on one end of the sofa. He proceeds to undo the cuffs of his shirt and roll his sleeves up to just below the elbow. He flashes those sexy wrists with absolutely no understanding of the way he's making my stomach flip. He unfastens the top two buttons of his shirt and collapses in the chair opposite me.

"What a day," he groans, shifting his body to sink back into the cushions.

"Okay, you go first. How was your day?" I ask. He reaches up to massage the back of his neck with his right hand, those sexy wrists calling out to me.

"Busy. It's very different to Portingale and Hughes, that's for sure. No sleazy Mason hanging around making everyone's life unbearable. But they don't have enough staff for the amount of work coming in. I'm not sure they can afford to take on anyone else, but I was thinking, should I ask on your behalf?"

"No, I'll be fine. I've made some calls today and something will turn up." I smile at him encouragingly. It's about time I did lighten up, as Sheena put it, and show Alex there is a fun side to me too.

"I'm glad you mentioned that. How do you feel about us moving in together? We already know each other pretty well. It's not as if we've just met. I like to think that the two years we've spent working so closely together would have shown up any disgusting habits either of us might have. I'm house-trained too." He looks nervous, hesitant and stupidly boyish for a guy his age.

"I know. It's one of the things I admired about you from the start." I try not to laugh. What I'm really thinking is that it was one of the things that made me think he wasn't into women. I've never known a man who pays so much attention to his personal grooming and is even tidier than I am.

"I've been mulling it over, and stop me if I'm running before I can walk here…" He jumps up and comes over to sit at my feet, placing one arm around my legs. It's a curious gesture, intimate without being overtly sexual. Loving. "But it would take the pressure off you having to find something straight away. We could rent out one of the apartments to bring in an income. Ceri, I don't want to push you into anything you don't feel comfortable with, but I feel I've wasted two years of our relationship by holding back and I'm not prepared to do that anymore."

I lean over him, sliding my fingers through the hair at the back of his head and down to rest my hand on his shoulder. The warmth of his skin through his shirt tells me his body chemistry is working overtime. The feel of him is strong and slightly tense.

"That's a great idea. I want this as much as you do, Alex, and I'm sorry I ran away. I guess you weren't the only one who was scared. I met up with Sheena today and she told me a few home truths. It made a lot of sense. I have to let go of the past and keep my sights firmly on the future."

He turns to kneel next to me, his lips brushing mine with a gentleness that's touching. He's a man who understands there are times for passion and times for loving reassurance. We're going to take this one step at a time.

***

We talked for hours, stopping only to take delivery of the Chinese takeaway, fill our plates, and to open a bottle of California's finest White Grenache. The alcohol wasn't necessary and we drank slowly, neither of us wanting to dull our senses. I recount the story of what happened after our argument. I told Alex about dashing off to France and meeting up with Sheena, about spending time on the coast and the long walks, during which I made myself face up to a lot of things that weren't easy to think about. I told him that while he sought advice from Ethan Morris, I turned to Mark Kessler. Alex hadn't heard about him, even though he's a celebrated local and an acclaimed psychic medium. He's also a motivational speaker. He travels all over the UK and his events are always sold out. I explained that I'd followed his website blog for a while and read some of his books. I went to one of his talks and afterwards I hung around to buy one of his motivational CDs. We began chatting and I signed up for a meditation tutorial. Mark and I connected immediately and I worried that Alex might misinterpret that, but he seemed fine with it. When I explained that Mark had offered to mentor me, the only thing he said was, "If you trust him, I trust your judgement".

I had to admit there were a lot of similarities in Ethan and Mark's beliefs, but on the one occasion Alex had taken me to meet Ethan I felt a strange sense of being frowned upon. As if he was judging me and found me lacking in some way. Mark might not have quite so much experience, but he's the sort of person you can discuss something with and he will listen. He takes time to consider the point you are making and is happy to discuss anything at all. I think that was what was wrong. Ethan obviously felt he knew exactly what was what and Mark saw everything as not necessarily being written in stone.

That was then, of course, and this is now. Meeting up with Mark for my next session will tell me a lot more, now that I can see things more clearly. I am worried that it will change the way I view him, but there are so few options open to me. At the time I was hoping Mark would help me hone my skills. Now, I need him to introduce me to the psychic community so I can begin my new task. I have to do that in a way that will not make it obvious something has changed. For now it's enough that Alex simply accepts, without question, things he doesn't fully understand. It's another reason why I love him so much. People are so judgmental at times and it's a trait that can seriously undermine a person's confidence. No wonder so many people are now opening their eyes and thinking less about the material things in life and more about the spiritual aspect. There's a global sense of change. You can almost hear the cry gathering momentum…

There has to be more to life than this.

CHAPTER SEVEN

Heaven Or Hell

As an angel I know there is no heaven or hell, there is only creation and everything that exists within it. Hell is a state of mind which exists only on this plane. It manifests itself in different ways. Lower vibrations—young souls with little experience—often flounder, trapped and unable to let go of whatever holds them back on their journey to the ethereal plane. On earth they busy themselves with causing mischief. They often do a lot of damage as they impede the work done by higher energies: those who are here trying to help people find their spiritual pathway. Unfortunately they cause serious confusion by sending out messages that have no meaning at all. In time they do move on. These are often the spirits that ghost hunters find, as few of the higher energies are disposed to help those who cannot believe without having proof.

However, I wasn't prepared for the very real sense of over-whelming happiness that I'm feeling now I'm with Alex. I was happy doing the work I did, but this is something completely different. I can't liken it to anything I have ever experienced before. We have a sense of oneness that takes my breath away. I trust Alex implicitly and when I'm with him I am a better person. Not just happier and more content, but complete and able to give more of myself to him and my ethereal life as well.

The passion is beyond giving; it's a fusion. It begins as a sensation of warmth, like basking in the sun on a glorious day, and ends with an explosion that takes me to another place. Somewhere that only Alex and I can go together. A place I've never been before, and at last I know what the word *love* really means. My previous experiences were nice, nothing more and nothing less. With Alex it has meaning, strength, and if there is a heaven then I'm in it now.

Something makes me stir and I roll away from Alex, turning onto my side. A chill hits me like a blast of icy cold air coming in through an open window on a winter's day. But I'm exhausted and my eyes are so heavy they won't stay open, no matter what my senses are telling me.

I drift into an uneasy sleep.

***

I awaken in the early hours of the morning, a cold sweat slick on my skin. I jump out of bed before I even have a chance to consider that I might disturb Alex. I hurry into the sitting room and open the laptop. The garish light from the screen blinds my sleepy eyes.

To: seb789@aol.com
Subject: Urgent
Message: Are you there? I need to speak to you. Please. Ceri xxxx

I look at the screen that confirms my message has been sent. A minute passes, then ten minutes, and my arms start to feel chilled. My phone vibrates and scuttles towards me across the desk top. As I reach for it, a tingle runs up my arm. The caller ID says *Seb*. My heart races. This is the first time I've spoken to him since Anna's death.

"Seb, are you okay?" The words come out in a rush.

"I don't know. I think I might be having some sort of nervous breakdown. I need to talk to someone I can trust, how did you know?" He sounds dispirited, isolated. Almost confused.

"I'm here and I'm listening." I can hardly keep the waver out of my voice. I want my brother to be here with me, not in some distant country that I'll never see. It's been too long. My instincts are screaming out *beware, tread carefully* and I wonder if he's been kidnapped or something. Life in Cambodia is hard, a strange mix of third world and modern life running in parallel. A few moments elapse and now I'm scared he's been involved in an accident. In his last email he briefly mentioned getting around in a tuk tuk. I Googled it and the examples that came up all looked like death-traps for the crazily busy roads. One feature I read said that traffic congestion in Phnom Penh was approaching a crisis.

"I...umm...don't know where to begin." He stops and there's a strange noise, then another, and it's clear he's sobbing. My stomach is churning and all of my senses seem to be kicking off all over the place. Whatever is behind this, I have to be careful about what I say.

"That's okay." I manage to keep my voice level and calm. "We all have moments where it's hard to find the words we need. Can I call you back? Are we in danger of getting cut off?" I'm unsure of his situation with regard to money, or whether he even has a mobile phone of his own now. I begin to panic. If we are cut off I feel a life-line is going to be severed.

"No, no. I have credit. I've been earning some money. It's good to hear your voice. I don't know why I didn't call you before." Another sob and the silent minutes pass, something deep down telling me to be patient and listen.

He lets out an anguished "Aaarghh," and I realise he's trying to pull himself together.

"Sorry, Sis, I have good days and bad ones. Today has been bad, that's when I miss you the most. I'm not angry anymore. I mean, about losing Anna. I don't understand it, but I'm no longer in denial. Shit happens, life is unfair sometimes. No point in asking why Anna or why me? Feels like I'm trying to shift the pain onto someone else's shoulders and I'm past that point now. Only I thought I was coping and now I know I'm not."

I don't jump in to answer him. Instead I wait a few seconds to see if he's going to continue. He remains silent and I soften my voice, hoping he'll feel the healing vibes I'm sending along with my words.

"I know Seb, it's so hard to bear and it doesn't make any sense. I wish you were here, you sound like you need a hug."

He makes a noise that sounds like a laugh and a sob combined. "Yeah, I thought I was coping until this morning." More silence.

"What happened? You know you can tell me anything."

Several more minutes elapse.

"I saw Anna last night."

I wait, with bated breath, wondering if he'll continue.

"She leant over me. I had just woken up. Or maybe I was still asleep. I don't know, it's not clear. How can I have seen her? She spoke to me, looked me in the eyes and said 'Don't give up', and I cried out. Then she was gone. She was real, at the time I really believed that, but then she was gone—as suddenly as she had appeared."

His words come tumbling out and I struggle to keep up with him. His emotions are all over the place, one moment reflecting desperation and the next sounding hopeful.

"You did the right thing calling me. Where are you?"

"In the commune. It's basic but we have everything we need. The new irrigation system is nearly finished."

"Okay, you need hot, sweet tea or very strong coffee. Do you have access?"

"Yes."

"Good. Are you on a mobile or land line?"

"Mobile, it's mine. My old one was stolen. This is a cheap one

139

I picked up."

"Okay, talk as you walk. Go make yourself something hot and strong."

I question Seb to keep him talking as he walks, about his surroundings and the people he shares with. His voice returns to a more normal level and I'm relieved as that frantic edge gradually subsides. I can hear him clattering about as he brews his tea. He walks back to his room and then I ask him to describe it.

"It's a box really, very small. Only a single bed, one cabinet and a small window. The walls are a dirty grey and the floor is permanently dusty. The road outside isn't made up, but compacted dirt. I have a red flower, in a glass jar. I bought it this morning," he sobs uncontrollably. I sit through the worst five minutes of my life, listening to the heart-wrenching sound. "I bought it for Anna, after last night."

I hear some gulps and assume he's drinking the tea. After a few more minutes he begins talking again.

"Ceri, when someone is dead, they are dead. Anna no longer exists and I know that. But she was here and I don't think it was a dream." It sounds more like a challenge than a statement. "Why did you email me tonight of all nights?" The tone is accusatory.

"It isn't anything I've done Seb, but I felt something was wrong and that's why I made contact. She didn't choose to visit me. Anna is worried about you and it would have taken a considerable amount of effort for her to appear, even briefly. It's too soon, her energy levels will still be depleted as the transition between planes is draining."

"How can you say that so calmly? This is in my head. All in my head!" He shouts so loudly I have to hold the phone away from my ear.

"Seb, calm down. Drink your tea. This is a blessing. You have to see it for what it is: a message that shows you how much Anna still loves you. I know you don't believe in life after death, or any of the spiritual stuff," I have to pause for a moment to wipe away my own tears, "but your denial doesn't change the fact that it does exist. You are my precious twin brother and I can't lie to you just to help you make some sense of this. I also wouldn't mislead you. Anna is obviously worried about how you are coping, so what's really going on here?"

"I nearly did it, Ceri, nearly had the guts to end it all. The tablets started sliding down too easily, then the alcohol, and it felt so right. The promise of an end to the pain was enticing. Then I drifted off and suddenly Anna was there. I thought at first it was the curtain next to the window, shimmering in the moonlight. Then I realised there is nothing up to the window and suddenly Anna was standing there. She was frowning and I shrieked so hard my throat constricted. I threw up everywhere and then I cried. I was back to square one and I'm not sure I have the courage to go through with it again..."

***

We talked for over an hour and after he disconnected I sat there for a few moments, staring at the phone. Then I sobbed. For Anna, for Seb, and for myself. What a mess this life was turning out to be. As twins, does this mean that both of our futures are destined to be blighted? Our soul mates paraded before us, only to be snatched away by death and, in my case, by the fear of ruining Alex's life?

Two hours later I received an email from Seb:

You saved me from myself Ceri. Is that what a twin with sensitivity does? Live their life half-feeling what the other feels? Because you sure know what's in my heart and in my mind. Seb xx

CHAPTER EIGHT

Earthbound

The weekly session I have booked with Mark Kessler tonight ties my stomach up in knots. It will be the first time I've seen him since I was called back.

The sense of duality I have isn't quite what I was expecting. I can see auras quite clearly now and sense the nature of the energy that lies deep within people. It isn't simply an intuitive thing, but a tangible sense of knowing. I no longer seem to have déjà vu incidents as I'd had before. What will tonight's session bring? Will I feel any differently towards Mark once I see him? This morning I asked Alex if he wanted to come along with me. He said he would have loved to come, but he's showing someone around his apartment and won't be back until late. I wondered if he purposely booked the appointment to coincide with my session to give me some space. I appreciate the thought. He doesn't want me to feel that he's watching all the time and it's his way of letting me know that he trusts me.

There's another email from Seb this morning.

She came to visit me again. I'm beginning to understand why you

142

believe what you do, but this isn't for me, Ceri. I can't accept that she's not here and yet she's around me. I did a very stupid thing and I'm sorry about that, I've put it behind me. I just can't believe in something that doesn't make any sense. Don't worry about me, I'm moving on and I'll keep myself active. No more wallowing.

Seb xx

It was a relief knowing that the worst was over. Seb was going to go through a time of change in the way he thinks and what he believes. He's on his own spiritual journey and eventually he will come home. After all this time of not knowing what would happen next, I offered up a silent prayer as I closed the email. I paused for a few moments, eyes closed and I saw a picture in my mind. I've never been to Cambodia, but suddenly I was there with him. The reality of experiencing the sights and sounds, the smells and a sense of disorganised chaos, was a shock. I came back with a jolt, wishing that Seb was here. I know it's not in his fate to permanently return to what would be, to him, a mundane life in this country. I think about his guardian angels and ask them to protect him while he seeks to find some sort of inner peace.

My phone kicks into life, disturbing my thoughts. It's Mark, and I wonder if he can sense my anxiety.

"Hi, Mark." I feel awkward, dreading that he'll know I'm not the same person and want to know the reason for the change in me.

"Ceri, sorry to interrupt, but the session I had booked before yours has been cancelled. If you are free, we could get together earlier. I'm here all afternoon."

"Yes, great. I was just about to organise my CV, so no great excitement there. I'll be with you in twenty minutes."

I run a brush through my hair, put on a smear of lipstick, and grab my coat and bag on the way out. I stop by the door and leave a note for Alex.

Gone to Mark's earlier than planned so we can eat together, see

Out in the open it's nice to fill my lungs, even if there is just a faint whiff creeping into the air from the car engines ticking over as they wait for the traffic lights to change. I walk quickly, deep in thought. What do I say to Mark? While I have knowledge now, I still don't understand the practical application of how it works on this level. Seeing the good and bad in people is one thing, understanding how to interact and use what I know is another. I'm rather embarrassed when I almost collide with a little old lady. I'm not sure whether she noticed me walking towards her, head down and mind elsewhere. Suddenly she's immediately in front of me and I let out a "sorry" as I quickly side-step to avoid bumping into her. We are both a little shaken and I reach out to take her elbow and steer her towards the low wall alongside the pavement. The moment my hand connects a bright light, similar to a streak of lightning, zips up into the air. I fall back slightly and she looks at me quizzically.

"Are you all right my dear?" Her voice is very genteel and soft.

"Yes, I'm fine, but I'm so sorry I nearly ploughed straight into you." I indicate for her to sit down and we both perch on the low wall.

"Bad day?" she asks, as if we haven't just avoided colliding but are chatting over a cup of tea.

"No, a lot going on in my head and I really do need to look where I'm going. I'm very sorry that I didn't see you until the last minute."

As I give her a reassuring smile to check that she isn't as shaky as I feel, a young woman walks towards us. She extends her arm in a half-wave.

I'm about to acknowledge her when I realise this is a spirit. She wants me to pass on a message, but all I have so far is her presence. She stands there smiling at me and the sensation of pure love emanating from her makes me tearful.

144

"How are you feeling?" I place my hand on the old lady's arm and give a little squeeze.

"I'm fine. I wasn't looking where I was going either." She has a soft, high-pitched laugh that is almost a girly-giggle. "It's such a pity the traffic is so heavy nowadays," she murmurs.

The young woman has moved closer, she's within reach. She keeps looking at me intently, as if she's encouraging me to say something, but I have no idea what she wants.

"Bide a while." The words come out gently and I have no idea where they're from. It's not a phrase I've ever used before. "Sit and remember."

"How lovely." The old lady looks up at me with sparkling eyes. "My daughter used to say that. I do want to sit and remember, often, but it's still too painful. Is she wearing a red woollen coat and black shoes?" She looks hesitant, glancing across at me nervously. "I'm not sure she's safe, you see, and I need to know it's really her," she whispers, leaning in anxiously as if she might be overheard. There is no one else around.

I notice that the young woman is now stooping and draping her arms around the old lady's shoulders. Instinctively I pull back, although there's plenty of space between us.

"She's safe and she's here. Yes, her coat is red and it has a heavy weave. She's wearing black leather boots though." Tears fill my eyes. The old lady reaches across to pat my hand as the young woman pulls away.

She's gone.

"That's her." The old woman's words are barely audible and I strain to catch them. "Thank you, my dear." Her voice is overcome with emotion.

We sit in silence for several minutes, her hand still placed over mine. Her fingers are cold. She reaches up to adjust the little brown hat perched on her head and smiles. I stand up and offer her my arm; she leans on me heavily to pull herself up, although she's so slight there's hardly any weight. With a little wave the old lady turns and walks away.

I almost run the rest of the way to Mark's, trying not to dwell on the strong emotions hovering around me. I can't do this, I can't do this. How can I survive if I feel everyone's deepest, darkest hurt as soon as I meet them? I'm shaking as I ring the bell and when Mark opens the door he can see something is up.

"Hi Ceri, that was a long twenty minutes. Are you okay? Come in."

Mark helps me take off my coat and suggests we have coffee first, so I follow him into the kitchen. He can see I'm a little shaken and he's giving me some breathing space. He makes polite conversation, telling me about his son and a football match he has coming up. Then I follow him through to his consulting room. It's a large, ground floor room that looks out onto a stunning garden. The grass is perfectly manicured and there is an abundance of flowers and shrubs. Quite simply it's a haven, and each time I come here I feel a sense of calm wash over me.

"Rough morning?" He gives me a few minutes to settle into the chair and tuck my bag to one side.

"Weird morning." I put my head down and stare into my coffee cup.

"An experience?"

I don't want to look at him because he presents very differently now. His aura is like a shiny gold band radiating out from him.

"Ceri, has anything unusual happened since I saw you last? Whatever you tell me is in confidence, but I have to ask...can you see my aura?"

I nod.

"Ah," he mutters, letting out a deep breath, "I thought something had changed. It's nothing to worry about. It happens sometimes, although it can take a while to become used to it. What do you see?"

"A gold band. It's very clear." I can't see any reason not to be honest with him. I can only hope he doesn't question me any further.

"That's good. Thank you. Gold reflects spiritual energy, that's a great compliment. Do you want to know the colour of your aura? Because it has changed since I last saw you."

Our eyes lock and a moment of recognition passes between us, before I avert my gaze.

"It's bright emerald green. It was a pale yellow the last time we met."

"Which means?" I have no idea what the relevance of each colour has, and wish I'd thought to research it beforehand.

"Well, you were an emerging energy, excited about new ideas, the changes to come. Your awareness has moved on and now you have the ability to be a healer. You are also love-centred, it's amazing. I can't believe the change in you."

I'm relieved he's regarding it as normal progression. I have no idea how frequently the colours of the aura change. I know the state of one's health affects it and I'm only too glad that he doesn't seem to want to dig any deeper.

"It's good, and you must remember that it's not my job to pry, only to assist you. I thought we'd talk about chakras today. The greater your understanding becomes, the more effective you will be in opening up and closing down when meditating. It's important to acquire a discipline that you adhere to every single time you meditate. Leaving yourself open, as it's referred to, will mean that lesser energies will be attracted to you."

I place the empty cup on the side table and settle back in my chair. "Is that something I should worry about?" Of course, I know all about lesser energies, the mischief makers who toy with those who have no faith, no sense of belief. Those who seek to either discredit the spirit world, or see proof as profit.

"Our sessions will help you develop the focus and strict regime you need, so that you have a framework within which to operate. You will work at a higher level than is required for mediumship, even. My belief is that while it does serve a purpose, it's merely to give encouragement to people who are searching, mindful only

147

that something is missing from their lives. A simple message from a loved one can be enough for some people to reach out for more information, and so their spiritual journey begins."

Mark stands, leaning across to grab my coffee mug and placing both of them on his desk. Then he takes a CD from a small stack in front of him and slides it into an open tray. Gentle music emits through the surround sound speakers and he turns the volume down very low.

Each session begins in the same way. I follow the example Mark sets as he adjusts his position. He straightens his back and draws himself up, as if someone is pulling an invisible thread above him. His feet are apart and flat on the floor, his arms loose in his lap, with palms open and fingers slightly curled. He arches his back for one moment and lowers his shoulders, taking a deep breath. In unison we breathe in through our noses and out through our mouths for a minute or two. The music is uplifting and my shoulders begin to feel lighter, all the tension in my muscles draining away.

***

An hour later I'm on my way home. Mark guided me through a much longer meditation this time. He took me to a woodland area and along a path. Someone was walking with me, but I couldn't recognise them as they kept to the edge of my peripheral vision. I only knew that it was an old friend and one of my spirit guides.

Afterwards Mark talked in depth about chakras and suddenly things seemed to slot into place. I immediately thought of Alex and made a mental note to talk to him about it tonight. I also told Mark about the old lady. I wanted to ask him about the spirit of her daughter. While I know so many things, there are lots of earth-bound traits that confuse me. I wanted to know why it was necessary for her to appear so clearly to me when the presence of her energy would have been enough. He explained that energy can choose to present itself in any way it pleases. The physical body only has relevance here on earth. So spirit presents in the form that will be most easily recognisable when described to the recipient of the message. It makes identification much easier and was one of the most effective forms of validation.

It made perfect sense, although a tinge of sadness hit me. I had a sudden longing for the ethereal plane. It's the place where energies exist, without form or substance. Being simply a vibration as intended and each unique in its own way. One thing I know for sure about life here on earth is that it's hard and I'm not surprised people often feel they have failed some sort of test.

CHAPTER NINE

In Love With Love

"Oh, you're back earlier than I thought. The viewing didn't go well?" I sidle up to Alex and cuddle into his back. He stirs something in a pan that smells of rich, buttery onions and tomatoes. I'm in for an Italian treat.

"On the contrary, we have a taker. I'm officially homeless as from next Saturday."

He lays the wooden spoon down on a piece of kitchen towel and spins around to draw me into his arms.

"Mmm…you taste nice!"

"You smell of garlicky onions," I laugh.

"How was the session with Mark?"

"Great, I learnt a lot about chakras."

"Well, grab the garlic bread and I'll dish up. If you can take the wine through I'll be there in a moment, can't wait to hear all about it."

Before he lets me go he kisses first one cheek, and then the other. His lips are warm and gentle.

"Let go of me then." I laugh and he squeezes a little tighter before releasing me. "I'm starving."

I have to admit that Alex's cooking is rather good. His attention to detail in all things means that, while it's simple, the taste reflects the effort he has put into the dish.

"Is it good?" he asks, almost as soon as I pop a forkful into my mouth.

"Mmm. Delicious! I wish you would cook all the time." I give him my best persuasive smile.

"A smile alone won't do it," he returns suggestively. His eyes linger for a few moments, as if he's seeing me for the first time. I feel my cheeks colouring up. "Tell me about Mark." He returns to his pasta, expertly winding his linguini around his fork.

"We did a woodland walk. I wasn't alone, but whoever was with me didn't come forward. I think it might have been my grandmother. I had a distinct sense of recognition. I thought I smelt her perfume…"

"Wow, that's a result. Perhaps I should try meditating, you can teach me."

It's wonderful to be able to talk to Alex about anything and everything. I reach out and slide my hand over the back of his neck, giving him an affectionate squeeze.

"I found out something about you, too."

He looks up as I pull my hand away. "You can't see all my secrets…can you?"

"No, nothing like that. It's to do with your chakras and your traits."

"Oh, the vibes that made you think I wasn't into women. Ceri, that doesn't do much for my self-esteem as a guy women find irresistible. Maybe that's why I've never had much luck on the dating front."

"Well, for a start I'm rather glad about that and secondly, your problem is that you are just too darned good looking. Women feel a bit intimidated chatting up a guy who looks like every woman would fall at his feet. No, it's about your attention to detail."

"Tell me more. What exactly are chakras, I've heard the term

151

but I'm not sure I understand what it's all about."

"Well, there are seven major chakras within the body and these are the energy centres. Opening them up allows a flow into and out of the aura. Mark explained to me that, equally as important as the opening up process to be receptive and reach a state of oneness, is the closing down process." I stop for a moment to scoop up some linguine and gauge Alex's reaction.

"Yeah, I've read a little and it's something to do with attracting negative energy or something, am I right?"

"Spot on. Lower astral energies, the ones who mislead and have nothing better to do. It's important to heed the balance within ourselves as it aligns the physical with the emotional and mental aspects of the life force. The seven points run in a line up through our bodies, ending with the crown chakra on the top of the head. Each is like a flower head with petal-like openings, invisible to most of us but energy workers can see them.

"What I didn't appreciate was that our surroundings can indicate when we have a problem with a blockage in any of our energy centres. I immediately thought of you." I stop to take another mouthful of food and give him a mischievous smile.

He groans. "Am I the textbook example of a walking chakra disaster zone?" His eyes twinkle.

"Quite the reverse, actually. I've learnt that dirty window panes might indicate a clouded third-eye perception and a dusty, cluttered bedroom can indicate negativity in one's love relationship. It seems cleaning really is cathartic."

"Well, I think we'd better finish up here and go dust the bedroom. I wouldn't want anything to hold us back now we're finally living together under the same roof."

***

I love having Alex around and I miss him when he leaves for work. Suddenly the apartment feels empty because his energy tends to fill every little space. It's lovely to laze around together, often in bed, feeling warm and cuddly after the passion we share so easily and without reservation. Being able to let down my guard and be myself feels like coming home after a long time away. He doesn't probe and I'm surprised that it's easier than I thought it would be. Why was I so worried? When something is right there is a natural flow and things around us both are flowing perfectly. I'm loved and in love, what more could anyone ask for?

I've had two interviews this week and both resulted in a job offer. It seems the universe is smiling upon me. One was part-time work and after a chat with Alex we decided I should accept that offer. I can spend a little more time on my psychic abilities, and that's becoming increasingly important. Mark has asked me along to one of his workshops and if he feels I'm ready, he's going to encourage me to take an active part. It will only be a small group, so I think I'll feel comfortable putting myself out there.

For the first time since my return I feel that life on this plane has something special to offer. Something that is worth being here for, setting aside all of the negatives about how unkind people and life can be. I begin to see that it's about avoiding the pitfalls: all the negative stuff that's in the media, fuelling a general air of disillusionment. People give up on their dreams, dragged down by incidents that are of no consequence whatsoever. I'd never really understood the glass half full/glass half empty thing, but now I do. I've chosen to surround myself with Alex's positive attitude, and it rubs off. Less and less I notice the harsh, cruel side of this life and more and more I celebrate the positives. No wonder depression exists here on this plane: it's hard to disentangle yourself from things that constantly seek to drag you down. There is no hell, but people choose to put themselves into a kind of hell because they lose sight of what matters.

Then something clicks.

That's what I'm supposed to do! Encourage people to let go of their negativity and embrace the positive. Send out good karma and it comes back to you a thousand times over.

CHAPTER TEN

First Impressions

Seb has emailed a few times. He thinks he's making some sense of his life, although I fear he is still very vulnerable at the moment. He's with a group of people who sound like a weird religious sect, trying to isolate their members from the real world. I've expressed my concerns but can tell he has to go through this and come out the other side.

Don't lose touch Seb, whatever happens. I respect your choices, but keep an open mind, please. That's all I ask. I'm always here for you, if and when you want to talk. Ceri xxx

Alex knows that I'm worried and has tried to reassure me. What I can't tell him is that in my work on the ethereal plane I can see Seb and I know exactly what's happening. He's being led down a path by someone who claims to be a higher being, but who knows very little. He's the worst sort of believer: someone whose knowledge is minimal although his ego is large. This man thinks he's God, or the closest thing to him on this earth. Worshipping false idols comes to mind and whilst it's clear to me Seb isn't swallowing everything he's being told, he remains curious. I can only watch from a distance, but I'm prepared to step in if necessary.

I seem to be managing my two very distinct worlds effortlessly. There doesn't seem to be any overlap and I don't think I've let anything slip.

"Are you ready yet?" Alex saunters into the bedroom and sashays towards me as if he's going to pounce.

"No, so don't come in here and start distracting me. I'm trying to do my make-up and I'll end up looking like a panda bear if I don't concentrate. I'm nervous. You can sit down and tell me some more about your boss if you want to help."

He sits on the edge of the bed, mindful not to upset the perfectly placed pillows, and I love that he cares about those little things. I never knew why ambience was so important, I simply knew it affected my mood and when everything was in order, I felt happier. After Mark's session on chakras it all became very clear. Cleanliness really is next to Godliness, and the reason is that dirt and clutter can stop the flow of energy. Since Alex moved in the apartment looks even better than it did before and, if that reflects our relationship, then this place is full of love and free-flowing energy.

"You know all about the company, Grey's Advertising, and Niall Grey is the kind of boss you'd stay late for to meet a deadline, even if he wasn't paying you. I've never met his wife but I assume they are going to be quite like-minded. There's no need to be nervous about meeting them," he's puzzled and concerned because I'm anxious.

"Technically I'm out of work, I'm a psychic and I'm not the usual sort of girlfriend someone would expect." I zip up my make-up case and choose some earrings. "How do I look?" I spin around for Alex to pass judgement.

"Bea-u-ti-ful. Much too attractive to take out on a work celebration dinner. You'll make Niall jealous." He gingerly places his arms around me. "I won't crush the dress," he murmurs into my hair. His body presses hard against mine and that little frisson of heat begins to flood through me.

"You're naughty, do you know that?" I turn my head, brushing my lips against his cheek. I move on to lightly tease his soft, gorgeous mouth. He kisses me back with a fierceness that makes me turn weak at the knees. I close my eyes and savour the moment, knowing full well any trace of lipstick will now have evaporated. I slide my arms down around his waist and Alex slides his hands down over my back, applying a slight pressure to pull my hips into him.

"I know, but you are just so, so sexy, Ceri. I can't keep my hands off you."

"I noticed," I reply, reluctantly pushing him away. I make my way to the bathroom to start again, brushing any vestiges of lipstick off my teeth. He follows close behind me and suddenly I'm in his arms, his body pressing mine up against the wall. I can't resist him and this moment is all that matters. Any thoughts about being late fade away.

***

"We're running a little late, Niall, my apologies. This is my partner, Ceri Adams." Alex slides his arm out from around my waist. I step forward to shake first Niall's hand and then his wife's, as he turns to introduce her to us.

"Alicia, this is Alex Delano. Hello Ceri, lovely to meet you."

Niall walks around the table to pull out a chair for me. Alex has disappeared with our coats. I feel slightly panicky standing here on my own, so I paste on a big smile and concentrate on friendly eye contact. Niall's aura is orangey red. He's a confident and creative individual, although I doubt he'll be very interested in anything spiritual. Alicia's aura is a very dark grey and it isn't opaque, but quite a solid band of colour. That isn't good, it means she's holding onto fear and that is causing her some serious health problems. There's a large cluster of grey around her temples and

I'm guessing she suffers from the most draining headaches. Maybe she has one coming now.

I look up from my thoughts, sensing I've missed something.

"I was asking what you would like to drink, Ceri."

Alex appears and answers for me as he settles into his chair. "Whatever you are having is fine for both of us," he says with a smile that looks a little forced. He looks nervously at Alicia and gives a little nod of acknowledgement, then back at me. Alex holds up my wine glass whilst Niall pours from a bottle sitting in a wine bucket on the table.

"Thank you." I take the glass Alex offers and raise it to toast both Niall's and Alicia's. Everyone is all smiles and I turn to Alex, to graze glasses. Something goes wrong and instead of a light touch, my glass shatters into a million pieces. Wine and shards of glass cascade down into my lap, making me jump. The look on his face startled me, something isn't right. Two waiters immediately come over and it's an embarrassing few minutes as they clear up the glass. Another waiter brings me some napkins to mop my dress and the table, then lays a new place setting.

"I'm so sorry, I don't know quite what happened," I'm mortified. "There really wasn't any reason why—"

"Faulty glass I suspect," Niall intercedes, obviously trying to make me feel better. Alex grabs my hand and gives it a gentle squeeze.

"One of those things, Ceri." He passes me the menu and there's a little light conversation about what to choose. It's a smart restaurant and very expensive, which makes this incident so much worse. I'm embarrassed and also confused about Alex. He's on edge and looks nervous. I wonder if he's disappointed in me and thinks I've let him down. I bite my lip, inwardly mad at myself for being so clumsy.

A waiter appears to take our order and things return to a more normal and relaxed atmosphere. I feel rather silly sitting here in a wine-splashed dress, only thankful that I wore black and it was white wine. The napkins mopped up most of it, but it's still damp in a couple of spots. A little wine goes a long way.

Thankfully the conversation begins to flow, dominated by the guys. Niall very kindly sings Alex's praises, which makes him squirm a little, and this time we air-kiss our glasses to toast Alex's promotion. Alicia says very little and only picks at her starter. The evening draws to a close very unexpectedly when Alicia suddenly turns very pale, as if she is going to faint. She admits to having the most awful migraine and virtually collapses, leaning into Niall, who puts a protective arm around her. He indicates for a waiter to bring the coats and begins apologising, insisting we stay to finish our meal.

It seems to have been a night of apologies, as we shake hands once more and bid each other goodnight.

Alex looks rather relieved as we make our way out of the restaurant a short while later, the evening in ruins.

Outside I can't help but ask the question. "What was that all about? For one moment you looked like you'd seen a ghost."

"It was nothing, you know me. I don't like attention and then when Niall started going on about my work...I'm just glad that's over. I'll be sure not to do anything to warrant another promotion," he adds, soberly.

"Well, when it comes to making a first impression, I think this is one evening we'll all want to forget!"

CHAPTER ELEVEN

A Little Doubt

Alex is rather subdued at breakfast the next morning and I'm wondering whether he's disappointed that last night ended up being a damp squib.

"Hey, I'm sorry about last night. I don't know quite what happened." My apology sounds pathetic.

"It's fine. Accidents happen. Socialising with the boss isn't a great idea, unless you get to sleep with her that is." He throws me a cheeky grin.

"Yes, but it spoiled your celebration. I'm so proud of you and I wanted it to go well."

"What was your initial impression? Any particular vibe you picked up?" He sounds casual, but there's an edge to his voice.

"No. Niall seemed like a nice guy. I couldn't really pick up very much from Alicia. I had the impression that she wasn't very well. I guess her migraine was hanging around from the start of the evening and that's what I could sense. She was pleasant enough, she laughed in all the right places before she began to feel really poorly."

"There's nothing for me to worry about then?"

I look up, wondering what prompted that strange question and why he's concerned.

"No, I don't think so. You aren't having second thoughts about being with Grey's, are you?"

"I get on well with Niall. He's a workaholic and so am I, we understand each other, but I'll have to see how it goes. It might have been a mistake taking this promotion and if it is, then I'll look for another job."

I can feel something is bothering him although I have no idea what exactly, so I change the subject. "I'm looking forward to starting work next week. We've agreed on alternate days, Monday to Friday. I've spoken to Mark, so he knows I'm available to help out with any workshops on the two days I'm not working. I thought I'd keep the evening sessions to a minimum. I don't want it to eat into our time together any more than necessary."

The fact that Alex doesn't immediately look up reaffirms his head is somewhere else. I wonder if the job is stretching him a little too far. I know he's not comfortable managing staff and that it hasn't been easy for him. He's encountering a little resentment, because he hasn't been with Grey's very long and Niall selected him as the best candidate over some longer-term employees. I know Alex hates ill feeling of any kind. He's going to have to ride the storm until it settles down, and it will. I walk around to his side of the table and plant a kiss on his cheek.

"They'll all grow to love you, as I do." I inhale and close my eyes, mentally invoking every strand of healing within my body to surround him.

"I sincerely hope not! I've discovered having one woman in my life is difficult enough." His mood is lighter and he stands, turning to wrap me in a bear hug.

"What did I do before you came into my life? Nothing else seems to count for anything at all. This is only work we're talking about and I'm not a total wimp. So don't worry your gorgeous little head about it."

"Alex."

"Yes?"

"Guys don't say 'gorgeous', it's camp."

"Noted, boss." He tips me a salute and gives me his cheekiest grin.

ALEX

CHAPTER TWELVE

Sometimes The Truth Isn't Pretty

I kiss Ceri, holding her for a little bit longer than necessary. Every time we part I worry that when I arrive home she won't be there. I know it's crazy. The reason she ran away before was because I said some awful things that weren't true. I was hurting, frustrated and desperate. It was hell being around her every day for two years, three months, and eight days without being able to acknowledge my love for her. Since she's been back and we've been together, everything is perfect. Until this damned promotion upset everything.

I keep walking, my head full of regrets, anger and desperation. What am I going to do? If Niall finds out that Alicia and I have a past together, I'm history. How will I explain that to Ceri? I hate lying to her—even if it is a lie by omission. But what can I say? Admitting the truth is going to be ugly and it was, but it sounds harsher when the words are spoken.

We were very young when we met and I really liked Alicia. We'd been seeing each other off and on for a couple of months when I received a phone call saying she was pregnant. She told me that she'd had counselling and was going to have an abortion. We were both in our first jobs after leaving university and the world stretched out enticingly before us. The news brought me down to earth with a bang. The day Alicia rang to tell me I was stunned, and I know she was struggling to hold it all together. We were dating exclusively but neither of us had said the word love, we weren't at that place. I can now see that we weren't ever going to fall in love. Not the sort of love I have for Ceri but, of course, you don't know that until you've experienced it for yourself.

There was no nastiness, no ugly scene, and that was the crazy part. When I said I would do whatever she wanted, that we could get married and somehow make it work, she laughed bitterly. "We can't even look after ourselves properly, what sort of parents would we make?" I hung my head in shame, thinking she was right and wondering how we could have been so careless.

We were just two young people who made the biggest mistake of all. I never saw her again after that. She refused to have anything to do with me. I tried to ring her several times, but it went to voicemail. Eventually a friend of hers sent me a text. She told me that if I had any respect for Alicia at all I would leave her alone and let her get on with her life. Alicia wrote me a letter a couple of months later, saying that we were both to blame and it was likely she would never forgive herself.

She was right in many ways, our relationship wouldn't have worked. We were too young to handle the situation. I've told Ceri everything about myself except this one thing. She's an angel and what the hell will she think of me if she finds out? I'm really scared that she can see inside of me, see what I'm hiding. I've been reading everything I can get my hands on to find out how it all works. Yes, a part of that is because I want to support her, but I'm running scared that my secret will be discovered.

I spoke to Ethan in a roundabout way and he says the rarity of an angel having an earthly life means it's difficult to imagine how that works. He believes that with lesser vibrations sent to this plane to help others, if they have an emotional attachment, it inhibits what they can see. But with angels, who knows? I've been working on the basis that Ceri would have said something by now, but I'm worried sick. If Niall had mentioned Alicia by name I might have caught on, but I still wouldn't have known it was her for sure, until last night.

I jump back as a car horn shatters my thoughts. I realise I'm stepping off the pavement and the crossing light is red. I'm anxious about seeing Niall today in case Alicia has said anything. A lot of couples share everything from the past before they make a firm commitment to each other. I know other people believe there's no point in raking over the details of old romances. Ceri's past was exactly as I expected. It made me feel sad to think that in the relationships she'd had the guys hadn't treated her with the respect she deserved. I know how much she loves me and how attracted to me she is, it shows in everything she does. She's a complex character, naturally, but there's an innocence and naivety to her nature that is refreshing. I understand the cautious side of her and I believe that's to do with her other-worldly connection. I never used to believe that there was more than one life, or one plane, but gradually I'm beginning to rethink the whole thing. At the moment I'm taking it all in my stride. People like Ethan, Ceri, and Mark are too intelligent to have the wool pulled over their eyes. Not only that, but I have my own gut feeling telling me that it's real, even though if someone asked me I couldn't explain it.

I'm beginning to wonder if a part of my desire to believe is because of that little soul, lost because Alicia and I had no relevant life experience and couldn't come to terms with what was happening. I should have done something, worked out a way to make it happen. I will admit, at the time, I was scared about the thought of providing a stable home environment for a baby and maybe also supporting a new wife. But it wasn't an empty offer, I would have managed somehow.

Niall and Alicia don't have children and I wonder if that was Alicia's choice? How can you think of bringing another baby into this world, when you failed to nurture a life that had begun to grow?

I have to shake myself and snap out of my reverie. I'm not in a fit state to walk through those office doors at the moment, pretending everything is fine. I need a large coffee with a couple of extra shots if I'm going to get through the day.

***

"Alex, hi. Thanks for coming in. Take a seat." Niall looks amiable, so I guess Alicia didn't say anything after all.

"Sorry about Alicia's headache, she suffers from these awful migraines. It's hormonal, you know how it is. It was great to meet Ceri. You're a very lucky man, Alex."

"Thanks, and I hope Alicia is feeling better today. It was a great meal and we both appreciated the gesture. Ceri felt awful about the glass."

"These things happen, probably some careless waiter not noticing a crack in the glass when they were laying the table. Poor Ceri, she handled it well and didn't make a fuss. I like that kind of woman. Can't stand melodrama. I wondered if you would be available next Wednesday evening. I'm wining and dining our biggest client, Jack Monahugh. It's more social than business, but it would be a great opportunity for you to meet him. Is Ceri available to come along too? What do you think?"

"It's a great idea but I know Ceri already has a meeting booked. It will just be me, is that a problem?"

"No. Not at all. Does Ceri work evenings? She's in advertising too, isn't she? I recognised the name."

"She starts a new job next week but she's also involved in a separate project and it means she's going part-time. She attends a few evening meetings now and again."

I'm tempted to cross my fingers under the table and hold my breath, really hoping Niall doesn't ask what exactly she does outside of her day job. He's a feet on the ground sort of guy and

I'm not sure he would understand. Heck, I'm not even sure what I would say. I need to think about it before I open up that line of conversation. He seems fine, though, and we briefly discuss what sort of background information the client would be interested in hearing. I like Niall, he's a straight talking guy and there are no pretences or half-truths. He does business the old-fashioned way, what you see is what you get, and that is value for money.

As I close the door behind me I sag a little. Nervous energy is eating me up and at this rate I'll run out of steam before the working day has finished. Ceri is attending a group meeting with Mark on Wednesday and I can't expect her to change her plans. Anyway, I'm thinking it will be much better not to involve her any more than necessary, certainly until I know whether Alicia is going to say anything to Niall.

I groan inwardly. Is this bad karma coming back to me because I did something so unforgiveable it doesn't even bear thinking about? Or maybe Ethan was right all along. What if I'm going to start paying the price for ignoring my dreams and making a life with Ceri? Or worse, Ceri is the one who is going to suffer. But why am I in love with her to my very core if it's not meant to be? Who would do that to someone, give them an all-consuming love and then snatch it away? I believe there is a God and I like to think he's compassionate, but I can't see any compassion in wrenching Ceri and me apart. If she knew what I'd done…a part of me deep inside crumples at the thought.

I realise I've been leaning against the wall staring into space for a few minutes and I make my way to the kitchen area for another strong hit of caffeine. My head is full of Ceri: her beautiful smile, those intriguing grey-blue eyes that melt my heart. I love the way her straight blonde hair flicks across her face when she laughs and she inclines her head a little, looking up from under her lashes. The times when she says little and I am left to fill in the gaps, knowing there's no point in talking. Maybe words just can't explain it sometimes. In sombre mood she is a little scary

167

at times but, given the burden she's carrying, that's only to be expected. How does someone live with that? I can understand why she's cautious with people, because the topic often invokes such a strong reaction. Non-believers decry it with such vehemence that it can feel like a personal attack. Believers want to know more. Either way it's awkward.

My mindset was that I believe in a God because we can't simply just "be", or have evolved from a state of nothingness. Someone created us and whomsoever it was had a far greater intelligence than any scientist known to man. I also struggle to accept that we end when we die, that the bit that makes each of us unique simply disappears. I literally grilled Ethan when I met up with him, wanting to know the answers to all my questions. Of course it wasn't as simple as that and yes, I have moved on and can now see why so many people believe in life after death.

But the angel thing was a shock. I thought angels belonged to that place we refer to as heaven, which is probably somewhere out there in the universe, where all our energy gathers once we're done here. The existence of multiple lives on earth sounds a bit too sci-fi for me.

Then there is Ceri, and Ethan was adamant his spirit guide told him Ceri is an angel.

Someone bumps my arm and my coffee mug splatters over the worktop.

"Sorry, Alex." It's one of the copy editors.

"No problem, I was deep in thought." I nod and make my way back to my desk.

The death of that innocent baby is a black stain on my soul, I'm sure. The fact that Ceri can't sense it means our love obscures her vision. I don't know whether to be grateful about that, or rather sad. How can I tell her something that is bound to alienate her from me?

The truth is that I love her enough to lie, and that's selfish. Totally selfish.

CHAPTER THIRTEEN

The Week From Hell

I'm beginning to wish that the moment I opened my eyes on Monday morning, I'd rolled back over and refused to play ball. I should have buried myself beneath the covers and disappeared for a week. Everywhere I turn there's a problem. One of the team at work is having a major meltdown over a computer problem that IT can't seem to resolve. Tempers have been frayed to say the least.

Ceri has been very subdued the last couple of days. On Tuesday evening we took a run over to visit my parents, as I knew it was about time I made the introduction. They were fine, but Ceri was very on edge. My parents are the kind of people who hug everyone and want to welcome them into their home whether they know them or not. I could see Ceri wanting to back away and I wondered if it was too much for her. I'm not sure whether she's withdrawn slightly because it obviously marks a turning point for us, or whether she's picked up something negative from me, regarding Alicia.

I'm having real trouble not blurting it all out. It sits on my chest like a heavy weight and I don't think I can carry on much longer knowing I'm deceiving her. I understand her stressing about not letting Mark down, but I have no idea if there is anything else troubling her. Despite everything Ceri has seen and been involved with, she continues to worry about getting it wrong. The idea of picking something up and misinterpreting it, potentially sending someone off in the wrong direction, terrifies her. I find myself doing the counsellor bit, which is a laugh. I told her that if our fate is predetermined, logic would dictate that we can't possibly stray too far from the plan. Her answer stunned me.

"You have been given free will, Alex. Willpower can be a useful tool, but it can also be misused. Whether the intent is good or bad, doesn't really matter. The effect is the same."

She wouldn't say any more. I almost had to sit down, I was so shocked. For a start she said 'you', as in humans, and not 'us'. Should I worry about that? Angels who come here live the same sort of life-span, don't they? She isn't going to suddenly disappear? And secondly, if she was referring to our situation, does that mean she's regretting it and there really is a reason we shouldn't be together? Has Ceri been shown something that proves we've made a big mistake? I try very hard not to ask awkward questions, but I had to know more. She became a little upset and I backed off, fearful of adding to her burden.

Then on Wednesday evening, I hadn't appreciated that the client was going to bring his wife along. Worse still, Niall appeared accompanied by Alicia. Not only was I a spare wheel, I was the centre of the conversation and all eyes were on me. Alicia kept looking away and I was fearful Niall would notice something was up.

At one point I couldn't take anymore. I'd chatted myself hoarse telling them about my career prior to Grey's and avoiding any reference to girlfriends or partners. After a long chat about formula one, which I felt was at least safer ground, I excused myself and headed for the cloakroom. I needed a break, to grab a few quiet moments to compose myself. What I hadn't banked on was Alicia excusing herself shortly after I left the table to waylay me in the lobby.

"I think we need to talk." She handed me a folded piece of paper and her look was one of gentle concern. As our eyes met a pained look passed between us. I nodded, pocketed the slip of paper and made my way back to the table. No one seemed to notice anything odd, but I was glad when the evening was finally over and the goodbyes had been said.

**

"You look totally exhausted," were Ceri's first words as she came through the door and saw me sprawled out on the sofa. "Have you been in long?"

"Ten minutes. A working dinner isn't much fun, I hope your evening was better." I start yanking off my tie and unbuttoning my shirt. I feel strangely closed in, my guilt hugging my chest like a ball and chain.

I watch as she skips around the room, putting her notepad and bag on the table neatly, slipping off her shoes. She's dressed casually tonight: a cherry red top and a great pair of jeans that make her small frame look taller than her five foot three stature. She turns and her hair flies around her face before settling down. One strand is caught by her lipstick and she swishes it away with her hand.

"It went much better than I thought it would. Mark was pleased to say the least!"

She's buzzing with excitement and there's a light in her eyes that seems to illuminate the whole area around her. How could anyone fail to see that Ceri is a very special person? She's an old soul in a young body. I'd heard that said a few times in the past and never really understood what it meant, but I do now. She has such depth of knowledge about some things and yet in other practical areas she often flounders. Her level of understanding is one thing; her ability to cope with life is another. She's strong when she feels she's on safe ground, in a work situation for example. Then with the

171

psychic stuff she seems to have all the answers, but struggles when it comes to dealing with other people's expectations and concerns.

She walks over to the sofa and lowers herself down, snuggling into me. I bury my face in her hair and breathe in the smell of her. Her perfume tonight is citrusy and there's a hint of bergamot which makes it musky. I can't help groaning as my body instantly reacts, wanting her. I know what Ceri needs at this precise moment is to tell me about her evening.

"Did you go solo?" My voice is even, but my heart is doing somersaults. I can't say what other parts of me are doing. Thinking about it will make it worse.

"Yes. After the meditation we sat around in a circle and there was a great deal of positivity flowing. I received two messages, both for people within the group. It wasn't that they were very clear and specific messages, but that I was shown validation that was meaningful to both of the recipients. Mark took me to one side afterwards and said he was astounded. He had no idea I would progress so quickly. He joked with me and said he must be a really awesome teacher!"

She's wriggling around in my arms and with the perfume and the contact this is too much for a guy to take. I disentangle myself and go into the kitchen to pour myself a drink. I'm still having problems trying not to over-think the 'having sex with an angel' thing. A part of me also doesn't want Ceri probing about tonight. I left the hand-written note Alicia handed to me in the car. It simply had a date, time and venue on it. It won't be a problem but I'm torn. I know I need to talk to Alicia, after all these years it's the least I can do. Lying to Ceri is another thing altogether.

I wish there was someone I could talk to as the guilt and remorse is over-shadowing everything I do at the moment. I can only hope that when I eventually find the courage to tell Ceri, she will be able to forgive me.

CHAPTER FOURTEEN

Facing The Past

The coffee shop Alicia named in her note was on the other side of town, well away from the office. I arrive half an hour early, which is a big mistake. I've been sitting here nervously fiddling with the menu, my eyes glued to the entrance, ever since I sat down. As she walks through the door she gives me a small smile of recognition and makes her way to the table.

She reaches out to shake hands and it all feels rather awkward.

"Thank you for agreeing to see me Alex. I thought it was best we meet face to face."

I pull out a chair for her and she sits, making no attempt to take off her coat.

"Would you like tea, or perhaps a coffee?"

"Tea would be fine, thank you."

I walk up to the counter to order our drinks and as I walk back to the table she looks away. Her eyes scan around the room and I think she's checking there's no one here who would recognise her.

I sit down and we eye each other nervously, neither knowing who should speak first. I decide it might as well be me.

"Niall doesn't know we...umm...know each other?"

"No, no he doesn't, and it would kill him if he knew. He isn't a jealous man and what is in the past, is in the past. We have tried for many years to have a child and it is his biggest disappointment. The problem lies with Niall and he feels he's robbed me of the chance to be a mother. If he found out…" She's shaking with the effort of holding herself together.

"Alicia, is there anything I can do? We were both guilty and young people make mistakes. I know that's no excuse—"

"I made the decision that seemed right at the time. What did we know about life, about anything?" The bitterness in her voice is tangible. She stops speaking as the waiter approaches the table, then continues after he's out of earshot. "I listened to the advice I was given and I was afraid of what my parents would say if they found out. My biggest regret is not talking to you about it before that decision was made. Would you really have tried to talk me out of it, if I'd given you a proper chance and listened to what you had to say?"

I sit back for a moment, taking myself back in time. I don't want to give Alicia some glib answer as if I'm emotionally detached from all of this.

"The truth is, Alicia, I know I said we could work it out, but I'm not sure I was mature enough at the time to cope with it all. Saying the words to reassure you was one thing, but providing for you and a baby? I was a kid with big ideas, but no life experience and no money. You can't blame yourself. We made this mess, you and I, but it wasn't intentional. We never set out to hurt anyone."

A haunted look appears in her eyes, a look that is so sad I can feel her pain.

"Will we ever be forgiven?" she whispers, her eyes searching mine.

"I don't know Alicia. I like to think that God really is forgiving and understands that if we had been even a couple of years older, it would have been a very different situation."

She looks around, checking no one is within earshot.

"Niall must never find out. It's hard enough that I've had to live with my decision all these years. Maybe I still deserve to suffer, but Niall is a kind and loving man. He would stand by me, but he would be torn into a million different pieces. I won't inflict this on him. You must understand that, Alex, and please promise me you will be careful. You can't tell Ceri, or anyone."

The look on her face is insistent and I feel a lump in my throat for the pain and damage that resulted from our carelessness.

"I'm so sorry, Alicia. This isn't something I've ever discussed with anyone. It's never left me though, not in here." The moment my hand comes to rest against my chest, her tears brim over.

"It's the same for me," her voice is so faint I can hardly hear the words. Her body language reflects the abject hopelessness she's feeling.

"Look, if there's anything I can do, any time at all. If you want to talk or—"

"I've spent my life talking to counsellors and even a psychiatrist. Some old wounds never heal and maybe this one isn't supposed to. Nothing good comes from something bad and I will never forgive myself."

She takes a tissue from her bag, dabs at her eyes, and pushes back on her chair.

"I have to go. But please, this is our secret and it must remain that way. I need you to do this for me."

I nod, unable to speak. She gives me her hand and I put both of mine around hers. I want to hug her, but I feel it would be inappropriate. Her words still ring in my ears as I watch her walk out of the coffee shop.

If I could change one thing in the whole of my life, it would be this, regardless of where that might have taken us in the future.

CERI

CHAPTER FIFTEEN

Feeling At Home

For the first time in my earthly life I feel a sense of peace, acceptance, and calm. I used to hate the fact that I never felt at ease, always the one on the outside looking in. Even when I was around people who were spiritually aware, I knew that my own path was very different. I just didn't know why. Many ordinary people proclaim an interest too, but when you start a real discussion you can see their perception of you change. Often it's because their minds are closed and what they are really hoping is that they can walk away thinking you are strange or deluded. Why ask questions if you aren't prepared to listen and evaluate the response? That puzzled me for a while, then I realised that people who shun any sort of belief—whether it's the existence of life after death, religion, or our in-born sense of belonging to something bigger—need reassurance. Unable to commit, they push everything away, but there is always that nagging doubt at the back of their minds. What if hell exists and it really is the place where non-believers end up? Well, hell on earth surely exists, although it's self-inflicted.

What has brought about the biggest change in me is being with Alex. Falling in love with someone is one thing, but when they love you back equally as fiercely it becomes something very different. I feel confident and it's nothing to do with my enlightenment. I'm valued, treasured and needed; that invokes a whole host of emotions I have never experienced before. I make him whole and knowing that makes me feel special.

We seem to be on the same level in virtually everything we do and the goodness in Alex's heart is very healing. He cares about the small things in life and he's sensitive to others in a way that is often missed, but I notice it. He tries to protect me without making it obvious and I love him even more with each passing day. The sun has never shined as brightly, the rain has never been so beautifully refreshing. It's all because of him. I have no idea how long we have together, but I treasure every single second.

Alex has accepted my friendship with Mark, who has been an amazing support and influence. The first time I sat in the group circle and Mark asked if I had any messages, I almost froze. All eyes were on me and suddenly it all became very real. Almost as soon as we had begun meditating a spirit had joined me and they were insistent. The message was for one of the group, Pete, and that concerned me as he had been very quiet all evening. I wished Mark had talked to me about the members beforehand, so I could gauge whether I needed to hold anything back. Messages can be pretty blunt and sometimes words come, but often it's more visual. The message for Pete had been very clear and it was from an older man.

"The gentleman who joined me had a walking stick, but he was swinging it jauntily, rather than using it for support. He found that amusing. We sat for a while on a bench overlooking a large grassy hill. He wore an old jacket with patched elbows and a smart silk handkerchief tucked into the breast pocket. I feel this message is for Pete."

All eyes in the group turned to look at Pete, who shifted in his chair.

"That's okay." He nodded in my direction, indicating that he was happy for me to continue.

"I think he might have worked with cars. I saw detailed drawings and what seemed to be test cars speeding around a track. Not racing cars, but saloon cars. They were all brand new but very old models, which would have made him in his late eighties probably. There was no name, but I know beyond a shadow of a doubt the message is for you. The only words I could hear were 'none of it matters now, so don't dwell on it my son', and he was insistent. The words kept repeating over and over in my head."

I looked up at Pete and he nodded curtly.

"Was there anything else?" Pete narrowed his eyes and I wondered whether he could read my mind.

"I'm not sure…there were some images from his life as we sat together on the bench. Most were to do with cars. There was one thing that was odd: a broken glass crystal rose bowl. I saw someone picking up the pieces, then cleaning up the flowers and water strewn over the floor."

Pete covered his face with his hands, running the heel of his palms back across his eyes. He sniffed and cleared his throat.

"It was my mother's treasured glass bowl. My father bought it for her on their fortieth wedding anniversary. I knocked it over when we were arguing, about a year after her death. He always had flowers in the house because he said it made him feel she was still around. I think it was the smell he identified with. We argued quite a bit and towards the end of his life I had to make some tough decisions. He refused to go into a nursing home, despite the fact that he wasn't really safe living on his own. He was also very sick and in a lot of pain. Often he refused to allow the doctor or nurses in to help. It's always weighed heavily upon me whether or not I did the right thing. Shortly after he died I bought a replacement rose bowl. I never put flowers in it, but it sits on the shelf and I think of them both every time I see it."

"I understand now that he was offering validation by mentioning something very special. He was concerned for you, that was very

179

clear. But I think he was also trying to let you know that he is around you. He is at peace with everything that happened and he recognised your gesture as a way of reaching out to him. There is no need to feel guilty, he's happy and he wants you to enjoy the rest of your life. The emotion he left me with was filled with gratefulness and love. It was touching because it was so strong."

The group sat in silence for a couple of minutes, then Mark asked me if there were any other messages.

"A special visitor," I mused, and everyone looked up at me. "He's a fairly big chappie, a golden retriever. This was someone who loved frolicking in the water, no matter what time of the year it was, and he would have been a very active dog. He kept running around me in a large circle. Can anyone connect with this?"

"Yes," the woman opposite was beaming and looking around the group. "It's Rufus. He was twelve when he died last year and we'd had him since he was ten weeks old. We miss the little devil so much, but we can't bring ourselves to get another pup. That's wonderful Ceri, thank you so much! I can't wait to go home and tell my husband, he'll be thrilled. We keep getting the scent of wet dog and we did wonder…nice to know he's still thinking of us too." She looked thrilled and shrugged her shoulders, as if giving herself a squeeze. "So glad I came tonight!" she added.

After the meeting ended, Pete came up to me and shook my hand.

"Thanks." He looked hesitant. "For what you said, and also what you decided not to share." Our eyes exchanged one meaningful look. What I hadn't mentioned was the fact that his father died of an overdose of medication. It was clear that Pete had been given an ultimatum: *help me to end it all, or get out of my house.* The assumption was made that Pete's father had been confused about the number of tablets he was supposed to take.

Mark said once that most people who sit in circle have a personal reason for wanting to know more. Sometimes it was due to an experience that was so traumatic it affected their energy, and their health. The further they progressed along their spiritual path, the greater the benefits as they learned to shed the burden they carried.

It wasn't the easiest of sessions and I would have preferred my first time solo to have been less intense. I did enjoy meeting Rufus and, as light-hearted as his message had been, it made someone very happy that night.

CHAPTER SIXTEEN

A Little Surprise…

Our first three months of living as a couple flew by and we celebrated the evening in style. Well, not quite—we had champagne and a takeaway. Even the champagne was an afterthought and something left over from a party last year. We were both really exhausted though. Alex has his hands full at work and I'm trying to juggle my new job, plus a steep learning curve being tutored by Mark. I accompany him on his weekly visits to a large number of psychic events. Some are informal and often I'm invited to stand up and do a small segment. Other times it's more formal, so I watch and learn. While we really wanted to celebrate, we admitted to each other that we were too tired and the promise of an early night to sleep seemed too good to waste. Alex yawned, then promised he would make it up to me.

A week later he came home from work buzzing.

"What?" I asked, as he bounced into the bedroom. His eyes were sparkling.

"I have a surprise." He waved a small envelope in front of me.

My hands were covered in moisturising cream after a relaxing bath and a facial, so he leant forward and kissed the top of my head.

"Are you going to tell me what it is, or will you make me wait until I've rubbed this in?"

He ripped open the envelope and pulled out a piece of paper, then proceeded to hold it up in front of me so I could read it.

"Alex, that sounds amazing! Why? What have I done to deserve three days in a beautiful French manor house? You do know it isn't my birthday for another two months…"

I stand up and fling my arms around his neck, holding my hands out to avoid covering him with cream. I give him a succession of short, sharp kisses. I can't wipe the smile off my face long enough to give him one long passionate one.

"You deserve it, heck, we both do. I know you booked some time off to spend with Sheena next month, but do you think she'll mind if I whisk you away for three days? I know how much you enjoyed your French trip, despite the circumstances. Niall recommended this place for a romantic getaway. I feel like spoiling you, and having three whole days together will do us both good."

"Of course she won't mind! You won't believe this, but I've been looking online at weekends away and thought I might surprise you. This is awesome. Thank you, thank you, thank you!"

He wraps me tightly in his arms and lifts me off the ground.

Alex buries his head in my hair. "I love you, my angel, and I can't wait to take you away."

The coincidence was yet another sign of how we seem to be on the same wavelength.

I know Alex has noticed that I haven't been quite my usual self. My work on the ethereal plane is hard at times and I wish I could keep everything totally separate. It's like having the radio on all the time in the background. If the music is gentle, then it's relaxing. If it's a pounding beat, it's distracting. Often I tune it out. The things I'm doing involve me flitting in and out of people's lives to help them.

With smaller problems, if their spiritual consciousness isn't awakened, they are often totally unaware that I'm with them. It's a case of subtle suggestion on a telepathic level. I send a thought vibration and that's the way I prefer to communicate, because it's easy. As soon as it comes into their minds they act on it and move on with their problem. On earth it's often referred to an inspiration and that amuses me. Do they never stop to consider that one moment their mind is unable to solve a problem and the next the answer is there? Often it's something that would never have occurred to them because they don't have the relevant knowledge or skills.

Then there are the other cases, those suffering a deep trauma that threatens to engulf them and drag them down to a dark place. Individuals with strong beliefs tend to fare better, used to reasoning both sides of a situation and tending towards a positive nature. Others are less grounded, having no sense of security to fall back on when times are tough. Suddenly it all becomes too much. It's referred to as depression and it's a state that only exists here on this plane. Dealing with those cases is much more intense and often the darkness surrounding them means they block out everything. It requires a lot more effort to help and sometimes that means influencing other people's actions to intervene. The problem then becomes complex, like trying to escape from a maze. One wrong turn and any progress made can be undone. I have a woman who has lost her husband after only five years of marriage and she's distraught. She can't see any reason to go on and the earthly part of me keeps getting drawn in as I think of Seb's situation. There is some movement, but each time I succeed in lifting her mood, it's so easy for her to fall back. A part of the problem is that she's taking some tablets prescribed by her doctor. It helps her to relax and sleep, but it isn't easy for me to deal with someone who can't concentrate. I have to work with her via her dreams and that's always difficult.

So many people don't heed the messages we discreetly weave into their dreams. I think, in all honesty, there is a design flaw. Sleep has many levels and on the highest one we interface seamlessly with our true energy on the ethereal plane. But on waking, the person has a whole range of mixed memories and, of course, leaving the body is not a memory that's supposed to remain. So things become garbled. Those who meditate will have a clearer picture than those who don't, simply because it gives them the ability to find that inner place more easily.

The lady I'm working with can only see a future stretching out ahead of her without the person she loves. Somehow I have to get her through this. I know she will survive, as it isn't her time to be called back, but that doesn't make the process any easier. Again, I can't help thinking of Seb and the way that he's being pulled into things that only serve to complicate his life. It's a time when it should be all about healing. Quite simply, it is hell on earth. In both cases, if they could just stand back and let go of their grief for one moment, they would have clarity. It would allow them to circumvent so much of the pain. Neither one of them is at a stage in their spiritual development to appreciate that, so it's purely wishful thinking on my part.

The things that I can't talk to Alex about don't usually cause me a problem. I will admit that when I'm feeling particularly drained emotionally it does affect this side of my life. Sometimes my thoughts are constantly elsewhere, even if that is only for very brief moments at a time.

"I can't wait for this break, Alex, and I promise I will try to totally switch off and concentrate on us."

"That's my girl." He brushes the hair away from my face and looks down at me intently.

"You work too hard and you do need this time away. I know that."

Looking into his eyes is like seeing into his soul. His concern for me is touching and it's a totally selfless act. It's the true sign of a soul chosen to visit this life to be instrumental in the fate of others. They do good works without being consciously aware of their purpose here, but their true vibration is one of healing and guidance.

"I think the universe is sending us back some of the good karma we've been sending out," I grin back at him. "I'm counting down the days."

**

Sheena's visit is relaxing and fun. I suppose Alex and I are like two excited children with our break coming up, so our evenings are light-hearted as we entertain our friend. After the evening meal we stay up late playing board games and laughing. Alex excuses himself around ten o'clock, as he has to leave for work at seven each morning.

"You two go together so well," Sheena remarks, late one night. "I told you there was a Mr Right out there for you. Alex is pretty special, I hope you appreciate him."

"You did and I do, appreciate him that is, all the time. There's a Mr Right for you too," I add.

Sheena looks at me with a slight frown.

"I'm beginning to think that isn't true."

Her aura is a beautiful clear red, indicating a powerful and energetic energy. However, the traits that are associated with that mean Sheena is also very competitive, sexual, and passionate about many things. Sometimes her work life stands in the way of her personal life. I wonder if now is the right time to point that out, because it needs to be said. Kelly is one of her guardian angels and helping to steer her in the right direction. It's obvious that everything will come in time and that there is nothing to fear. Her fate is such that she won't settle down until a little later in life, but I can't see anything untoward, unless that is being hidden from me.

"Your life revolves around your work at the moment and that makes you happy, right?" I throw in, cautiously.

She leans her head back, taking a few moments to contemplate.

"Yes, I love what I do and the fact that I travel extensively and have different experiences. But I know there will come a time when I will tire of this, Ceri. What then?" A sadness creeps over her.

"Then your life will move on when the time is right." I reach across and touch her hand. The life-force I feel is vibrant and positive.

"Don't worry about the future, there's nothing bad. I would tell you if I could sense something to worry about, and you aren't alone."

Immediately she looks at me and I realise I've said something without thinking.

"I don't have spirits around me, do I?" She looks freaked and I detect a hint of fear.

"I didn't mean that." I try to downplay my words, as if she's misunderstood me. "I'm here for you always."

Sheena looks relieved and our attention returns to the Scrabble board. As I pour her another glass of wine I make a mental note to be more careful. Sheena is the closest person I have, after Alex and Seb. She is like a sister to me, but she knows much less about the other side of me now than Alex does and it isn't something she's meant to be involved with.

CHAPTER SEVENTEEN

Time To Kickback

As Sheena flies off to her next job, Alex and I are busy getting ready for our own trip. She was slightly emotional when we parted, hugging me and making me promise I will ring her when we are safely back home.

There's a slight chill in the air as Alex and I quietly pack the car and it feels as if we are the only ones up and about. At five o'clock in the morning it's a very different world. There's something slightly decadent about being so wide awake and excited. There is little traffic on the road as we begin our journey to the channel tunnel. The miles speed by before the early morning rush hour begins to slow our progress.

We chat, listen to music, and once we are safely aboard the shuttle, we both fall asleep. It's only just over half an hour, but the gentle sway of the carriages speeding along on the rails is blissfully relaxing. Only the announcement over the loudspeaker that we are about to arrive in France stirs us, and our holiday is about to begin.

The manor house, Le Jardin dans le Parc, is truly wonderful. Standing at the entrance to the sweeping drive leading up to the house, it's amazing. The view of the eighteenth century building, set within the beautiful grounds, feels like a glimpse of heaven on earth. With its grand windows and detailed stonework, even on a grey afternoon it's too beautiful for words. Most of the extensive grounds are covered in forest. Only the areas immediately surrounding the house have been cultivated. Rolling lawns, perfectly manicured flower beds and the most stunning display of topiary inspire this image of classic French style. It is indeed a garden within a park and beyond the trees there is a lake that runs close to the rear elevation of the house. Our room is at the front and overlooks the beautiful lawns and rose beds. Walking around to the terraced area, there is a sheer drop down to the edge of the lake. The stone flagstones are covered with a display of potted geraniums. All are still in bloom, although the leaves are beginning to fall as the chilly morning and night air reminds them winter is coming. The pinks, reds, and whites are a mass of blazing colour.

We settle in and realise that communication is going to be a problem. The couple who run the hotel are both Dutch and do not speak any English. Our French isn't the best, so there is a lot of nodding of heads when we go down for dinner.

It's too chilly to eat out on the terrace, but the dining room is very elegant. A cut-glass chandelier graces the centre of the room and doesn't look at all out of place. The floor is varnished and with age is now a dark walnut colour. It creaks as we walk across it, in the comforting way that old floors do. Somehow it makes it feel more like being in someone's home than being in a hotel.

The décor itself is more modern. The circular tables have pale green linen tablecloths and the chairs have cream brocade covers, tied with matching green bows. The attention to detail is both romantic and pleasing to the eye. Each place setting has an array of sparkling crystal glassware and the table centres comprise a white candle rising up from a ring of fresh flowers. It's enchanting as the flickering candlelight reflects off the chandelier and the crystalware, sending little prisms of multi-coloured light everywhere.

Alex pulls out a chair for me, before seating himself.

"Well?" he whispers, leaning forward across the table.

"Perfect! It's wonderful and I love it here."

And perfect it was. The evening was a succession of wonderful food and some amazing wines neither of us had tried before. Everything was served with a genuine respect for the dining experience and great attention to detail. Each of the five small courses was accompanied by a different wine. The glasses were huge and only an inch or two of wine was enough to savour and not obliterate the wonderful flavours of the delicate cuisine. The menu was in French and Dutch, so we decided not to worry too much about the translation and to let each course come as a surprise. It ended with the most delicious tarte tatin—the pastry base caramelised to perfection and layered with apples so thinly sliced they were almost transparent.

The meal wasn't heavy, but we decided to grab our coats and walk around the gardens simply to stretch our legs. Neither of us wanted the evening to end, it was as perfect as a scene from a film. Alex was looking so handsome in his dinner jacket and I felt at ease wearing a long evening dress. As we walked we held hands and then Alex pulled my arm into his.

"You look amazing tonight," his voice sounded heavy with emotion. "Not that you don't look great all the time, but you know what I mean," he added.

"Thank you, I feel good and I think we both brush up rather well!" We laughed. The wine was pleasantly softening our mood, without overwhelming our senses.

"I think I can safely say that this has been the most memorable evening of my life. It's all down to you, my lovely angel. Thank you for agreeing to come away with me."

I burst out laughing.

"It's a hard task but someone had to do it."

He playfully tugged at my arm, safely tucked into his.

"Is it time to head back? There's an incredibly comfortable bed awaiting us and a Jacuzzi for two…"

"Mmm, I think it's that time. Wouldn't it be lovely if life was always like this?" I looked up at the starry sky. From that vantage point, in the middle of extensive grounds and with only a little light pollution from the house spilling out into the darkness, there were millions of little twinkling lights. I wondered how anyone could ever believe there was only the here and now.

"Come on." Alex encouraged me to begin walking back to the house. He pulled my arm a little closer into his body. "I can't wait to find out what you are wearing beneath that gorgeous dress."

"Alex," I admonished, "there you go again."

"I can't help being in touch with my female side." He laughed. "You do look gorgeous and I'm not apologising for using that word. I also can't wait to get my hands on what's underneath and show you what it does to me."

"Okay," I replied meekly. "Sounds good to me."

CHAPTER EIGHTEEN

A Moment In Time

Sunshine peeks through a gap in the blind and I open my eyes suddenly, remembering we aren't at home. I close them again, snuggling up a little closer to Alex and savouring the peace and quiet. Not a single car or honking of a horn to be heard; only the birds and nothing else.

Alex rolls into me, his eyes still closed. "Wondered when you were going to wake up. This is bliss, isn't it?"

"Mmm, what time is it?"

He props himself up on one elbow to glance at the clock. "Just before seven. Our breakfast in bed will be here soon. We ought to have a bit of a tidy…"

A brief knock on the door and it swings open. I pull the covers up to my chin, but Alex lays there, naked to the waist looking sleepy but cool.

"Bonjour." The patron calmly waltzes in, placing a large tray on the writing desk with hardly a glance. As the door closes we both dissolve into a fit of giggles. I hastily look around the room. I'm sure there isn't anything he hasn't seen before, but the trail of clothes leading to the bathroom is a bit of a giveaway about our evening pursuits.

"I can't believe we left the room in this much of a state." I sit up and survey the rumpled clothes.

"Hey," Alex says over his shoulder, as I adjust my seating position and he hops out of bed to collect the tray. "We had other things occupying our thoughts at the time. A little chaos doesn't hurt once in a while."

However, on his traipse back he places the tray at our feet, then stoops to gather everything up in his arms and deposits the pile on top of an armchair.

"Is that better, Madame?" he enquires.

"Yes, now come and eat breakfast. You said we need to be on the road by eight o'clock and I need a hot shower."

Alex had planned a visit to Versailles and I was thrilled when he suggested it. It's a place I've always longed to visit and even suggested it when I spent time in France with Sheena. I couldn't convince her as she isn't into history, or old buildings. Le Jardin is just north of Paris, so it's an easy journey if we avoid the city and the suburbs, taking the longer route. It's pleasant driving with long stretches of road interspersed with roundabouts and a few small towns.

We expected Versailles to be grand and to have the proportions of a palace, but the size, grandeur and opulence is overpowering. At a time when many people lived in hovels, this was another world entirely. We decide to wander around the grounds before taking the tour inside of the Palace. The sheer scale is bewildering and I'm so excited, wanting to soak up the ambience. You can feel the intrigue and the place is alive with a sense of the generations who have lived, loved and suffered here. Alex purchases a guide book in English and I read out aloud to him as we walk.

"Versailles was regarded as the ultimate example of a royal residence for over a century. It began with Louis XIV and continued to the time of Louis XVI. Versailles is a wealthy suburb of Paris now, but originally it was merely a country village. It became the

centre of political power from the late 1600s. How's your history?"
I take a peek at his glazed look.

"Not too good."

I skim the pages and then flick through. In the middle there's
a map of the grounds.

"Okay, we'll head in this direction. You've heard of the Petit
Trianon, Louis XVI gave it as a gift to his wife, Marie Antoinette?
She was only nineteen at the time. The small château was meant
to keep her occupied and she whiled away her time redesigning
the garden in the latest English fashion. The Petit Trianon was
originally built for Louis XV's mistress, Madame de Pompadour,
but it became famous for being associated with Marie Antoinette's
extravagances. Only the Queen's inner circle were invited as it was
reputed to be a place of intimacy and pleasure, away from the
prying eyes of court life. Imagine someone so young having all
that responsibility, she was only fifteen years of age when she was
married. Alex, thank you for bringing me here, I absolutely love it!"

"I can tell," he replies, smirking. We stop at the top of several
flights of sweeping stone steps to survey the Grand Canal, which
the guide book tells us is an incredible sixty two metres wide and
fifteen hundred metres long. It seems to stretch endlessly into the
distance and even Alex is speechless. He stands at my side, taking
in a scene that simply cannot be described. Grand or magnificent
seem to hardly do it justice.

We wander along the gently curving path that takes us away
from the astounding view and find ourselves surrounded by manicured lawns, vast flower beds, sculptures, and ornate fountains.
Everywhere there are little hidden corners and my mind conjures
up pictures of clandestine meetings between lovers.

"You love this stuff, don't you?"

I laugh. "It shows, does it?"

We've been following a tall hedge and it opens up to a little
vantage point, a simple terrace surrounded by a stone wall and
with a wide stone bench.

"Sit," Alex commands and at first I laugh at his tone, then I see his face is serious. I put the guide book down, feeling guilty I've bored him. It's easy for me to submerse myself in the history and my romantic imaginings of life at court. But then, as a teen I was an avid reader of historical romance mainly because, I suppose, it was a form of escapism.

He turns away from me as I sit, to look out across the view. When he turns back to face me he has something in his hand.

"Ceri, I brought you here today for a reason." He walks towards me, kneeling at my side on the dusty ground so that our eyes are level. "I can't imagine ever being without you. The point of bringing you here was because I wanted to show you that, in terms of this life, we are a dot on the timeline of history. This dot, though, is the most important thing in the world to me. I'm not saying to you that what you know about everything out there isn't relevant, but our togetherness has a place too. Will you accept this?"

He takes my hand and turns it palm upwards, then places a ring in the centre of it. It's white gold, with one single diamond in a square setting. It's beautiful. I sit here for a few moments as tears fill my eyes. This little corner is protected from the wind and the hedge stifles any sounds from the grounds immediately surrounding the main buildings. It's as if we are alone here and time stands still. His eyes have not moved from mine, but words are hard to find.

"Alex, are you asking me to marry you?" I whisper, my throat hoarse from holding back a full flood of tears.

"I know we could just go on as we are, but I need 'us' to be official. I want to tell the world I've found my soul mate and I don't intend letting her go. Is that selfish of me?"

"Alex, you don't have a selfish bone in your body. But do you know what you are getting yourself into? We're still feeling our way along and what if something gets in the way? I don't want to think of hurting you ever, and I don't want you to have a false sense of security. I can't see our future. I just hope and pray it's one that sees us being together until this life is over."

He bends his head and I can feel the emotion within him. He throws his arms around me and hugs me so tightly I can scarcely breathe.

"I'm not asking for guarantees, I'm only asking you to accept this symbol of my love for you. It's a promise that when the time is right we'll make it official, God willing."

I nod, wiping away the tears that escape, despite the enormous effort I'm making not to let them flow. Tears of happiness and sadness too, hope for our future together and prayers that this is something our fate will grant us.

"Alex, as long as I am here on this earth I am yours, that's my promise," I whisper into his ear. It's enough and we sit entwined, while the wind playfully messes our hair and the magical backdrop of Versailles casts a spell over us both.

This was meant to be.

CHAPTER NINETEEN

Announcements

Alex's proposal was a total surprise and I didn't see it coming. He admitted to me that he had confided in Sheena about his intentions and asked her opinion. That worried me slightly—what if he'd let anything slip? Obviously that wasn't the case, or Sheena would have said something, but it was yet another sharp reminder that our situation isn't straightforward.

We are both excited to share our news, of course, although we've decided not to set a date or to feel any pressure about arranging a wedding. It also presents me with a headache. Telling my parents is going to be a problem, but more importantly sharing our news with Seb. It's not something I feel able to do by email and when I ring him I'm rather relieved to hear he sounds more like his old self.

"It's lovely to hear your voice, Sis," his words reflect warmth and he's genuinely pleased.

"I wondered how you were doing. And I have some news."

"I'm fine. You have to stop worrying about me, I'm surviving. Quite frankly, with some of the things I've seen since I've been travelling, it serves to remind me that I still have a lot for which I need to be grateful. I've moved on again and I've met up with a group doing work for a social enterprise agency. It's unpaid, but there's free accommodation and a small allowance. So what's your news?"

"Alex and I are engaged, we aren't setting a date or anything heavy like that. It's just the next step."

He immediately replies and I can hear he's happy for us. "About time! He's a great guy, Ceri, and I thought that from the start. Wish I knew him a bit better, but such is life. Do I sense some hesitation though? I always thought you'd be the one to tie the knot first and not me."

The irony of that is so sad, but I know what Seb means. I want to be excited and do the bride thing, although I would choose to do that in a low-key way. Seb has no idea that it isn't that simple. I still find it hard to believe that fate is smiling upon us.

"Life is busy at the moment and we both have new jobs. There's so much we should catch up on, you know. Do you see yourself coming home, even for a short visit? I could send the money for the air fare?"

He pauses and I can feel he's torn, but the answer is said without hesitation. "No, I have to discover who I am so I can move forward. I think I'll know when I've found something that feels right. For now I'm happy to try anything that comes along. At least at the moment I feel I'm being useful. Every single day I see hardship that you wouldn't believe. It's a sad world at times."

"I know, but always remember that you can only do so much. Don't take the weight of the world on your shoulders, do your bit and try to live with what you can't change."

"The only way to survive here is to understand you can only help to relieve the suffering for a few. Sometimes even that is a temporary thing. It's better than doing nothing at all."

"I'm proud of you Seb, and I love you."

"Don't run away from the marriage thing, Ceri. Embrace it. You take life too seriously at times and you never know what's around the corner, take it from me. Grab the good things that life has to offer and feel blessed."

It strikes me that my brother is changing in ways I hadn't even considered. From being a man with a totally closed mind, he is gradually learning that life is multifaceted. What you see depends upon where you are standing and what your life experiences have been. He has taken the first step on his own path of enlightenment.

***

"We should have a party," Alex mumbles, his mouth full of potato chips.

"Why?"

"Because it's a bit mean-spirited simply sharing the news. We're doing everyone out of all the free food and drink that usually accompany an engagement party."

I groan.

"Seriously, Ceri, think about it. We can invite your parents and that will be so much easier than travelling down to see them. I know you've been ignoring it, but you can't keep them in the dark forever. Especially now that you've told Seb, it seems unfair. We can still keep it small, but it would be nice to invite a few work friends too. Niall has already asked if we are having a party."

I feel as if my back is up against a wall. When I said "yes" I was only thinking about Alex and myself, forgetting that other people around us will have expectations.

"All right, but we keep it to the minimum." Alex moves in for his trademark hug, picking me up and twirling me around. "Now put me down and go and find a venue. I'll organise the food, but that's it."

"You must be a little bit excited, admit it." He flashes me his stupid grin.

"No, it's all a pain and it means I have to phone my parents sooner rather than later. See what you've started?"

"Ring them after we've eaten, don't let it cast a shadow over things. Remember that everyone else at the party will be there because we want them to be, they'll be happy for us. You never know, your parents might feel the same way too."

***

When I ring to break the news I'm glad Alex is in the other room. My father answers the phone and without saying anything other than "Hello Ceri," he immediately puts down the handset. There are a few minutes of silence.

"Hello?" Clearly he didn't bother to mention who was calling.

"It's Ceri, Mum."

"Oh, hello Ceri, that's unexpected. Seb doesn't have a problem, does he?" Her voice becomes anxious.

"No, he's fine. I spoke to him yesterday. I'm ringing with some news of my own."

"I do worry about him so and we miss Anna, she was such a lovely young woman. Is he talking about coming back home?"

"No, not at the moment. Give him some time Mum, he isn't ready quite yet. He's discovering who he is and thinking about what he wants to do with the rest of his life."

Her voice turns cold. "Why is he suddenly so unsure of himself? You haven't been advising him, have you? Seb was always the one who knew where he was going. Look at the wonderful experiences he's had and now he's reached the point in his life where he needs to settle down."

"Look Mum, when you find someone to love it never crosses your mind you will lose them. What Seb's going through is quite normal given the tragic circumstances." I wish I hadn't dialled the number. Alex can't understand how every time I talk to my parents it turns into a disaster.

"You are hardly an expert, but Seb going off to discover himself sounds more like you talking, than Seb. He needs to move on and find someone else."

I'm almost speechless with anger. Not least because in one breath she is dismissing Seb's loss as if it's one of those things, suggesting he should now look for a replacement.

"I haven't called to argue. I want to tell you that I'm engaged and Alex and I are throwing a party. I will send you an invitation in the post. If you are both free it would be an opportunity for you to meet him. Work is very busy at the moment and I can't really take off any time to come and visit."

There's a moment's silence.

"Oh, I see. And who exactly is this Alex?"

"The man I've fallen in love with. I'll send that invitation out to you this weekend."

I hit the end call button and sit, my nerves on edge. There seems to be absolutely no connection whatsoever between my parents and myself. I will have to sit Alex down and explain that he can't have any expectations when it comes to meeting them, or he's going to be in for a big disappointment.

CHAPTER TWENTY

When The Past Catches Up

"Time to party." Alex stands over me as I'm leaning in to straighten the flower arrangement on the drinks table.

"Well, the buffet looks great and the room is perfect. Let's hope the guests behave themselves." I grimace. I'm not a party person at the best of times and the thought of introducing my parents to Alex's family makes me want to roll my eyes. It will be fire meets ice. Alex can tell I'm worried and I will be so glad when this night is over.

"Come on," he taunts, flashing me his grin. "Relax. It's supposed to be a celebration. Let me see that ring." He grabs my hand, holding it up for inspection. "Divine. And the ring isn't bad either." He laughs.

"It is beautiful and you look awesome." I lean into him and plant a soft kiss on his neck. "In case I forget to mention it later, I'm very proud to be engaged to you, Alex. I love you more than I could ever have thought possible."

We hug for a few minutes, drawing breath before the guests begin to arrive.

"Any last minute instructions?" he asks nervously.

"Yes. You are doing the intros for the parents and I'm staying well away. Rescue your parents before the conversation deteriorates and that's an order. How about you? Anything I need to be wary of?"

He looks at me as if he's giving it some serious thought. "Hey, I was only joking," I add.

"Consider it done," he says, as he heads off to the reception area. "By the way, did I tell you that I am the luckiest man alive?"

"Many times, now go!"

I pop up to the room The Bell Inn have set aside for us to change in. My dress is laid out on the bed and I take my time getting ready. I figure it's a little bit like practising to be the bride, everyone will be expecting me to arrive fashionably late. There's a knock on the door and I hear Sheena's voice.

"Come in!"

"Hey, how are you doing girl?" She waltzes in looking very glamorous and with shining eyes. "I've brought a plus one as instructed and he just might be someone special!"

Her excitement is infectious. It seems the party has begun.

***

Sheena does my hair, piling it high on top of my head with one single tendril curling down around each side of my face. It's a new me and it looks good. She helps me to slip on the floor length gown, and standing back to look at myself I feel elegant. The colour on the label said nude. It's a very soft pink with a strappy top, falling in simple folds from my waist to the floor. A thin silver belt matches the silver necklace and earrings Alex helped me choose.

"You look amazing, Ceri!" Sheena sighs. "You'll be a bride next and that means I'll be a bridesmaid yet again."

"Not for a long time yet, so there's still time for you to beat me to the altar." We burst out laughing.

"Now there's a thought." She chuckles. "Are you ready?"

"As ready as I'm ever going to be. I really need a drink though."

"Follow me, I know a man who might be able to remedy that little predicament for you."

As we descend the staircase the buzz of music and laughter filters up from the function room. There are already about twenty people inside and we head over to Alex. He's talking to someone I don't know and Sheena immediately introduces him as her plus one.

"This is Sam, we work together." We shake hands and I manage to stop myself from saying that Sheena has kept this very quiet. She hasn't ever mentioned him to me before and I flash an inquisitive look her way. She blushes.

"Great to meet you, Ceri. Congratulations on your engagement. Alex was just telling me that you recently visited the palace at Versailles. I'll have to remember that for the future if I ever decide to get engaged."

I take an instant liking to him.

Behind us the room is filling up and people are searching for us, gifts and cards in hand. Alex steers me away and in the direction of Niall and Alicia, who have just arrived. Niall is carrying a large, beautifully wrapped present.

"Ceri, Alex, congratulations you two! Alicia chose this, I have no idea what it is, but it's heavy." He hands the parcel to Alex to place on the present table, which I notice already has a small mound of boxes and a stack of cards. Niall kisses my cheek and shakes Alex's hand. I lean in to air kiss Alicia and she says a quiet, "Thank you for the invitation. I hope you two will be very happy."

"Our pleasure, and you really shouldn't have," I add, feeling slightly embarrassed.

"I hope you like it, Alex mentioned you love cooking." Before I can reply with a quip that I'm sort of banking on Alex being in the kitchen more than I am, Alex is at my side and whisks me away to meet his work colleagues.

It's one long round of meet and greet. Then I spot my parents arriving. I nudge Alex and he leaves me to chat whilst he takes care of them. Following behind is Mark and his wife, Sarah, so

I excuse myself. As Mark introduces us, I look up to see Alex's parents, Tony and Helen, wander in. I grab Sheena and ask her to sort out drinks for Mark and Sarah, then make my way over to Tony and Helen. They both hug me as they would a daughter and I can tell they are thrilled to be here celebrating our engagement.

"Alex is over here, talking to my parents." It's the worst scenario: I was hoping I wouldn't be around for this bit. Alex has already spotted us and heads across the room with my parents in tow and we meet in the middle.

He gives his mum a kiss and a hug, then shakes his father's hand vigorously. His father leans in to put his hand on Alex's shoulder and give a hefty pat. At that precise moment three of the people I work with arrive and I make my apologies, leaving Alex to deal with it. A sigh of relief escapes my lips as I walk away and I only hope no one has heard it.

I sort out drinks for the guys, and walk them across to Sheena's little group to get acquainted. It's a juggling act and I'm exhausted already. I'm about to grab myself a big glass of wine when I see a familiar face appear in the doorway.

"Seb!" I screech and run the length of the room, jumping into his arms. Tears of joy run down my face and I wipe them away with the back of my hand. "How did you get here? You never said..."

"I asked him." Alex is at my side as Seb releases me. I turn and Alex throws his arms around me.

"I knew it would make you happy," he says and leans across to shake hands with Seb. I study my brother's face. He's heavily tanned and he looks well, but much slimmer and tired. Gone is the carefree guy who meandered through life and standing in his place is someone who is a survivor. There is a new sense of strength about him. Maybe determination is a better description. My mind is whirling and then I remember that Alex has left our respective parents alone.

"Come and say hello to Mum and Dad," I say, dragging Seb across the room. As we head in their direction it's obvious they

205

are making polite conversation that is a bit strained. As soon as my parents see Seb they stop talking and there are a few tearful eyes. Everyone is interesting in hearing about the latest project Seb's been involved with and it's a relief. It breaks the ice.

Alex and I slide away to grab two glasses of wine.

"Alex, that was a totally amazing thing to do! Seb told me you sent him a return ticket, you are the best, do you know that?" I reach up on tip toe to kiss his cheek.

"What makes you happy makes me happy too, angel."

Alex's father suddenly appears at my side, carrying two empty glasses to be refilled. He smiles at me and inclines his head to Alex, indicating a group of people standing by the window.

"Alex, I just bumped into Alicia. You didn't mention you were in touch after all these years. What a lovely surprise."

The colour drains from Alex's face and he shoots me a glance. I open my mouth to speak, but I can tell from Alex's reaction that now is not the right time. I help his father top up the glasses and he walks back to the group gathered around Seb.

"Alex?" I don't know quite what to say to him.

"It's a long story and one I should have told you when we first met. I'll explain later, I promise." We kiss briefly. I'm still a little stunned, but pull myself together. Not least because I'm anxious to check on what my parents are talking about and whether the subject of their difficult daughter has yet raised its head.

I leave Alex and walk back to them. The room is buzzing with laughter, soft music and happiness. We're getting through this and another two hours and it will all be over. Seb is home for a while at least and I'm feeling happy. The only worry is that Alex is uncomfortable and I don't know if I should be worried. I purposely walk past Niall and Alicia, who are still talking to Sheena and Sam. I walk straight past, but as I do Alicia suddenly turns, totally unaware I'm behind her. We bump slightly, she apologises and I smile as she heads in the direction of the cloakroom.

Something inside me groans, oh no, not that. I continue walking.

That moment of intense pain, guilt, and desperation that hit me when Alicia and I touched remains with me. I look around for Alex and our eyes meet across the room. He stares at me for one lingering moment and absentmindedly runs a hand through his hair in a solitary act of desperation.

No words are necessary. His soul is crying out *forgive me*.

FOREVER

PROLOGUE

Ceri isn't meant to fall in love, as she is here for one purpose only. Alex is supposed to cross her path briefly and give her the confidence to move on and fulfil her destiny. It's meant to be a turning point for them both – but in opposite directions.

Ethan Morris, a well-respected medium, gave Alex a warning after receiving a message for him from the other side. Ceri receives her own warning when it's made very plain to her that she is responsible for her own actions and will have to put right anything she changes in error. Alex begs Ceri to meet with Ethan, but she refuses to believe what he has to say and manages to convince Alex that he could be wrong. Psychic medium Mark Kessler becomes Ceri's spiritual mentor. Her confidence begins to grow as she gains an awareness of her work on both planes of existence, something that can only be granted to an angel.

As Ceri and Alex cling to their relationship things begin to unravel and, at their engagement party, Alex's past catches up with him. At the same time Ceri faces the stark reality that fate cannot be cheated...

ALEX

CHAPTER ONE

You Can't Run From The Truth

"She's gone, Ethan. Ceri's disappeared and I think it's because of Alicia." There's silence on the other end of the phone and I can't stop myself from pacing back and forth. "Are you there? Hey man, I really need your help."

Ethan lets out a sigh. "Alex, I tried to warn you. You can't mess with fate and I know you both felt you were meant to be together, but clearly this is telling you something. You lulled yourselves into a false sense of security. Call it wishful thinking. I don't know what else I can say to you." He sounds grim.

"No, this is different. Honestly, this isn't about our being together, it's about the abortion that Alicia had. If only I'd told Ceri everything at the very start... I'm a complete and utter fool!"

"How did she find out? I'm rather surprised it should come to light after all these years. What were you, eighteen or something when it happened?"

"Yeah and I know it's a long time ago, but my parents recognised Alicia at the engagement party. I think Ceri put two and two together, and then suddenly she was gone. When I went back to the flat some of her things were missing, but there was no note, as if she had been spirited away." My voice cracks and I grit my teeth, trying to stop myself from shaking.

"I think you are forgetting one thing," Ethan's tone is forceful.

"What?"

"Ceri is an angel. She would be able to connect with Alicia's emotions on a much deeper level. Nothing can remain hidden, unless she has a close and personal involvement with the other person."

"How could I forget—man, I've blown it!"

CERI

CHAPTER TWO

Facing Facts

The split second I bumped into Alicia it was as if the inside of my head had exploded. I saw the energy of a baby and felt the love. That bond between mother and child. It was only meant to briefly experience the wonders of those early weeks of growing, safe inside the shell of someone with whom she will forever be linked. Out of all of the zillions of energies, we each have a 'family' in tune with our own unique vibration who are with us forever. No matter what happens, or which plane we are on, that bond never weakens. That's why the power of love is so strong and miracles sometimes happen, fuelled by an emotion that can transcend everything.

I knew instantly that I had to leave the party, to walk away from Alex before he had the chance to officially place that ring on my finger. It would link us with a promise that I couldn't make, simply because I knew it was wrong. My heart was in pieces, but my ethereal mentor was calling me and directing me to leave.

It was an impossible situation and at first I seriously doubted I had the strength of character in this mortal body to obey. As I pushed clothes into the holdall and gathered the things that I would need I knew that I wasn't just leaving Alex, but also Seb. It was unfair on my dear brother who, despite the sad memories, had come home to help celebrate our engagement.

But I wasn't running away. This wasn't something of my choosing.

"Why?" I asked the voice with no name, as our minds linked and his thoughts filled my head.

"Because it was never a part of the plan for your earthly life, Ceri. I think you knew the moment you touched Alicia that she is the next person you have to help. In order for Alicia to heal and forgive herself for the decision she made about that young soul, she needs to hear Alex say he understands. That will bring them together once more, because that is their true destiny."

"No!" The sound that came forth was hardly recognisable as my voice. "I can't give him up. I can't survive here without him. Please, I'm begging you." As fast as my feet were taking me away from the apartment, a part of me was hoping I would soon be making my way back. "Please don't wrench us apart."

"I'm not the creator. It isn't in my power to change anything and you know that's not how it works. No one questions the path, it's simply there and in each life it's different. Alicia has suffered for many years and it's now time for the suffering to end. Destiny is a part of creation, everything evolves through experiencing emotions and when Alicia returns to spirit she will be able to help others along their path. She will have empathy and understanding that can only come from experiencing something first-hand. You are destined to understand the loss of true love. There is no turning back, Ceri. As an angel you know that."

His words spoke the truth, but my human form was much frailer than my spirit energy and one was overpowering the other.

"Pull yourself together. You have important work to do. You will have to work at sorting out the situation you have made so much worse than it need have been." The tone of his voice was more of a reprimand than his words. I know I created this mess.

If I had listened to my instincts, or even the guidance I'd been given, Alex and I would simply be good friends. Alicia coming back into his life would not have been a problem. I hung my head in shame. There is no such thing as a fallen angel... or is this yet another earthly anomaly?

CHAPTER THREE

A Message For Me

I knew each step towards building my new life was going to be mercilessly straightforward. I would have welcomed a battle, if only to have an excuse to let rip the horrible mix of emotion within me. The path mapped out before me is clear. The plan was merely to disconnect myself from Alex completely, so that he would realise it was over between us. Alicia is his future, but it's too soon for him to understand that. The circumstances have yet to unfold.

I threw my SIM card away and purchased a new number as soon as I'd found a place to rent. It was on the other side of town, so there was little likelihood of bumping into Alex and it meant I could still keep my day job. It is all happening so instinctively, now I'm really listening to what my core vibes are telling me, that I hardly have to tune in. This isn't about starting over again, only correcting one painful mistake: sleeping with Alex, oh, and falling in love with him.

I try to accept the inevitable, simply because I – of all people – should know better. Alex's pain wears more heavily upon me than my own. He emails me dozens of times each day.

I will never stop loving you until my last breath...

I need you, I can breathe without you. I can't sleep, I can't eat...

I know you would not do this to us unless you had no choice...

I forgive you, but I cannot believe in a divine power who would think of our love as anything other than something extraordinary and meaningful. I go on because I'm too cowardly to take the easy way out...

I lie in bed at night and my hands remember your body, my mouth longs to kiss you just one more time...

Nothing matters to me now, without you by my side. I will accept it because I know how much you love me. You can't hide that from me. We belong to each other no matter what...

There has to be something we can do, Ceri, I can't accept this. I don't care if I go to hell, if that's the price I have to pay...

His emails are long, his mood swings reflect the emotional rollercoaster he's on, one moment desperate and the next forgiving. Each one tears another hole in what's left of my heart.

If only Alex could understand there is no heaven or hell, no price to pay as such. But if I hadn't walked away I would have robbed him of a future that has already been mapped out for him. Imagine the repercussions as this one major change ripples outwards, affecting future generations. There is no hell Alex, my soul cries out to him silently, only the whole of creation and the universe. This life is just a tiny part of that.

But I've come to understand something else. Something that I don't think even my ethereal mentor can see. And that is the fact that this life counts for everything when you are here. Alex is a much younger soul than I am, so our paths might never touch again on any plane. The tears I shed might as well be blood. Each little droplet represents a part of me that is dying, once lost, never to be regained – on either plane.

I mark Alex's emails as spam so they no longer drop into my inbox. I cannot delete them, read or unread, and change the setting to never auto delete. I don't know why, because all is lost and there is no turning back. It's not that I fear being punished, it doesn't work in that way. No one checks the work we do. It's all instinctive and the emotions that bring out the worst in humans – jealousy, anger, hatred – simply don't exist other than here. Everyone works quite happily for the good of the universe and with joyous intent; it's really so simple I can now see it's almost laughable. Earth life is like a film full of special effects and when the film is over everyone goes home to reality.

My new reality is cold and stark. It is a life without Alex.

***

Weeks have passed and each day has been a struggle for my human persona, although my spiritual self is progressing in leaps and bounds. So much so that Mark has admitted I've outgrown his mentoring.

"You're a strange one, Ceri. I've never had a student like you before. At the start I realised you had a very intuitive sensitivity, but within such a short space of time I can't believe how you've developed. Things that took me a long time to adjust to, and skills that required honing to a fine degree, seem to come so naturally to you. There's nothing left I can offer. You have outgrown your teacher." He sounded in awe and also a little sad.

"You helped me find myself Mark, and for that I will be eternally grateful. You taught me to stop fighting my instincts and listen to the inner me. I feel like I've been reborn." I reached out and touched his arm, giving it a gentle squeeze. I wanted this man

219

to know I was indebted to him. I still felt guilty that I couldn't explain how exactly my eyes had been opened and that I live my conscious life on two very different planes. He understands that we all visit the ethereal world when we are in a deep sleep, but in this life he will not have knowledge about how angels work. It's so frustrating, as he has his suspicions, although his theory isn't quite correct.

That's what scared me so much when Alex went to see Ethan. Ethan is a more highly evolved being and he knows exactly how angels work. That's why he told Alex we were not meant to be together. He could see the path stretching out before me, even though I seemed intent on changing it.

"It will be strange not having you there when I'm on stage. I've enjoyed calling you up and you must be delighted with the reception you've received. You must stretch your wings now and confirm the bookings you've been offered. People warm to you instantly when you are on stage receiving messages. I think a large part of that is down to the way you so easily tap into the emotions coming through. I'm so proud to have been a part of your development, it's been a privilege." Mark isn't usually an overly emotional man, but tonight he's opening up the most sensitive part of himself.

"Thanks, that means so much to me! Now, go and meditate. Clear your head, because you're on in fifteen minutes."

We exchange smiles and part. Mark heads off to the quiet room and I walk back into the hall to sit in the audience.

He has a great session. His messages are clear and well received by all. There's hardly any negativity amongst the audience, which is unusual. Fortunately, the vast majority of people who attend an open evening with a psychic medium come hoping for a message from a loved one. Each will be seeking something in particular, whether its confirmation their loved one has safely passed to the other side or forgiveness for something they regret. A handful will be there merely to prove to themselves it's fake.

People don't realise that the message in itself is not important, because in spirit nothing that happens on earth is of any consequence. It's a training ground, where we learn about right and wrong, hope and disappointment. Emotions make the soul grow, and some of the awful things that happen here on this earthly plane happen only for the reason of allowing a soul to grow and gain understanding. Humans have the power of free choice and it's the same in spirit. No one controls us, but then again there is no need. Earth is the only plane where bad things exist.

Free will was given so that people could experience having to make choices. On the ethereal plane that isn't an issue, we are all simply involved in fostering harmony and spiritual growth. But a part of our job is also to support those on the earth plane, as it certainly isn't an easy existence. For those energies that come back repeatedly to help others on their path, each life can be very different. No life is entirely easy, but some are incredibly hard and that level of experience is always a sign of a more evolved soul. The extreme experiences are reserved for those who can utilise and share their learning, upon their return. My ethereal mentor once told me that being in the presence of someone even closer to the centre of creation than him was a truly humbling moment. His words were "the purity brought tears to my eyes".

A round of applause fills the room and it takes me a moment or two before I realise one of the other guys on the stage is pointing directly at me. As the hall falls silent I feel the colour rising in my cheeks. The man walks down the steps at the side of the stage and approaches me from the centre aisle.

"I'm sorry." He apologises as he walks towards me, eyes firmly locked on mine. "I have one more message and this man isn't going to let me go until I've delivered it. Are you happy to accept it?" He seems concerned and I know he will expect me to answer; we all want verbal confirmation from the recipient as we never like to offend.

"Of course." My voice sounds a little uneven. I'm nervous to be on the receiving end.

"He says that there is no looking back. That you have done well, but you must not weaken. He keeps repeating that because it's important." He's silent but holds up a hand to me, as if to say 'wait'. "Let go, he's saying, but I'm not sure what that refers to. And, oh, there's some validation. You recently returned something—it was in a small box. He's touching his heart with his hand. I think this means that it was a really important moment. Like a turning point in your life. That's all I have, he's withdrawing. Thank you for listening."

I nod my head and say a quiet thank you. He walks back to the stage, hardly aware of the power or meaning of his message. I glance across at Mark, who stands up to address the audience and say a final goodnight. He indicates for me to join him as he descends the steps.

"Are you okay?" He places his hands on my shoulders. I see an instant reaction: he senses something but says nothing.

"I'm fine, really," I try to reassure him. I'm still shocked at having received a message in an open forum. It seems someone is intent on making sure I don't fall back on my commitment and that I stay focussed on the task ahead. My heart constricts and I have to swallow the lump that suddenly appears in my throat. My outward appearance might seem calm, but my heart is crying out to the universe. Forgive me, I meant no harm...don't let Alex suffer because of me.

CHAPTER FOUR

Moving On

"Seb, it's me."

"Ceri, where are you? Alex is demented with worry. Why did you disappear and what's wrong with your phone?" He sounds worried and a little angry.

It's understandable, and I feel guilty that he's still in the UK. I know he had only planned a short stay and the fact he's still here means he wouldn't leave until he knew I was safe. But there was no way I could make contact any earlier. I had to organise things and allow enough time to pass, so that it would be very clear to Alex that I'm not going back to him.

"I've found a place to rent. It's a long story Seb, but I'm safe and well. I can't be with Alex anymore and you must encourage him to move on and accept that. I'm so, so sorry for what I've done and the way Alex is hurting, I know it's entirely my fault. I'm really glad you're still here, because he needs you. Thank you."

Seb lets out a loud sigh. "Ceri, we called the police, but fortunately someone saw you only a couple of miles away and rang us. They were travelling on a bus and by the time it stopped and they went back to find you, you were gone. If it wasn't for that sighting, the police would be dragging the river and your photo would be plastered everywhere. What were you thinking? How irresponsible!"

As he vents his anger I know all I can do is listen. He's right, but then he doesn't know the situation I'm in. There was no choice in it for me and that sighting was divine intervention. Everything happens for a reason—and I have to stifle a laugh. So many people say that phrase. Few understand what it really means.

"Look, I'm sorry and I'm fine. You didn't fly back—" I can't hide the guilt that echoes in my words.

"Are you kidding me? My twin sister goes missing from her own engagement party. I've heard of cold feet, but this is insane. Alex is a great guy, Sis, and you've hurt him in the worst possible way. You owe him an explanation at the very least. What's gotten into you all of a sudden? You're supposed to be the sensitive one! I know he should have told you about his past, but he was very young and he made a mistake. It was a long time ago and I'm sure he would have told you in his own time. Since when did you become so unforgiving? This makes no sense to me at all."

He finally runs out of steam and I let a moment or two pass without answering.

"Believe me, Seb, if I could turn back the hands of time, I would. Alex and I should have remained friends and no more. I can't really explain, but I wanted something that I wasn't meant to have and now I have to make amends. Alex needs to find someone... less complicated. Please don't repeat any of this to him, just say we've spoken. Tell him I'm safe, but that it was a mistake, and if he really loves me he will understand when I say that it could never work for us. It's better we split up sooner rather than later. We have to accept that and move on. Seb, I need you to do this for me and it's vital you convince him I'm serious. It's important, and you are the one who can do this for me." I think the begging tone in my voice is enough to convince him.

" I thought I'd lost you too..." His anger has dissipated and he's referring to losing his precious Anna. My heart bleeds for his loss and the pain that I can feel, despite the distance between us. But he's healing, albeit slowly, and I wonder if having to support Alex during the last few weeks has been cathartic for him. Maybe it took his mind off his own problems for a short while.

"Look, I'll text you my current address, but only on condition you don't give it to anyone. The same goes for my new number. I'm going to ring Sheena next."

"Now I feel awful. I've quizzed Sheena because I couldn't believe she wasn't in on it. I thought she was hiding what she knew about your whereabouts. You really are okay, aren't you? Should I be worried about anything?"

"I can't pretend this hasn't knocked me for six. This is so not what I wanted to happen, but sometimes we're not in control of our own destiny. Alex must be convinced that this is what I want, or he won't move on. I can't allow him to suffer that way, so please, be the friend he needs at this moment in his life."

"Okay. I'll do what you ask on the condition that you pick up whenever I ring and you agree to meeting up with me soon. I want to check out for myself where you're staying. There's going to be a lot to sort out as Alex's apartment is let for another two months."

"He can stay there as long as he wants, tell him that. I would like some more of my clothes though and I'm going to ask Sheena to call in and pack them up for me. Do you mind being the one to break the news to Alex? It's not fair that I ask Sheena, but I also feel it will be easier for Alex if it comes from you."

Seb lets out another long sigh. I can tell that he thinks I'm making a big mistake, but what can I say? If I told him the truth he would probably call in a psychiatrist.

"You're breaking Alex's heart, and treating him this way is out of character, Ceri. I thought you would understand. A young, naive couple made a mistake and having an abortion has scarred Alicia for life. Alex didn't have a say in it and I understand that doesn't matter, it takes two to make that sort of mistake. But did you stop to think about the reason *why* he didn't tell you about it in the first place? It changed him, and has affected every relationship he's had since. This isn't simply old baggage, it's an old wound that has never healed."

This is a sensitive side of Seb that I haven't seen before, he's almost pleading on behalf of Alex. It sounds like Alex has poured his heart out to Seb and yes, I knew from the start that Alex carried some old wounds, but I had no idea what had happened. Seb doesn't understand that this isn't about Alex's past, but his future. I can't explain that, so I have to cut short this conversation before I let something slip.

"What's done is done. I'm sorry if it seems cruel, but I have Alex's best interests at heart."

"I never thought I'd ever describe you as cold, Ceri. I think you seriously need to examine why you are doing this, for your own sake, as well as Alex's. Don't forget, I want to meet up with you soon. I'll tell Alex, although what exactly I'm going to say, I don't know."

He disconnects abruptly, before I can say anything else and I lean back against the wall, my eyes closed as my whole body begins to shake. Is it possible to cry without tears? My body is crying out in agony over the unfairness of this situation, for the love I have for Alex that will never die.

"I love you Alex and I always will. If we can't be together in this life, then I'll do whatever I have to do to ensure we are together in the ethereal world. I don't want to be an angel if it means I lose you forever."

The room around me is silent.

***

It took me two days to recover enough to call Sheena.

"Oh my poor Ceri!" Her sympathy was tangible the moment she heard my voice. "Seb called and said you were fine, that he couldn't tell me anything else other than you would be in touch. I can't tell you how many times I've checked my phone each day. Are you safe? What do you need?"

The part of me that I've struggled to hold together begins to unravel as her concern touches my core. Sheena has known me for so many years and even in the midst of this mess, when the whole world will think I'm being cruel to Alex, she's worried about me.

"It's horrible. I want to curl up and die. Everything's such a mess and it's entirely my fault. I couldn't face anyone, even though I knew you would all be worried. Seb is so angry with me and I know I've broken Alex's heart. He's paying the price for my selfishness but please, believe me when I say I'm doing this for him." I can't stop the tears escaping, and trying to keep myself from outright sobbing is difficult. I'm an empty shell, hollow inside where there used to be love and happiness. I can sense that Sheena understands the enormity of my situation and that there is more to it than I can convey.

"My dear girl, whatever has happened is complicated. I know you well enough to understand that. You wouldn't walk away from the man you love unless you had a good reason, and I know it's nothing to do with Alex's past. He believes that you hate him for his part in what happened, but it's the psychic thing interfering, isn't it? Look, I know how accurate your instincts have been in the past, so do what you have to do. I'm here to help pick up the pieces. Whatever I can do to help, you only have to say, and Seb is being a tower of strength in supporting Alex."

"I don't deserve your kindness. I've done something very wrong accepting Alex's love and it's his future that I'm fighting to protect. Why did I think I knew best? Better than the advice I'd been given... free will is a bad thing. It can mess everything up."

"Ceri, I don't understand. You aren't making much sense. Look, I'm going away tomorrow for three weeks, but when I get back we'll spend some time together. If you need me I'm only a phone call away. You won't do anything silly, will you?"

A moment passes as a memory flashes through my mind. "No. You don't have to worry on that score. My life isn't my own."

Sheena exhales slowly. I've failed to reassure her, but what else can I say without breaking even more of the rules?

I've been told that I will live this earthly life for another fifty-two years. While death is a welcoming thought, it isn't in my fate and I know that willpower alone can't overturn what has been decided. I thought I could change things, make it happen because it felt so right but, as the saying goes, pride comes before a fall.

CHAPTER FIVE

A New Normality

My reputation as a psychic and medium is growing. It's largely due to Mark spreading the word. All of the venues where I accompanied him have offered me slots in their annual programme. I'm also beginning to receive bookings for one-to-one sessions and although the thought terrified me at first, I haven't had a difficult one yet. I was concerned I might find myself sitting across the table from a client and my mind would be blank—no messages, no vibes—and what would I do then? Say "sorry, there are no messages for you" and send them home? I'd voiced my fears to Mark, thinking he might laugh, but his answer demonstrated my fears were only natural.

"That's not a problem you are going to have to worry about, Ceri. Some people go out there before they are ready, or with such a big ego that they don't listen as carefully as they should to their spirit guides. It's teamwork channelling messages, and there's no 'I' in team."

His confidence in my abilities was rather difficult to handle. I didn't have the same level of optimism. Then, suddenly, here I am—doing what I'm supposed to do and every step forward is so easy, I can't make a wrong move. Even I'm surprised by some of the things that I hear myself saying. How do I know all of this? From time to time my work on the ethereal plane is more difficult and demands my conscious time. That's the only way I can explain it. Some days I'm hardly aware, unless I sit and meditate and then I'm there, on the other plane and living it. When it's a difficult problem I'm dealing with, it can overlap with my consciousness here and I feel like I'm actively living two lives at the same time. Two sets of thoughts at the forefront of my mind competing for attention. A repeat of what happened that first morning after I talked Alex into believing we could have a relationship. I was here, but I knew I was also somewhere else at the same time. Even worse, I chose to totally ignore everything that Ethan had said in the message for Alex, as if it didn't count.

What worries me now is that I can't avoid Ethan forever. He's a working psychic medium on the same circuit and our paths will cross at some point. What will I say? "Sorry I snubbed you, when I knew everything you had told Alex was correct. I thought I could change what fate had in store for us"? I knowingly tried to sow seeds of doubt in Alex's mind about a man whose abilities far outweigh Mark's and I feel ashamed of myself. I had the worst motive for trying to discredit his words. I wanted Alex to love me without reservation.

In the ethereal world there is only good intention, and there is no ego or need for self-preservation. Energies don't put themselves first, because it isn't necessary. But the earthly part of me feels very real at times and I was fighting for something so precious it was almost heart-stopping. I wanted Alex's love in this life, more than I respected the laws of the universe. Why? This earthly life is harsh, cold and cruel at times, and yet it's also full of emotions that can overwhelm the senses. The suffering some individuals have to bear seems extreme and tortuous. Why have such an intense training ground? Maybe the centre of all being is admitting that creation and the ongoing perpetuity of the universe is missing something?

The power created by emotions that can be all-consuming, that can make a weak person strong, and it doesn't exist anywhere other than here. I now understand that I am a splinter, a part of the spark of life that is creation. It lies within us all, of course, but some sparks are instrumental. Few angels experience an earthly life because our powers do not require that input: we are highly evolved, but are we emotionally evolved?

So here I am, alone, with my heart torn to shreds. Alex is no longer a part of my life and I have no choice but to accept that with grace and humility. It was my transgression that caused the pain both Alex and I have to endure, and the weight of that lies heavily upon me. The load is lightened every single time I pass on a message for someone whose life will be altered by what they hear. Sometimes it's very sad: in this world where there are atrocities that are hard to stomach there is also a wonderful sense of nurturing, compassion and sacrifice. Tonight I saw a woman who had nursed her mother through her final months of life. She was totally unaware that her mother was around her all the time and will be until the day she dies. They are kindred energies from the same family, and will be together throughout all of time.

While the message was positive and very personal, those on the ethereal plane are not allowed to share detail about their non-earthly existence. Therefore the messages are mainly validation, to give comfort, or guidance when someone is in danger of losing their way. The woman who came to me was looking for forgiveness. Towards the end of her mother's life she was required to make some tough decisions about her care, and the guilt she was feeling was overwhelming. In truth, the answer should have been that it didn't matter when her mother was here, and it most certainly doesn't matter now. Her mother's energy is back working on the ethereal plane and helping lower energies, and even humans, achieve their full potential. But her eye will always be on her daughter, because they are one and the same and always will be. For those energies that have experienced at least one earthly life, I can now understand the level of compassion they feel. I know my life here will never be the same now that I've known, and lost, my beloved Alex. I will never get over having to walk away from his love. Am I destined to be the first angel to harbour regret? The thought scares me beyond belief, because that reflects the human side of my nature only. I fear it means my ethereal energy is now damaged. Is that what is referred to here as a fallen angel? If that is the case, I have fallen into the depths of earthly hell and if it was within my power I would end my life here and now. The truth is that life without Alex isn't worth living.

It's strange that in the depths of misery the sun still shines and the birds still sing. Nature continues to surprise and delight, whether that's a glorious blue sky or heavy rain sweeping across barren fields. There is beauty everywhere and in everything, if you take a moment to notice what's happening around you. Now I spend my days showing others how to see with open eyes and passing on messages that are positive, meant to bring comfort or direction. However, what is important isn't the fact that it often helps to make their grief more bearable, but that it's a step towards their spiritual awakening. It strikes me that those who care the most, suffer the most. Earth logic is so hard to understand at times.

CHAPTER SIX

Pain

I thought I had felt pain...and then I linked with Alicia. The pain of losing the man I love is nothing compared with the pain in Alicia's life. That fateful decision is the first thought in her head each morning as she awakens and the last thought on her mind at night. She isn't in love with Niall: she tries hard to convince herself she is, because he has shown her such kindness. He recognised in her a need to be protected and he does that with love and devotion. She is everything to him and the fact that he is unable to father a child and give her what he feels she longs for eats away at him. Everything he has achieved pales into insignificance, when the one thing he really wants in life is beyond his grasp.

They are together in their unhappiness and that is their common bond. Ironically, if they had succeeded in having a child, I feel that the differences between them would have divided them over time. Irrespective of that, their fate does not steer them along the same path. Niall cannot help being business-focussed and that trait will never change. Alicia knows that money and material goods do not bring happiness. It's almost too much for one human to bear and it's clear to me when I visit her, that she cannot continue like this for much longer. Something is going to break and that's why this task has been given to me.

Alicia has strayed off her life path because she can no longer identify with her inner voice, which is pitifully full of self-loathing. She stays with Niall because he clings to her and that isn't good for either of them. He deserves to be with a woman who can love him just as deeply in return. The fact that Alex has been determined as Alicia's soul mate is testing me beyond belief. I am an angel, but a part of me is human while I'm here doing my work and it's that part I struggle to control. Feelings of jealousy and resentment are new, alien emotions that are much stronger than I could have thought possible. I have to keep zoning out the human pull on my nature and concentrate on the task in hand.

My heart bleeds for her pain and real sense of loss. She's a practical woman in many ways. She understands that regretting her decision doesn't mean that having made a different one would have been the right answer. She's not spiritual and doesn't practice a religion, but there is a seed of belief within her. She finds herself having conversations with "whatever is out there" and it's the way she's managed to keep sane, despite the pressures. She has only paid lip-service to the years of therapy she's undergone, aware that the healing comes from within. But the stumbling block is always that inability to forgive herself.

What hurts me most is that I can now see so very clear that Alex too has suffered. He has carried this around with him for a long time, unable to admit how he feels to anyone, even me. His share of the guilt is as real as Alicia's and it made him the man he has become. Subsequent relationships never lasted very long, because after the abortion he felt inadequate. He had failed to inspire a belief in his ability to be a provider and make a commitment, which he feels is the reason Alicia made her decision without consulting him. Suddenly everything falls into place, and the fact that he fell in love with me is even more incredible.

I've been told I have the strength to complete my tasks, I hope that's true. At the time I had no idea at all how deeply my personal beliefs and emotions would be tested. The worst is yet to come and I know I cannot fail.

***

"Seb." I wrap my arms around him and we hug each other with a sense of sadness. The last time we embraced was supposed to have been an occasion of celebration and joy, but it ended so abruptly when I had to leave the party.

His own pain is still visible in his aura, his daily fight to keep on an even course continues. One slip and he risks losing his grasp on the new life he is beginning to build. That is the greatest fear he has ever had to face, greater than the mountains he has climbed or the heights he has scaled. It breaks my heart, and I know that an angel's life on this plane is never going to be an easy one.

"You look tired," he admonishes. He stands back and scrutinises my face. "And you've lost weight."

I stand aside to let him enter and his eyes flick around the tiny entrance hall. I wonder if he thinks I've left Alex for someone else and he's looking for subtle clues.

"Coffee?"

"Yes, thanks."

Seb follows me through into the tiny kitchen. "How long are you renting for?"

"Three months, it's someone I know at work. It's going on the market once the painters have been in to freshen it up. They're moving in together..."

"What a mess." Seb takes a seat at the bistro table.

"How's Alex?" I can't help myself asking the question.

"In pieces. He hasn't been to work since the day you left and he's talking about handing in his notice. He's in no shape to even pretend his life is normal and I'm encouraging him to think about freelancing. It will be less pressure if he can work from home, and doesn't have to face the world if he doesn't feel up to it." He grimaces and I understand how bad it must be.

"He will get over this. There is someone out there for him. It just isn't me."

"Well, we all have to trust your judgement on that one. You broke his heart not once, but twice." His tone is clipped, he thinks I'm wrong and he doesn't approve.

"I know I'm not the one for him and I bitterly regret that fact. Believe me, if I could change this I would." A tear trickles down the side of my face and I turn away.

I stir the coffees and carry them across, sitting down next to him. "I've missed you so much and I'm sorry you were dragged back, only to have more grief. Thank you for stepping up and being strong for Alex. I don't know what would have happened if you hadn't been here." I reach out and place my hand on his arm. Our eyes lock for a brief moment.

"I figure I owe you, Sis. You've always been there for me." His voice is softer, emotional. "Is there any way at all you can see yourself getting back together with Alex? This isn't just cold feet or something?"

"No, Seb. I tried fighting my destiny and look how many people have ended up getting hurt. Free will is a dangerous thing and I'm being taught a difficult lesson. If Alex can get through this, there is a bright future ahead for him. Much happiness and love."

Seb absentmindedly moves his coffee mug around the table.

"I'll do what I can. I'm flying out again next week, but I'll be checking in with Alex every day in case he needs to talk. He's a very private guy, we both are really. I've listened to him baring his soul about his past and his feelings for you, and in return he's listened to my problems. It's been cathartic in a way and it takes someone in the depths of their own sorrow to understand another person's pain."

"I'm proud of you, Seb. Your silver lining is there, I promise you."

"But is there happiness for you?" His eyes reflect his concern

236

for me. His frown is like a question mark. He's asking me if I can see my own future, but the answer is no.

"Lots of things bring happiness. Sometimes getting what we think we want doesn't make things right. What's that saying? Be careful what you wish for, it might just come true." I laugh with the irony. "I can't grab my happiness at the expense of someone else. It goes against everything I believe."

"That's why I'm an atheist." Seb says bitterly. If I believed his words I would be horrified, but I can see what's happening inside him and it's an awakening. "Do you need anything?"

"I'll survive. I always do."

CHAPTER SEVEN

Learning To Forgive

Working with Alicia is tiring. Thankfully my day job is going well and I'll be moving back into my own apartment very soon. I received an email from Seb to tell me he'd found himself a salaried job with an aid agency. Then followed the words I had been dreading. Alex moved out a few days ago and Seb told me Alex had posted the keys back through the letterbox. Our final link was severed, but I was too numb to react.

It's strange to be working on so many different levels at the same time. I'm being given guidance and support which has allowed me to stand back and assess things with a new clarity. I hadn't mentioned anything to Seb, but Alex leaving Grey's is a part of the next step towards growing closer to Alicia. The relationship between herself and Niall is floundering. Not because he has any suspicions about what happened in the past, but because one-sided love doesn't work. She cares for him and idolises him in many ways, but the spark isn't there. Niall is beginning to realise that and he will let her go.

I focus mainly on sending her positive and healing thoughts. Connecting with her mind and making each step forward clear and concise. That is bolstering her self-esteem and she is beginning to listen to her inner self again. She can make good decisions and she can move on. We are both benefitting and the connection we have is helping to heal me. The raw emotions after my split with Alex are beginning to heal over, as I accept my earthly fate. Ironically Alex has had a hand in that, although not quite in the way I think he meant.

Shortly after Seb flew out, Alex contacted Ethan again. He asked him to talk to me. Alex doesn't have my telephone number, but he knew Ethan would be able to find me. The psychic network is a close group and avoiding Ethan hasn't been easy for me, but he sought me out.

"Ceri, it's been a while."

I was thrown when I heard his voice and turned around to see he was holding out his hand. We shook and his handshake was firm. I was taken aback by his aura. Why had I thought he was judgmental when I met him before? He's an old soul and I cringe, thinking that the last time we met things were very different. I hadn't been called back at that point and I only had my intuitive understanding. My angel work was not a part of my consciousness. Seeing him now I feel guilty for the way I dismissed his advice and tried to talk Alex into questioning his theory. He knew the truth: that no good would come of trying to enforce what we both wanted over what fate would allow.

"Ethan, I didn't know you were here tonight." I feel awkward, but I know he will understand the change in me and hopefully forgive the way I acted.

"I'm not here working. I heard you were going to be here so I thought I'd pop in and see how you were doing. Could we meet up afterwards for a drink?"

He's being very casual and it would be rude of me to refuse, but I know Alex has asked him to come.

"Okay. I'll meet you at the wine bar in the High Street, about nine-thirty?"

"Great, hope you have a good session." He flashes me an encouraging smile.

"I hope so too."

***

It was a great night and it reminded me that my angel work is essential. So many messages, so much hope to foster and corrections to make that will allow the true course of destiny to follow through. Granting free will to those who have lost touch with their inner wisdom has been damaging. I'm sure there are those who wonder why the creator doesn't make sweeping changes and over-ride a decision that seems dubious.

It doesn't quite work like that. Take fate, for example. All of the little things I correct have to be done subtly, or the ripples caused will actually do even more damage. Once a change has happened, it impacts on other things. Managing it isn't straightforward. The only recourse at a higher level would be to dispense with the earth plane entirely, and it does serve a valuable purpose. I really believe that it is required to keep everything in balance by teaching valuable lessons. I once jokingly thought there was an inherent design flaw, and I could feel my ethereal mentor's disapproval. What made me think I could ever grasp the whole concept of being? I felt humbled and determined to work even harder to fulfil my part in the process. But now I've lived the theory and I have a story to tell that is stranger than any fairytale.

It means something to me that I have the power to make a real difference to people's lives. I know I have to come to terms with losing Alex's love and let go of the resentment I often feel. Even anger has coursed through my veins, in the early hours when I lie awake wanting him, needing him. He must hate me now and maybe that's not such a bad thing. It doesn't stop my heart from aching and my body from missing his touch, but at least he will no longer harbour hope. Hope, I've come to learn, can be a soul destroying emotion.

As I find myself walking towards Ethan, I wonder just how much he understands about me. I suspect it is much more than anyone else I know.

"Ceri, that was great!" He pulls out a chair for me to sit next to him at a small corner table. "I didn't order drinks as I wasn't sure what you might want."

"A glass of white Grenache would be lovely, thank you."

He disappears and returns a few minutes later. He's carrying one large wine glass, a pint of local ale, and a selection of things stuffed into his two jacket pockets. I give a nervous laugh.

"What?" He shrugs his shoulders, puzzled at my reaction. Placing the glasses on the table he empties his pockets, like a magician pulling rabbits from a hat.

"How did you know I was going to be hungry?" I ask, still stifling laughter.

"I always am after a session—all that nervous energy. Big changes for you, I see." He settles himself down, slipping off his jacket. I sit back and study him for a moment. What can he sense? When Alex initially introduced me to Ethan, I didn't take to him at all. With hindsight, was that down to the fact that he was trying to tell me something I didn't want to believe?

"What do you mean, getting up on the platform? I've been doing it for a couple of months now and each time is a little easier than the one before. I've surprised myself and yes, I suppose you could say some things have changed quite significantly."

He lays out the snacks in front of me. "Ladies first."

I pick up a packet of crisps and give him a grateful smile. I guess we have a few things in common, and maybe he isn't as condescending or judgmental as I first thought.

"Thanks." I give him my best polite smile. "What did you want to talk about?" I watch his face and his reaction is a mix of emotions. He feels awkward and he raises his beer glass to his mouth, taking a generous slug.

"We both know why I'm here, and I told Alex I didn't think it was a good idea. I've been thinking about our first meeting, Ceri, and feeling rather guilty. I didn't handle it very well, which is unusual for me. I'm used to giving bad news and I should have realised how shocked you were going to be. I misread the signs."

I stop munching and look at him intently. "What signs? Are you saying your theory was wrong?" I hold my breath, although I know full well he was right. But hope leaps in my heart to think there is even a slight possibility.

"No, sorry, I can't change what I said. The message was very clear. I simply mean you are a different person now. I don't know what's happened but your aura is amazing. The Ceri I was talking to then probably couldn't grasp the concept of warnings via a dream. Something has been awakened in you. I feel you can read me like a book. The tables have turned. I'm astounded."

I have to be careful what I say. Even though Ethan's vibration is a wonderful thing to behold, he isn't an angel. I have no idea if he's ever met one before, although I doubt it.

"I had a good teacher, and this is my path. I understand now and all I want is for Alex to be happy. I want him to find the person he's destined to spend the rest of his life with. I really wish I was the one, but I'm not. I'm also sorry I took my disappointment out on you. It was nothing personal."

"I know. No explanation necessary, let's call it quits. It reminded me that I can never make assumptions, even when I sense someone is spiritually enlightened."

We sit looking at each other for a few moments. He's a very tall guy, although he's rather self-conscious about that. I like that he's a straight talker and he isn't glib. I can now see why I felt uncomfortable around him, because the truth is all I did was challenge everything he said. I feel embarrassed, despite the way he's trying to smooth over the awkwardness.

"What will you say to Alex?"

Ethan raises his eyebrows in a sad way. "It will sound like more bad news I suppose. There's no point in giving him false hope. I'll be gentle though, and I don't think he really expected anything to come of this chat. Mainly he wanted some reassurance that you are okay. He loves you so much it's still his first concern."

"Life can be very cruel sometimes, you understand that more than most. I can't hide how this has torn me apart, but it's the right thing to do. The only thing."

It's weird, but psychics rarely talk about the messages they receive and pass on. Mostly that's because we have to open up to be receptive. It's like preparing to meditate. There is a process of opening up the chakras so that the spirit world can connect. Afterwards there is a similar closing down process. When in a receptive state, the channel is wide open, but once we finish our work it is indeed the same for anyone else—we leave it all behind us. The personal stuff we pass on isn't ours to mull over or contemplate, we are simply the spokesperson. We are the medium that handles the communication process. Often, after a session, there is little I can remember and at first I found that very strange. I wonder what Ethan remembers. Obviously enough to know there's no point in giving Alex any hope.

He downs half his pint and sits back. "There was a lot of negativity in that room tonight," he reflects.

I nod. "It still terrifies me every time I stand there. I wonder if my mind will go blank and nothing will come."

"Smart lady." He smiles. "Never take anything for granted. No one ever said it was going to be an easy line of work and there are times I know a message will be wasted. It falls on deaf ears. I'm relieved you've found your niche though, and that you can accept what's coming. It's time to move on."

"It will become easier, but some days it's still tough. Alex has a friend, Alicia, has he ever mentioned her?"

"Ah, you know..." He pretends to be distracted, as someone squeezes past his chair.

"He told you the story. He's such a sensitive guy, and it's only recently I've come to appreciate the link between his past and the way he perceives himself. He still feels he failed in some way and I'm hoping that together they can move forward. Be instrumental in healing each other..."A meaningful glance passes between us.

"Understood." His tone is accepting. "I'll do what I can."

"Thanks. I'm so relieved Alex has you to talk to, Ethan. I know how busy you are."

"I don't mind being busy, although the travel gets me down sometimes." He's beginning to warm to me and I'm pleased about that.

"Can't make home life very easy."

"Well, after a very messy split a couple of years back, I can vouch for the fact that working evenings and weekends isn't conducive to keeping a partner happy."

"Oh, I'm sorry. I didn't know."

"It's fine, I'm over it, and I'm not always the easiest person to live with. Jess wasn't a believer and as time went on that came between us. When the question 'how was your day?' crops up, it isn't easy to answer when you are sitting opposite someone who wishes you would go out and find a proper job."

I burst out laughing. "She didn't say that, really, did she?"

"Yep, after fifteen years of studying and honing my craft, countless interviews, talk shows, twelve published books and a busy schedule, every single argument came back to the same thing.

"The lesson I learnt was humility. It's easy to be fooled by all the praise and the positive feedback. But never forget that this is something we are given as a blessing and that it isn't something of our own making."

The more I hear, the more I'm liking this guy. He's a little rough around the edges compared to Alex. Nothing about him is sleek: he looks a little worn. He's the sort of guy who might dress in the morning and forget to look in the mirror to check his appearance. I bet he hates formal interviews.

"Some lessons are best learnt the hard way," I mutter.

"Amen to that."

CHAPTER EIGHT

Picking Up The Pieces

As the months pass I'm increasingly caught up with my psychic work and travelling further and further afield to attend events. I can foresee a point when the day job will have to go, as even working three days a week is becoming a juggling act.

With no significant other in my life, and my new friends being mainly mediums I tour with, I've had to find a hobby. It was Ethan who suggested it would be cathartic for me to write a journal looking back over what has happened. He told me the idea had been "given to him" and that means someone in spirit put forward the suggestion. He indicated that there might be another reason that people out there would connect with what I was saying. He also talked about spiritually-inspired writing. It wasn't something I was familiar with, so he lent me half a dozen booklets written by a medium from the US. It was a series of discussions with various angels and I was surprised by the level of accuracy. There were inconsistencies, but I wondered if that was purely misunderstanding, poor communication, or intention. Some things are not meant to be known and fully understood in this life. If I had read any of this prior to my eyes being opened to my spiritual life, I would have sought out this man. His words were astounding and clearly he wasn't merely talking from personal knowledge, but from detailed interaction with the spirit world. Ethan said if I was interested in spiritually-inspired writing, he could help me tune into the process. It wasn't something many on this earth were offered and he said I should feel flattered.

He's actually a very nice man. Well, nice sounds rather bland, as he can be quite forceful at times because of his beliefs, and he can be impatient. Initially I mistook that as being judgmental, but I can now see it's often because he's frustrated by people's reactions. He genuinely wants to help when he can see someone struggling. If the messages he receives fall on deaf ears, he takes it as a personal knock. I can see why his partner thought he was difficult to live with at times, especially if she didn't share his passion. He lives for his work and is so focused he often forgets to eat. He works too hard and over-commits in his attempts to reach out to anyone who comes forward. Often his diary is full of meetings and sessions with little thought given to him having some down time to relax.

A part of that is an occupational hazard I suppose, and I'm beginning to be affected in much the same way. Even my normal day job doesn't really help me to establish a separate life away from spiritual things. When you work part-time, people are used to you being there less frequently. They often forget to invite you to some of the social after-work sessions. I'm glad about that at the moment. It's really hard not to feel depressed about the fact that the only person I will ever truly love is Alex. It sort of defeats the purpose of even thinking about relationships. There's a guy, Tom, who keeps asking me out, and I've told him straight I don't date toy boys. He laughs, but I am serious. He's five years younger than I am. It isn't solely that, it's also because there's no spark and there never will be. If I said yes because I'm lonely at times, that wouldn't be fair on him.

Sheena flits in and out of my life according to her work schedule and keeps hinting that it's a shame Ethan is alone. I know Madame Voleta said I wouldn't be alone forever, but she didn't qualify that in any way. I don't know if angels who visit earth can have a normal, human life. Perhaps that's because it would be too much of a distraction. Our role is not to be a part of creating future generations, only to correct the things that go wrong.

When Sheena came across my journal, she made me tell her all about it. That was an awkward moment, as she only knows a small part of what has happened. For some reason I felt that there would be no harm in telling her a little more. I never mentioned the word angel but I explained that my life had an agenda and she assumed I was talking about destiny.

Well, that's sort of what it's all about, so I didn't bother to enlighten her any further. At least now she has some understanding of the reason behind my behaviour.

"Don't you feel that maybe you and Ethan have been thrown together for a reason?" she said one day, when we were walking home from the cinema.

"No, why?"

"Well, you weren't very complimentary about him when Alex first dragged you to his office, and after that I felt you were simply looking to pick a fight with him."

I laughed. "Oh, really? It was a case of not agreeing with what he had to say and he was a little abrupt. Not the best start."

"Do me a favour and give him a chance."

I looked at her suspiciously. "Don't try to match-make, Sheena. Anyway, I'm not sure I'm his type."

Sheena smiled, and then tried to hide it. "I'm not suggesting you marry the poor guy, he knows your reputation. I'm simply saying that a relationship can be many things and sometimes companionship and shared interests are a good base upon which to build a friendship. He could be your BSB, no strings attached." She raises her eyebrows.

"What the heck is a BSB?" I'm clueless.

247

"Best sex buddy—some put it a little more bluntly, of course! Wake up girl, are you in the real world or not?"

"Is that what happens with the singles set now? I'm not sure I approve," I admit, rather shocked.

"Oh come on, if some of us had to wait for Mr Right to appear there would be a chance we'd never, ever have sex. It isn't like a mindless one night stand with someone you don't know. It avoids that horrible moment when you wake up next to someone and find yourself wishing you were anywhere other than in bed with a virtual stranger. I'm talking nice, comfort sex between two mutually consenting adults. Someone you can trust, who is in the same position as you are, waiting to see if their soul mate is around the next corner. Someone who can help take away that feeling of loneliness on a mutual basis."

"Sounds rather pathetic to me," I mumble. I'm mortified that my best friend has been thinking about my sex life.

"I know your situation is a bit different, Ceri, but what if it's the same for Ethan? If you are both going to end up lonely workaholics on a mission, why not see if there's a deeper friendship lurking underneath? Having a BSB stops you making a mistake because you're—"

I hold up my hand. "Stop right there! I don't need you to organise my personal life, even if you think you have my best interests at heart. I can sort whatever needs sorting and I'm not that desperate. Really." I feel myself colouring.

"Sex with Ethan is out of the question, then?" She looks concerned and I feel guilty. My response sounded rather snappy.

"Why are you suddenly so intent on getting me to jump into bed with someone?"

She looks at me, guiltily, as if she's hiding something.

"Because Alex has been sleeping with Alicia for a little while now, I think. He's moving on and I don't feel that's the case for you. Not deep down inside. You're stuck and afraid to let go of that last little thread."

I shut my eyes and bow my head, trying to quell the pain that stabs at my insides. I have achieved my task, they are getting back together and the healing guidance has not been wasted. All of the hours I spent watching Alicia and sending her positive little thoughts, gradually rebuilding her self-esteem to enable her to feel whole again. I haven't opened any of Alex's emails, which have continued to fill up the spam box on my laptop. Stupid, I know, not to have emptied it and even to have withdrawn the automatic monthly deletion. I check it regularly, half hoping they will continue to appear and yet knowing I should be hoping they will stop. I can't read his words—for both our sakes. I have no link whatsoever to Alex, other than the dreams I have, which are more like a fantasy playing out in my head. While my spiritual side carries out the work I have to do, the dream-like state before and after deep sleep is obsessed with the need to be with him. It's enough to keep me going, but I'm ashamed of the way I can't let go. It's the only piece of me that is totally mine, a time when no one in spirit can enter my thoughts. Even my ethereal mentor cannot link with my mind when I'm in that sleepy state—neither fully awake, nor in a deep sleep. It's the private part of my mind where I can imagine a wonderful life of doing good things, but with Alex by my side.

"Ceri, I'm sorry. I shouldn't have told you. Are you going to be okay?" I open my eyes and Sheena looks fraught with concern.

"I'm fine. I'm glad that Alex and Alicia have found each other again, that's good for them both. I was...thinking about Ethan. Maybe you are right, but if anything happens it will have to be initiated by him. Then I'll take it one step at a time."

Sheena leans across and puts her arms around me. "Now I've found my Mr Right, I want you to find some happiness too," she murmurs.

"I know you mean well, but maybe I'm not ready yet to move forward. And I have my work, which I love."

"You were the one who always used to warn me that being

married to your work isn't good for you." She laughs, raising one eyebrow in amusement . "I admit I've wasted years on the romantic front, but that was my fate. Now I have Sam, I know he's the one." Her words fade to a whisper and I can see that she feels guilty talking about her happiness at a time when I'm in limbo.

"There are only so many times you can be a bridesmaid before eventually it's your turn. Sam is perfect for you and he was worth the wait."

"Yes," her voice can't hide the depth of her feeling. "He was worth the wait."

"Can I ask you one thing?" I hate to pose this question, but I need to know.

"Fire away." She sounds hesitant, despite her words.

"Is Alex in love with Alicia?"

"Oh, Ceri, my darling girl. I suspected as much. He isn't lost to you, is he? Would you sacrifice your spiritual work to be with him, if it wasn't too late?"

"That isn't a choice I can make. If it was that simple, the answer is yes, I would. But you misunderstand me. I want him to be happy, I'm just not sure he knows what he wants after what I put him through. Is he clinging to Alicia because it appeases his conscience for what she's suffered all these years? Or has he rediscovered whatever they had?"

She stirs her coffee absentmindedly, deep in thought. "I can only pass on information that has come my way. It's not as if Alex confides in me, but he maintains contact. It's been like that ever since I sent him that email after he upset you—that seems like a distant memory now. It's always brief, asking how I am, and he never mentions you but I know he's hoping your name will crop up. He said that he didn't want me hearing it from anyone else and that Alicia has left Niall. She's staying with him, although he said it was only for a short while. I think he was being diplomatic and I assume he wanted me to let you know. Maybe he thinks it will jolt you into action and make you realise that sometimes you

250

have to listen to your heart."

"I wish you could understand, Sheena, I really do. You have to live my life to grasp how little control I actually have over everything that happens. Sometimes I feel like a passenger on a train that's heading for a crash and there's no way I can halt it. I'm frightened and alone, but still the train thunders on. My heart wants you to say that he doesn't love her, he's simply looking after her. My head tells me that I want him to find peace, love and contentment. I know Alicia is capable of that, and more, if she can find the right person."

"I don't know, Ceri. I just don't know, and that's the truth."

***

It was one of those days when it rains endlessly and you find yourself stuck indoors because there's no real reason to venture out. A part of you is glad about that, but it begins to feel as if you are cut off from the world. I lean my head against the window pane and watch the rivulets of water cascade down, hitting the window sill with force and spraying outwards. The grey day reflects my mood. I've just had a session with Alicia and she's doing so well I can scarcely believe it. I am glad for her as the tension leaves her body, and even her migraine attacks are now under control. She is blossoming and a part of that, I'm sure, is down to Alex. The irony of the situation is not lost on me.

Sheena is in Germany at the moment and life is quiet. It's the slow season in the run up to Christmas and so there are fewer psychic fairs and evening audiences. My one-to-one sessions are still very busy. It's all about personal recommendation and my name is being passed around. A lot of the sessions are happy ones, positive messages for people who only need pointers to keep them on the right path. Now that my work with Alicia is less intensive, I feel something is missing. My ethereal work ticks over in the background and seldom bothers me.

The phone rings and I drag myself back into reality.

"Hello?"

"Ceri, it's Ethan. How are you?"

I haven't seen him for two weeks. He's been up in Scotland attending a conference. "I'm good. How did it go?"

"Productive, useful." He seems a little preoccupied. "Are you busy this evening?"

"No, free as a bird." I try to sound upbeat, but my voice doesn't ring true.

"I'm going to a talk. It's about sleep problems really, but it will also go into detail about the various stages of sleep. I think it might be of interest to you. I was given two tickets and I wondered if you'd like to come along?"

"That sounds great. What time?"

"I'll pick you up at six-thirty?"

What's actually going through my mind is Sheena's reference to BSBs and I feel uncomfortable. Then I get a grip. It's not a date. It's merely a lecture he thinks I'll enjoy.

"Thanks for thinking of me." At least my words reflect a genuine thank you.

"It's entirely my pleasure. See you in short while." The line goes dead and I find myself looking down at the phone. He's not an overly polite sort of guy, because he focuses on the practical side of life. He often forgets the commonplace niceties that other people think of as essentials. The fact that he's making an effort is worrying, but I realise that time is short if I'm going to have any chance of making myself look presentable. With messy hair and jogging bottoms and tee-shirt, I look like I've dragged myself out of bed. In fact I've been on the computer writing since six a.m. and Ethan was right, it's cathartic. Letting my emotions spill out onto the page is a harsh wake-up call, but after each session I feel calmer. There's almost a sense of relief and release. Once the words are there in black and white they aren't quite so insistent inside my head. I know I have to thank Ethan for his guidance.

CHAPTER NINE

Just Another Rainy Day

As I shower and dress I keep thinking about what Sheena said. She's right in one way, as I am lonely, and yet it isn't easy for me to open up to new people. The crowd I work with in my day job have no idea that I'm a medium and I need to keep it that way. It's less complicated and means that I'm not dragged into awkward conversations. There are three different points of view: those who believe, those who don't, and those in the middle. People who don't believe often feel they have to challenge you the moment it comes up in conversation. I refuse to be drawn into those sorts of discussions as it can become very heated. People start going on about proof, as if that means something. It makes me shake my head, although I should know better and that it's simply not their time to gain an understanding. It becomes annoying though, to say the least.

That leaves me with only my personal life to talk about. As my psychic work takes up the vast majority of my time outside of the office, there's little I can meaningfully discuss. I need to have some sort of life and the only way I'm ever going to do that is to socialise. I need to mix with normal people. The thought of having

Ethan as a friend sort of defeats the purpose but, then again, it's probably safer. The more I think about it, the more I see that maybe I should let down my guard a little when I'm with him.

I push any thoughts of Alex away. I've learnt that I can't allow myself to let him seep back into my thoughts for even one moment, because he is my Achilles heel.

***

"Oh, you've dressed up," Ethan says as he steps through the door.

I instinctively put my hand up to my hair, wishing I hadn't bothered to scoop it up into a clip. Perhaps it looks a little too formal.

"I thought with the rain I'd play safe. I don't want to end up looking like I've been dragged through a bush backwards." I laugh to cover my self-consciousness. Ethan doesn't usually make personal comments

"Don't mind me, I was teasing." He steps inside, looking rather uncomfortable.

"Where are we heading?" I grab my bag and begin slipping on my coat. Ethan steps forward to hold it for me.

My heart misses a beat. If this is a date, I'm not sure I'm ready… despite mulling things over after Sheena's little talk.

"The other side of town. It's a twenty-minute drive to Charlton Hall, which is a great venue, and there will be drinks and canapés." He holds open the door for me and follows behind. As I lock the door he bends to pick up my bag which I dropped at my feet, and stands there holding it for me. When I take it from him with an awkward thanks, our hands touch and I freeze.

I look up at him: he's at least a foot taller than me and I wish I'd worn heels instead of flat shoes. As we walk to the car he makes polite conversation, and I wonder if he's regretting asking me along. It doesn't flow easily, but I think that's more to do with the fact that I feel so self-conscious.

"Look, Ceri," he says, stopping to turn around and gaze down at me. He frowns, furrowing his brow as if he's battling with a tough decision. "I hope I didn't put you on the spot about tonight. I genuinely think this will be an interesting talk, but there's another reason why I called you. I sometimes struggle to have normal friendships, with women. Heck, that makes me sound like I'm some crazy guy. What I mean is—"

I put up my hand to stop him. "I know exactly what you mean. It's the same for me. In fact, my best friend has been lecturing me about it today. Being serious all the time makes for a dull life, but in our line of work that isn't easy. We are both in the same position, Ethan, so let's not feel awkward. Everything happens for a reason, so let's enjoy an evening out. Drinks and canapés sound perfect to me, and I'm actually very interested in learning more about stages of sleep." I give him a rueful smile, and he laughs out aloud.

"I'm not much good at this, am I?" he jests.

It's enough to clear the air and we manage to chat away quite happily on the drive. He tells me a bit about his family and his ex. He has one son who is six and he really misses him, as he only manages to see him in the school holidays. His partner moved back to be with her family and it's a five hour journey each time he visits.

"I'm sorry it's so messy." I genuinely feel for him.

"How about you? Are you surviving?" He glances at me and then looks straight at the rear view mirror as he indicates and pulls into a car park.

"I manage one day at a time. Sheena thinks I've closeted myself away, and I have to say that loneliness is an awful thing. But sometimes it's easier than having to put all that effort into making new friends. Sorry, I wasn't referring to you, of course. I suppose it's different though, as we know quite a bit about each other already. It's easier filling in the gaps, if you follow my drift. You probably know more about the other side of me than even Sheena does. That does feel a bit strange, but it's actually a good thing."

He raises one eyebrow as if I've said something surprising.

"Couldn't have put it better myself. We oddballs have to stick together."

The easy banter continues as we head inside. It's a large Georgian house set on probably an acre of land. It's now used entirely for corporate functions by the looks of it. The car park is huge and well laid out. We enter a grand reception area, and there are three different talks taking place. We drop our coats off at the cloakroom and wander through in search of The Clarence Suite.

I'm actually quite pleased that I took a little trouble with my appearance and opted for a little black dress. Ethan looks smart but casual in his jeans, pale blue shirt, and navy jacket. We check the meetings board and the talk is in one of the side rooms on the ground floor. The room can probably hold around eighty people. It has an enormous glass chandelier hanging elegantly from the ceiling, which is slightly off centre. It's clear this was originally one half of a much larger room. I think it would have been a magnificent ballroom once. On the other side of what is now a dividing wall is probably an exact mirror image of this room.

"Great place, isn't it?" Ethan stoops to whisper into my ear, but I notice he doesn't move in too close. He grabs two tulip-stemmed glasses off a silver tray and nods for me to move on into the room to find a seat. "Over there, on the right? Near the back, just in case it's boring and we can slope off early."

I shush him as a few heads turn and look in our direction, but I don't think anyone heard what he said. His voice is quite deep and he is an attractive looking man, I've noticed women often look his way. His height too, gives him an instant presence.

"Well." He settles into his seat and has to push his chair back to accommodate his legs. "Thanks for coming along, Ceri. I hope it's going to be worthwhile." He hands me a glass and we both take a sip, then immediately place our glasses under our chairs. Trying not to grimace, he shrugs his shoulders and heads off, returning with two glasses of orange juice instead.

The talk is fascinating. Professor Karl Shultz is impressive. I will admit that when we looked at the three events displayed on the board in reception: Sleep Disorders, Keeping Fit & Active over 60 and Marketing & Consumerism, I was tempted to turn around and keep walking. I immediately assumed that this was going to be a rather dry presentation with lots of pie charts, statistics and references to detailed research work. Well, it was all of those things in small measure, but this man is completely fascinating to listen to and watch. His body and hands never stop moving. He's passionate about the subject and his energy, and aura, is incredible. His vibration level in the ethereal world must surely be on a par with my own, although clearly he isn't an angel. He's simply an energy who has been working here on earth for a long time.

Stress is a direct result of the way life here works. It doesn't exist anywhere else, and the moment Karl Shultz steps out onto the small raised platform at the front of the room, I connect with him. He probably doesn't sense it: his ethereal side is reserved for deep sleep, and the irony of that isn't lost on me. His work is obviously to educate people and try to alleviate some of the unnecessary suffering. I glance at Ethan to gauge his reaction. Clearly he's impressed, although I'm not so sure he can see everything in quite the same way I can.

Whilst a great deal of the talk revolves around sleep disorders, his introduction gives detailed background on the various stages of sleep. I have to stifle a laugh, wondering if he will mention that it is only in deep sleep that we all return to the ethereal plane. I give Ethan a sideways glance at that point and he has to turn away from me, as a laugh is brewing. He comes back with a glare that says *behave yourself.*

I've never really understood the differences between the various stages of sleep. I suppose I look at it simplistically. You are either asleep or you are awake.

Professor Shultz explained that originally there were four non-REM stages, with REM being the fifth stage. However, over time two of the stages were combined. The science of how it works had never interested me before; but as he continued it explained many of the problems I'd experienced when working with people via their dreams. Much of the healing and guidance I do happens in the non-REM stages, as these can be remembered by the individual. What happens in the REM stage cannot, simply because this is one of the rules of the universe. Science seems to bear this out, without understanding the reasoning behind it.

What I'd often assumed was someone withdrawing from me, was in fact a part of the natural sleep process taking them further away from me and towards REM sleep. They weren't being unreceptive, but were simply affected by rhythmic brain activity, their heart rate slowing and their muscles relaxing as they moved through the sleep cycle. We exit the room after a wild round of well-deserved applause. I turn to Ethan and start saying how impressed I am and how glad I am that he invited me along, when the look on his face stops me mid-sentence. I turn to follow his gaze and am stunned to see Alex standing a few feet away. He looks shocked and very pale. The eye contact between the three of us is frantic. No one knows how to react. Ethan pulls himself together and turns me around, gently leading me outside.

My legs don't want to work and he ends up putting his arm around my waist to support me. I turn my head to look back at Alex, but one glimpse and he's gone. I lean into Ethan in despair.

Ethan leads me to a quiet bench and then heads back inside. He returns with two glasses of wine.

"Here," he places a glass firmly in my hand, "you need this. I'm sorry about that Ceri, I had no idea Alex would be here. It wasn't planned, this wasn't a trap. Alex is devastated, I can't believe this has happened. He assumed I'd taken you to a psychic talk and he told me he was working. He is, I just didn't know it was at the marketing talk here tonight."

I can feel he's mad with himself, but there's also something else: confusion. Everything happens for a reason, but why now, when the pain is beginning to lessen? Well, I say that lightly, as if it means something. It doesn't, but after all these months you learn to quietly accept what you can't change. Poor, poor Alex.

Ethan's mobile kicks into life and he checks the caller ID. He rolls his eyes. "Sorry, I have to answer this, it's Jess". He immediately stands and begins pacing back and forth. Clearly it's not good news. The call ends and he walks back towards me looking ashen.

"My son has been admitted to hospital with suspected appendicitis. They are taking him down to the operating theatre now." He stands there, not sure what to do.

"Go. Your son needs you. I can call a taxi. You have a long journey and you will want to be there when he wakes up."

Ethan looks relieved. He thanks me and leans forward to kiss my cheek. "I hate leaving you like this," he admits, and I can see he feels torn. Something else is unsettling him, but I give him a hug and say "Go. Be a daddy."

I sit for a while after Ethan's car disappears out of the car park. I can't face drinking the wine and walk back inside with it. I approach the reception desk to book a taxi and within a minute or two a small queue forms. Another of the talks has just finished. A woman standing directly behind me in the queue touches my arm, and leans forward. She asks whether I would mind sharing, she's overheard me giving my address and says she lives on the other side of the park.

"I don't like travelling on my own at night," she offers, apologetically. It's rather nice to have some company and I ask the driver to drop me off on the corner of the street, bidding my companion goodbye.

I walk slowly, deep in thought. As I approach the building I begin searching for my keys and when I turn my head to delve inside my bag, I glimpse a shadow. I snap back into the moment and begin walking a little faster. It's hard to tell, without turning around and staring, whether this is a real person or a spirit. The traffic on the main road obscures the sound of footfall, despite the lateness of the hour. It isn't fear I'm feeling though, no, it's something very different that I can't quite explain. I hurry inside the building and close the door firmly behind me, but as I step into the lift I hear the door click open. Whoever it is has the security code, so I relax a little, but the feeling in the pit of my stomach remains, like a ball of nervous energy.

The front door to the apartment opens on the first turn of the key and I step inside, feeling slightly breathless. For some unexplained reason I don't reach for the light switch. I drop my bag and jacket on the floor and stand for a moment in the twilight. The moonlight streaming in through the sitting room windows filters into the hallway. I realise the door didn't click behind me and I wonder why I was so careless, but my feet refuse to move. I could easily push it shut, simply by stretching out my hand, but something prevents me, even when I see a shadow hovering in the hallway. It steps inside. The door closes and I find myself standing within inches of the one man I can't resist.

We don't speak. Alex wraps his arms around me and pushes me gently back against the wall. His mouth is hot on my neck and I find myself holding my breath. My legs feel shaky and I'm glad to have the wall behind me for support. His body presses up tight against mine and there isn't one part of my body that isn't on fire.

As our lips find each other, I close my eyes and the voice is in my head. "Be careful, you are doing the work of an angel, but you have the temptations of a mortal." It's real enough for me to know I'm being guided, but every single cell in my body is screaming I want this, I need this man…

Alex scoops me up into his arms and carries me through to the bedroom. He lays me gently on the bed and stands over me. Even in the gloom I can see his face is full of love and passion. As I tug off my clothes, he drops his shirt on the floor and our eyes don't leave each other for a second. It seems like moments before we are lying next to each other and this isn't about right or wrong, fate or making mistakes. Rules mean nothing. This is about us and at this precise moment it's bigger than fate or the universe. Like a thief in the night, Alex has stolen my heart again, but this time he's taken my soul as well. Whatever the price I'm going to have to pay, it doesn't matter anymore.

***

We awake just before dawn. I'm not sure who stirs first, but suddenly our eyes are open and we're gazing at each other. Not one single word has passed our lips in the time we've been together. Words are inadequate, and what could we say to each other? We both sit up and I look at Alex nervously. He looks back at me with sad eyes, full of sorrow and pain. He leans forward, kisses my forehead and within minutes he's dressed and walking out the door.

I am incapable of moving, so full of distress at the emptiness he's left behind him. Not just from the loss of his physical presence, but the love and desire that filled this room which is now totally desolate. My body still tingles with the joy of loving the only man with whom I can be whole. The places he touched, the kisses and caresses, already memories of pleasure that might never be revisited. My mind relives the feel of his body, the warmth of his skin and the firmness of taught muscle as passion swept us both away. I let out a wail, like an animal in distress, and the sound is barely human. If the ethereal plane hasn't already registered my transgression, it will sense my pain now. My heart has been wrenched from my body yet again and I don't know how much more I can take. I shiver, as it dawns on me that I did nothing. I let him walk away...I let him walk out of my life as if he doesn't belong. Just a thief in the night.

ALEX

CHAPTER TEN

Accepting The Inevitable

I feel feverish. Whether it's the adrenalin, or fear, I don't know. A dry sob wracks my body and the pain feels like there's a huge lump of iron stuck inside my chest.

Like a drug addict, I'm full of self-loathing because I fed my addiction, but it doesn't only hurt me: it hurts the woman I love. How could I be so selfish? I hear a key turn in the lock. Alicia is back and she'll wonder where I've been. I glance at the clock. It's just after eight in the morning, so she's probably been down to the local store to pick up milk or something for breakfast. I quickly grab the clothes I dropped so carelessly on the floor and head into the bathroom, locking the door behind me.

I switch on the shower, then turn and stand in front of the basin, staring into the mirror. As I pull off my clothes I take stock of what I see reflected before me. Man, you're in hell and you look like it. My body is mottled, almost bruised in places from the passionate clinches as Ceri clung to me. I've just spent an entire night making love to an angel. I disgust myself. I couldn't even speak to her, because if I did it would have been to say one thing:

"I don't care about what's right or wrong anymore."

I can't face work, even though I'm now freelance and all I have to do is take six strides and I'm at my desk. Pathetic. The day passes and sounds of the outside world filter in through the partially open window, serving only to remind me that everyone else is functioning normally.

By mid-afternoon I need to get up, my body is sore from lying in bed. I force myself to go out for a five-mile run, leaving the iPod behind because my head is already too full of stuff to tolerate music. I don't think, I try to switch off and let the rhythm of my feet pounding on the pavement calm me. When I begin to lapse, and thoughts creep back in, I run faster until the cramp is so painful I have to drop down onto a bench at the side of the road. It's chilly today and I cool down very quickly.

Suddenly, I hear my name. I spin around and there's someone standing back against the tall hedges behind the seat.

I blink and they are gone. Turning back around my mouth is still open. I was about to ask how they knew my name. As I sink back against the bench there's a pressure on my shoulders that feels slightly uncomfortable. Like someone has grabbed me, albeit with mild force, but as I grow accustomed to the feeling I find it strangely relaxing. A sensation of warmth spreads up my shoulders and into my neck, creeping up and over my head. I close my eyes.

How long I've been sitting here, I don't know, but my arms are covered in goose bumps as the sweat has chilled in the cool air. I feel like I've been asleep, but because I didn't wear my watch I have no idea of the time and decide to jog back home at a gentler pace.

As soon as I unlock the door, Alicia calls out to me.

"You're back." Her voice is full of concern. "Are you okay?" She walks out of the kitchen, drying her hands on a towel. "Coffee?"

"Please. I'll jump in the shower. Back in five minutes."

I shower and change. Walking back into the sitting room I feel relaxed and less stressed.

"I'm glad you're running again." She smiles at me, anxiously.

"I think I need to settle back into my old routine again. I become lazy when I don't exercise. Thanks." I take the coffee mug Alicia hands to me. She's looking brighter these days and it's good to see. "How was your evening?"

"Great! I'm meeting up with a couple of people from work tonight, down at the local pub. Do you fancy coming along?"

"No, you go and enjoy yourself. I'm going to work. I've taken too much time off lately and that has to change now. Life doesn't owe me anything and I've been acting as if it does."

She looks at me, shocked, and I realise it sounds a little harsh.

"I mean, I'm running behind on some deadlines and now I'm working for myself I have a reputation to build. I can't expect my clients to wait while I sort myself out."

I'm not sure the explanation helps, Alicia's face still registers concern, but she doesn't say any more.

I carry my coffee through to the study and it's three in the morning before I pull myself away from the computer to slink into bed, exhausted.

CHAPTER ELEVEN

Turning The Corner

What triggers a change in any person? Does it have to be something monumental, or can it be a few very small incidents that add up to a revelation? Seb, Ethan, and even Ceri, have been directing me to take control of my life and move on. Alicia still needs support but, even with the battles she has to face every single day of her life, she finds time to offer me advice or simple encouragement.

Now I'm back in my working and exercising groove, I feel I have a sense of normality. I don't give myself time to think, I do something instead. That means I'm flying through the work projects and clients are really beginning to sit up and notice me. No one ever submits something ahead of a deadline, but I'm on the case now and I work late into the night to ensure I deliver well before time.

There is a sense of satisfaction from picking up the pieces and trying to claw my way out of the mess that I made.

I begin putting things right by talking to Ethan. I rang him to find out how his son was doing, since that fateful night when I bumped into him and Ceri.

"Ethan, its Alex. How did the operation go?" I feel like a heel,

266

knowing that's not the reason why I'm calling, although I really do hope his son is over the worst.

"Great, he's doing well, thanks for asking. They managed to operate before it actually burst. Jess's parents have offered to put me up for the weekend, as Aaron is coming home late Friday afternoon. How are things with you? I can't apologise enough for what happened. I explained to Ceri it wasn't staged and she seemed to accept that. It only happened because I had been given two tickets and I knew Ceri would find the talk interesting. It wasn't a date, I know it looks bad now I come to think of it—"

"Ethan, it's none of my business. I'm moving on now and realise that's something I should have done months ago."

There's a moment's silence and the awkwardness is tangible. So he fancies Ceri.

"Look, I contacted her a while back after you and I chatted, I stuck to pretty much what you wanted me to ask her. After that it was work related. We move in the same circles and we couldn't avoid each other forever. You know my situation. I can't get involved with another woman because my ex, Jess, is very insecure at the moment and not happy to be back living with her parents. It's been hard for her, well, for both of us. Ceri is a great person, but she's not looking to hook up with anyone and neither am I at the moment."

He's given himself away. "At the moment" sounds like a warning shot to me. Okay, this really *is* none of my business, as I can't repeat the mistake I made the other night.

"I think Ceri might appreciate spending time with you, she must be lonely. I have to go, I'm on a tight deadline today. I'll catch you later and I'm glad Aaron is on the mend."

I wonder briefly if something in me has died. I feel disconnected from the emotion I know is there, after hearing Ethan talking about Ceri. He's getting to know her well in a work situation. Ha! Where have I heard that before? A man is supposed to be strong. Well, maybe I've learnt my lesson and my heart now has a shield around it. What better match for an angel, but a man who is a spiritual teacher? My fist makes a ball, but instead of pounding on my chest it comes to rest very gently over my heart. Ceri deserves happiness, no matter where it comes from, and there's no point in feeling bitter. Ethan is probably the person I would choose to be with her.

I'm done with overthinking things. Now I'm simply moving forward one step at a time.

CERI

CHAPTER TWELVE

Facing My Demons

I knew it was wrong. I move the mouse down over the list of folders and click on Spam. The number next to the heading reads two hundred and forty-eight in brackets. As I scan down I can only find a handful that aren't from Alex, until the day after our illicit night together. Something has changed and there is now one solitary email, which is already forty-eight hours old.

I hover over it. It was sent at 3.23 AM. My hand clicks before I have time to think about what I'm doing.

A cold chill runs down my back. I look at the words without reading them, as if they are merely hieroglyphics, patterns on the page. My eyes focus and the colour drains from my face.

We're done and I know it. It's over. A relationship can't be solely about the passion, it has to be a two-way street where both parties are fully committed. I don't know what came over me and I sure as hell don't know what came over you. Throwing me out at the start would have been a good move, unless you couldn't resist one last goodbye and it's my fault for making it impossible for you.

So this is me signing out. Ethan's a great guy. You are both on the same wavelength. I hope for your sake fate smiles on you both, because he's had a rough time too. You both deserve better in this life, never mind about the next one.

Alex

I read it, then read it again and again. At first it stings more than a slap in the face, then I think it can be read in two very different ways. He's telling me to move on and he's blaming himself.

Tears obscure my vision and when I wipe my eyes I see that I've deleted the entire contents of the spam folder. I put my head down on the desk and sob. We're done and, this time, it really is for good.

***

Having successfully brought Alicia and Alex together I wasn't expecting a reward, but maybe some respite from the hell of human emotions might have been a nice gesture. Instead, the days following Alex's email are filled with a whole range of ugly thoughts and feelings. Bitterness doesn't even begin to describe it. I rant and rave, shout and scream, but nothing helps. No one comes to my rescue—whether that's ethereal or mortal. Does anyone care if I go mad inside these four walls? Where is Seb or Sheena? They are busy living their lives and five days pass with no contact from anyone. I sink into a depression.

Sunday morning there's a knock on the door. I drag myself up to answer it, putting the chain on so I can only open it a few inches. I look a mess and am in no fit state to take in someone's parcels.

"It's Ethan, Ceri. Let me in, I need to speak to you. Please."

I have to steel myself to unhook the chain, knowing full well he'll be shocked at what he sees. I open the door and walk back through into the sitting room. He closes the door quietly and follows me in. There's no loud exclamation, no pointed comments about the state of the room or the mess I'm in. Instead he puts both of his arms around me and holds me. Even when the tears have stopped, he continues to hold me. When the strength goes from my legs he lifts me up and lays me down on the sofa. Two minutes later he's back with a cold, wet flannel for my forehead, then he disappears again.

"Here. Hot, sweet tea, and don't say you don't want it, because you are going to do as I say. I'm only sorry I've been away spending time with Aaron. I should have realised there isn't anyone at hand to talk through what happened."

Ethan means bumping into Alex. My mind flashes back and I'm looking up into Alex's eyes as he lowers his body onto mine. Ethan shakes me.

"Ceri, drink this tea. Now. It's an order." He physically picks up my legs and swings me around into a sitting position.

"How did you know I wasn't well?"

"You didn't turn up for the event last night, but don't worry, I covered for you. I went along because I wanted to surprise you. It turned out you surprised me."

His voice is hard. He doesn't suffer fools gladly and I'm a fool. Ethan has a deep well of sympathy, but he won't waste it on people who won't help themselves.

"Ceri." He looks at me sharply. "Do you think you are the only person to suffer? You of all people should abhor the waste of self-pity. Depression is a luxury you can't afford. You should be helping other people who aren't as well equipped to cope as you are."

I reel from his words. He's right, and guilt wraps its ugliness around me.

"I need a shower." I swallow the rest of my tea and pass him the cup. "I'll be back shortly."

He watches me as I walk away, then I hear him opening the door into the kitchen. I return fifteen minutes later, refreshed, dressed, and with my hair neatly brushed and pulled back in a ponytail. The smell of bacon wafts past my nose.

"There isn't much in the fridge. I'm defrosting some bread for some bacon sandwiches. I need to talk to you about a few work-shops I'm arranging. I want you to take part."

He acts as if nothing has happened. I'm not sure what I was expecting, but I think this is precisely what I need. My only concern is, why is Ethan the only one who understands?

ALEX

CHAPTER THIRTEEN

Escaping Into My Dreams

Life is easy. I work hard and the business is growing. Success brings money, which doesn't concern me, but it's also making me see that not everything I touch falls apart. I can be successful in something. I don't wake in the morning feeling depressed anymore, although there's a good reason for that.

I spend my nights with Ceri.

I can't remember one night since that final time together when she hasn't filled my dreams. I can touch her skin, breathe in the scent of her body, and I'm there with her. It's enough to keep me going, because I know that before the day is out we will be together again.

Alicia more or less has her own life now and I'm pretty sure she will be moving out soon. I've felt privileged to be here for her during her split with Niall, when she faced up to the fact that she doesn't need a man in her life. She's a competent woman and I truly believe the hurt within her is healing. She went to see Ethan for a private sitting and afterwards she wouldn't tell me what happened. It was clear when I picked her up to bring her home that she had been crying. Her cheeks were dry, but her eyes were puffy and red. Whatever messages he gave her, she was different after that. I gave her the opportunity to talk about it, but all she would say was that nothing is lost forever and understanding that had helped.

While it's been nice to have company and to feel I've helped a little, I won't be too sorry to lose my flatmate. I know she's moving on to begin again and appreciates the fact that I gave her the space she needed at a crucial point in her life.

Seb contacts me frequently, but we don't talk about Ceri anymore. He's enjoying his new job and now goes out in the field as well as being part office-based. I think it's important to him that he doesn't lose touch with the harsh reality of the job. His input means things really do happen out there on the ground and people's lives are changed in a very real way. He mentioned he's involved in some fundraising over here and I offered to help out if he thought there was anything I could do.

Sheena emails me from time to time. It's always light and friendly. Neither of us ever mentions Ceri.

However, there's one last thing I have to do. I've been putting it off for quite a while. Ethan and I lost touch: it was too painful talking to him knowing that he's the man in Ceri's life now. Eventually I let go of my jealousy because it was eating me alive, and that was liberating. I can now think of Ceri and smile, instead of wanting to hammer down her door like a caveman and claim my woman. Basic instincts are hard to ignore, but there's a real sense of triumph in proving that you are in control. I can do this for her. If I could just see her, to know that he's made her happy, then I could be at peace.

I look at my watch and smile. Another fourteen hours and we'll be together in my dreams. No one can take that away from me, not even fate.

***

My head hits the pillow and the sheets feel cool against my skin. The darkness is comforting. I imagine the stress of the day flowing down through my body and out through my feet, willing my muscles to relax. My mind calls out to her.

Ceri, Ceri, come be with me. I'm here and I'm waiting for you.

I start to breathe deeply, holding each breath and expelling it slowly, counting in a rhythm that lulls my mind.

It's a bright morning, very early, and I turn when I hear her footsteps. She smiles at me shyly and wraps her arms around me. It's gentle and I kiss her shoulder, then lift her hand so that my lips can work down her arm. I kiss her finger tips and hold her hand to my cheek.

"I missed you." My voice is hoarse with emotion.

"I'm always here. I never leave you. If you relax you will feel me. Our hearts are entwined because we are one." She smiles up at me from beneath brown lashes. The breeze lifts her hair and she absentmindedly brushes it away from her eyes.

"I believe you, but it's hard at times. I feel I don't belong here anymore. No one understands me, only you, my love."

Her eyes are sad and she holds me tight against her. "Come, walk with me. Let go of your negative thoughts. Here we can always be true to ourselves, and that's my gift to you. Never fear, you do not walk alone."

Our hands lock. The warmth of her flesh reassures me and, as we walk, I wonder if this is heaven.

CHAPTER FOURTEEN

Happiness Is Seeing The Person You Love Smiling

I had my final glimpse of Ceri. They say everything happens for a reason, well, this one was too big a coincidence not to have a much deeper meaning. I think the universe decided to throw me a break. Did I deserve it? Well, I think the jury is still out on that one. You see, I sent her an email. Well, it was probably the three hundredth one, or something, but it was special. I doubt she opened any of the others, but after our final, totally unplanned night together I knew she would give in. Did I declare my undying love? Tell her how much being with her excited me and made me feel fulfilled? No, I alienated her in the only way I could think of that would allow her to let us go. It was the point of no return, so I wasn't surprised when I was granted this one last thing.

I don't mix in psychic circles, so I have no idea when either Ethan or Ceri are in town for the regular clairvoyant events. To be honest I'm terrified by it all now, and I don't know what I believe anymore. So it's the last place I would go, even to satisfy myself that Ceri's life is a happy one.

I was skimming the local paper over a leisurely Saturday

morning breakfast and I saw it, an advert for a fun run in aid of charity. There was a photo of Ethan and Seb, then some photos of the overseas projects Seb has been involved with. Ceri was mentioned by name in the article and it seems they have also been raising funds by selling tickets to special psychic events. I won't pretend a part of me didn't feel gutted that I wasn't the one chosen to help Seb and Ceri, but Ethan is a good man.

I've come to terms with the fact there was absolutely nothing I could have done differently, that it wasn't my fault and I didn't fail. It was never meant to be, but for a while the bitterness and longing ruled my head and my actions. I've had no choice but to become a stronger person and that final email was my gift to Ceri. The depth of her love meant she would never let go, and our final night confirmed that. She didn't hold back for one second, she abandoned everything she believed in without fear or thought. It was enough for me and I will always treasure that knowledge.

In my attempt to move on I've had a few dates with one of my clients. It started with a meeting over a drink and progressed to a few meals out when we're both free. It's very casual at the moment, as she has a four year old daughter and she's understandably cautious. Macy knows I'm still very raw from the breakup of my previous relationship, but she doesn't know any of the details. It suits us both at the moment and it's a way of socialising without feeling any undue pressure.

I asked her if she was interested in taking part in a fun run and she loved the idea. Macy offered to complete our application and did it in her name with a plus one. As I said, it was too big a coincidence to be merely that.

It was a huge turnout with over two thousand people congregating at the starting line in the park. It was easy to be invisible in the throng of runners clustered in groups as everyone warmed up. Macy is easy to chat to and for the first time in quite a while I felt like a normal guy having fun doing something he enjoys. I kept scanning the sea of faces, not lingering on any one in particular in case I found myself eye to eye with Ceri.

It wasn't until after the race began that I saw Ceri and Ethan. We set off in small groups and as people slowed their pace on the uphill hauls, the groups dispersed and spread out. I sensed her presence before I saw her, something inside me kicking my senses. They were pacing themselves, running side by side, and every now and again they glanced at each other and smiled. I could tell that Ethan was watching her like a hawk, making sure she was running at a comfortable pace. Macy and I began gaining ground, so I had to fake a cramp in my calf muscle to avoid getting too close to them. We stopped at one of the drinks stations and Macy good-naturedly marked time running on the spot while I grabbed some water and did a few stretches. Then we were off again, but I made sure our pace meant we were far enough behind Ceri and Ethan not to be noticed by either of them.

"I've enjoyed today," Macy said when we said goodbye. "You're the first guy I've dated who shares a love of running. My ex was into the gym and was obsessed with lifting weights, but he wouldn't do anything that involved being out in the fresh air." She frowned.

"Oh, the heavy stuff! I admire the dedication, but for me it would be too boring. I enjoy nature and I love being out in the fresh air, so what's not to like?"

She studied my face as if seeing something new in me that interested her. "My thoughts exactly." She smiled. "We must do this again. Maybe not such a long distance next time."

We parted company with our usual smile and a wave, but she hesitated and I wondered if she wanted me to hug her. I'm not ready, yet. Maybe one day soon, but not today. In the car driving home I kept picturing Ceri's face. She looked tanned and happy. When she smiled at Ethan her eyes lit up, as they had when I first knew her and before things became so mixed up. I replayed her smile over and over in my head, like the frames from a series of camera shots...it's just a pity the person she was smiling at was another man.

Enough, Alex! She's happy and that's all you needed to know. I said a silent thank you to whoever had taken pity on me. Then I turned my attention to the next project I was about to start working on later this afternoon. Finally I'm in a place where everything feels neutral, no excessive highs or lows, and that's a good point to build a new future from.

***

The following morning I awake with a start from a deep sleep. I open my eyes and the daylight is harsh, making me squint. I turn onto my side to replay my dream, except that there's nothing there, no memory of being with Ceri to start my day. It's the strangest feeling and I'm truly lost, set adrift in a world I no longer understand. I drag myself out of bed and into the shower to stop the sensation of panic rising in my chest.

CERI

CHAPTER FIFTEEN

The Circle Of Life

Why did I think Ethan wasn't a patient man? He has been by my side constantly, either in person or on the phone, talking me through each day. Every single hurdle and setback I've had, he's listened and kept me moving forward. Without him I would have no focus. At times he's been hard on me, pushing me relentlessly and refusing to let me dwell on regrets and fears. We've grown closer in so many ways and a part of that is due to the fact he has shared all of his own fears with me. His son Aaron is the one thing in his life that brings him pure joy. He admitted that he always felt he'd failed his ex-wife, Jess, who hated the work he did. Towards the end they fought about it constantly. From what I've seen so far though, he drops everything whenever she needs something. Maybe they both need to accept the inevitable and move on.

A bitter laugh escapes my lips. Who am I to talk?

His work is fulfilling, but also full of frustrations. At least in that respect we can meaningfully share our trials and tribulations. Many of the people I help grab onto what is offered, but there are others who brush all help away. Human nature seems to encourage people to hold onto hurt and it is only having a belief that can break the endless circle. Ethan feels each disappointment acutely: he takes each rejection as a personal failure. He laughs at me, good-naturedly, as if I'm well-meaning but missing the point.

"We're on different levels, Ceri. There's so much I don't understand, so I can't look at things in quite the same way that you do," he admits in a regretful tone. There's so much I can't tell him… it seems unfair.

I give up my part-time job and, if I'm honest, it isn't without a hint of sadness. However, there is no point in pretending that my future isn't going to be totally caught up in spiritual work. Ethan has pulled me into several projects which are rather exciting. Not least are a series of workshops and a fun run raising funds for the project Seb's involved with. I didn't realise how I'd pushed everyone away for a short while and it felt good to put that to one side and pick up the threads again.

Seb is going from strength to strength. He's happy and has a wide group of new friends. He never mentions anyone in particular, but I feel he has someone with whom he can talk meaningfully. I see that as a start and I know there is happiness for him in the future, although he will be on his own for a few years.

The doorbell rings and I take one last look in the mirror to check no stray tendrils of hair have escaped the hairclip and I smile back at the reflection I see. These days I am feeling more and more comfortable with the person I am in this life.

"Sheena, you're late."

She steps inside and we hug, her face is glowing.

"I have news…*big* news. I can't wait to tell you," she shrieks. I usher her inside and she literally throws her bag and coat down on the chair impatiently.

"Well?" I ask, my senses instantly picking up the vibe.

"I'm pregnant!" Her face is a picture of happiness and we hug like the sisters we have become.

"Oh my goodness! Congratulations, I can't believe it!"

She looks at me and chuckles. "You knew, didn't you?" she

peers at me accusingly.

"Well, maybe I had an inkling. Coffee or juice?"

"Ah, juice please, I'm thinking healthily now. Can you really believe I'm going to be a mum?"

"And I'm going to be an aunt. It's about time someone had a baby, I can't remember the last time I held a newborn in my arms." As the words escape my mouth a tinge of regret courses through me, but I put it to one side. This is a time to be joyful and count our blessings, and a baby is a blessing indeed.

"How's Ethan?"

I hand Sheena her juice and stir my coffee. "Great. He's been amazing. The fundraising is going really well and we've had a lot of fun with the workshops. Each one has been sold out and the demand has been so great that once it's all over Ethan and I are going to run a regular series of sessions. It seems there are a lot of very stressed people out there looking for guidance on how to make significant changes in their lives. Not all of them are interested in mediumship and clairvoyance, so this is the perfect vehicle for them."

"I can understand people being cautious about the heavy spiritual stuff. I am too, so it's good to hear that the two of you are recognising that. Maybe I'll come along to one of your motivational meditation sessions. Is it a bit like Alcoholics Anonymous? Hello, my name is Sheena and I'm a compulsive workaholic, show me how to relax."

I start laughing and she joins in.

"I like to think it's a bit subtler, but in essence, you aren't far wrong. It's as if people are looking for someone to say it's okay to step back and not feel you have to be productive every second of the day. We've had some fantastic results already."

Sheena rests her elbows on the table and places her hands beneath her chin. She's in serious mode. "Have you slept with him yet?"

"Sheena! I can't believe you've asked me that. We're just good friends." My face colours, despite the fact that I'm trying to remain cool about our relationship.

"Oh, so you're thinking about it then," she dismisses my comment and raises her juice glass to me in an air toast. "To the future," she says, with a wry smile on her face.

***

Sheena insisted that the four of us go out for a meal tonight and a quick call to Ethan confirms he's free. When he arrives there's something different about him. I think he's had his hair cut, or maybe it's because he's looking quite smart this evening. For one moment I have a flashback of Alex, which I dismiss as quickly as it comes. Ethan leans forward to kiss my cheek as I hold the door open for him.

"You look very smart," I can't help commenting.

"I thought I'd make an effort to impress your friends," he jokes, but I can see he's pleased I've noticed.

"Maybe I'll rethink what I'm wearing. I'll be back in a moment."

"I'll make coffee," he calls over his shoulder as he walks off towards the kitchen

I look at myself in the mirror and think how lacklustre I look. I slip off my jeans and top, then grab a couple of dresses from the cupboard. I hold each one up and then discard them. I remember something I bought a while ago that I've never worn. It's a plain knit dress, knee length in a deep purple, and I remember it felt good when I tried it on. As I delve into the back of the cupboard there's a knock on the door and I automatically say "come in". I spin around and realise I'm in my underwear, and I quickly grab the first thing to hand to cover myself.

Ethan stands there looking rather shocked, coffee mug in hand. His eyes sweep over me, slightly embarrassed, and then he turns away to put the hot drink down on a side table.

"Sorry," he mutters and exits as quickly as he can.

My heart is thumping and I feel both hot and cold at the same time. Don't be stupid, Ceri, I reprimand myself. It's unlikely you are going to go through life without another man looking at your body.

I find the purple dress and quickly pull it over my head. I run my hands down over my hair so that it's perfect again and grab the mug. Ethan is standing by the window, watching the traffic go by. He looks up the moment he hears the bedroom door open.

"Sorry," he apologises, unable to look me in the face.

"My fault, I forgot what I was doing and I told you to come in. It's no big deal."

His eyes meet mine and I give him an encouraging smile.

"That looks really good on you. Purple is your colour." He smiles back. It's a grateful smile, but then he frowns. "Ceri?"

"Yes?"

"Can I kiss you? I don't mean a peck on the cheek."

I don't know how I feel about this, but I guess I'll never know if I make an excuse. I walk towards him without answering his question. I put my mug on the table and then turn to face him. Standing on tip-toe I kiss him, and it's a real kiss. It lasts for several seconds and he kisses me back gently. He puts his arms around me to take the weight off my toes and as we pull apart he lowers me to the floor.

"Reaction?" He gazes down at me, his question honest.

"Nice," is the only word that springs to mind, and then I realise that might be a disappointment to him.

"Well, that's a start. I'll try harder next time."

He's sending me a message in very clear terms. There are two options and he wants me to consider how I feel about him before he makes his next move. I'm a little flustered because I'm not ready and I know I've purposely been avoiding thinking about it. I don't know how I feel about taking our relationship to the next level.

***

The pub is packed, but Sheena and Sam are already seated in a booth. It's the first time Sam and Ethan have met, and they shake hands before we all sit down. Sheena has an orange juice in front of her and there's an open bottle of white wine in a chiller with three glasses.

"Wine okay?" Sam asks, pouring out a glass. "Or would you prefer beer, Ethan?"

"Wine's fine," he confirms and I nod. "I hear congratulations are in order for your two, or should I say, three." Ethan holds up his wine glass and we toast. Sam and Sheena are all smiles and the buzz between them is awesome. Sheena is right, Sam was worth the wait. Ethan looks at me and raises his eyebrows, then touches his glass against mine.

"To good news and good times," he says. He places his glass on the table and then slips his hand over mine, which is resting on my leg. Sheena notices and her left eyebrow raises a fraction as she shoots me a glance.

"Pregnancy is an amazing journey, enjoy every moment. After they are born the years go by way too fast," Ethan says.

"You have children, Ethan?" Sam sounds surprised.

"One son, Aaron, with my ex, Jess. He's the best thing that ever happened to me, until I met Ceri."

Sam and Sheena raise their glasses to him in acknowledgement and I give a nervous laugh. Ethan squeezes my hand gently and then moves his arm gently around my shoulders. He's relaxed and happy. I tune out of the conversation around the table as two inner voices discuss the pros and cons of making my decision.

I feel like I'm watching everything through a window, like an interloper. Sheena and Sam are very much in love and in tune, happiness radiates from them both. A sideways glance at Ethan and I feel I'm seeing him for the first time. An attractive guy, he's amazingly gentle despite his tall and powerful frame. He has soft, curly black hair that never really looks groomed. He talks in an animated way, using his free hand to express himself, but content to have one arm curled protectively around me. He's happy to share Sheena and Sam's excitement and it's clear he's connecting with them in a very personal way. I don't think I've ever seen him this relaxed, or this carefree. One of my inner voices says decision time, Ceri, and I wonder if it's my subconscious voice, or whether I'm being guided. I lean in closer to Ethan and he instantly squeezes my shoulder, beaming down at me.

I think I've made my decision.

CHAPTER SIXTEEN

The Next Step

We all end up back at Ethan's place. Sam is a little tipsy from a few glasses of wine at the bar as Sheena is driving. Ethan and I only had a glass, the tension between the two of us mounting throughout the evening.

Ethan takes us through to the kitchen, which is on the ground floor of his three-storey house. Sheena hasn't been here before and enthuses over the décor, so Ethan suggests she and Sam do a tour. "There's a balcony on the top floor," he calls out to them, as they disappear into the hallway.

Ethan pushes the door so it's ajar, then turns to me. He places a hand on each shoulder and stares down at me intently.

"Have you made your decision? I don't think I can't wait any longer."

I take a moment, before raising my gaze to meet his.

"Do you feel this is the right move for us? I'm scared that I'll make another mistake and misread the signs. Maybe I'm supposed to be alone forever. I don't want to hurt you Ethan, not like—"

He places a finger against my lips to silence me, then lowers his head until his mouth is on mine. There's a powerful urgency to his kiss.

"I can't see your future, or mine, Ceri. You know how it works, but I'm not taking this lightly. We have to both feel the same, so no one gets hurt."

"Then I've made my decision."

"So you'll stay the night?"

I nod as the door swings open and Sam stumbles in.

"Nice place, Ethan," his words are slightly slurred, and Ethan immediately flicks the switch on the kettle and opens a cupboard to grab some mugs.

"Do you see yourself having more children, Ethan?" Sheena asks, as I take over making the coffee.

"At some point I would love to settle down and I think Aaron would love to have a sibling. At the moment he's surrounded by adults. His grandparents look after him when Jess is at work. He has a wide circle of friends, though." He flashes me a look.

"How about you, Ceri?" Sam asks.

It's an innocent enough question, and Sam doesn't know the circumstances. Sheena frowns and her demeanour says a silent "sorry, should have warned him".

"You never know what the future might hold. I think most people like to think they will be able to enjoy family life at some point. I'm not close with my own family, which my brother and I always thought was a shame. Families should be close."

It's an honest reply, although I don't think I've answered it the way Ethan might have hoped. He knows why I can't simply enthuse and say I'm looking forward to having children of my own. I can't control my destiny, it isn't up to me.

Sheena tactfully changes the subject and encourages Sam to drink his coffee quickly.

As we see them out she turns to hug me and holds it a second or two longer than normal. When she pulls away her eyes are tearful, but she says nothing.

Closing the door behind them, the house suddenly seems very

quiet. Ethan grabs my hand and leads me upstairs.

"Sheena and Sam are a great couple. They're very lucky."

"They deserve each other and I'm thrilled for them both." My words come out a little breathless. I'm nervous.

"I meant what I said, Ceri, when I answered Sam's question. I'm ready to commit."

He pushes open his bedroom door. It's the first time I've been inside this room. It's very neutral, distinctly lacking in feminine touches, but everything is extremely neat and clean. There's a Zen theme going on and it's a tranquil setting.

I'm going through the motions, following Ethan's lead. He stops in front of the bed and turns to me, tipping back my chin with his hand so that he can stare into my eyes.

"Are you sure about this?"

"Yes, I'm sure."

He pulls down the zipper on the back of my dress and it falls to the floor. I step out of my shoes and lie back on the bed. He strips down to his boxer shorts and lowers himself down next to me. He rolls on his side and places a hand on my stomach, it feels strange. As he leans in to kiss me, he suddenly recoils sharply. A haunted look appears in his eyes.

"What?" I ask, dreading what he's going to say.

"This is all wrong, Ceri. I left it too late. What an utter fool I've been!" He rolls away from me to stand up and begins dressing.

"Ethan I don't understand…?"

"I'm still in love with Jess. I hope you can forgive me, Ceri, but I can't do this. I was scared because I thought you were the one who was going to back out. Talk about a revelation…I sure as hell didn't see this coming!"

CHAPTER SEVENTEEN

Pride Comes Before A Fall

It wasn't until Ethan dropped me home that the relief flooded over me. Who was I trying to kid? Someone on the other side was protecting me from myself tonight. Maybe they were protecting Ethan's feelings as well. How could I try to fool myself like that, when I know what's still in my heart?

I stand under the shower, letting the water cleanse me as if it is washing away the vestiges of another big mistake. When I lie down on the bed I want to hasten into my dream state, there is a question I need to ask.

***

Transition now takes mere moments, living as I do with the ability to be on both sides of this earthly life with ease. I open my mind and know that my ethereal mentor is here for me.

"Why?"

"Because you were about to make big a mistake. You were using your head and not your heart, which was not only disappointing but totally out of character. You were taking the easy way out, Ceri."

"Can you blame me, given what I've been through?"

"Spoken like a true mortal. You are an angel. You are above the pulls of human emotions. You know better." His words sting.

"I've failed."

"Yes."

"How will I learn the new lessons so that I can move on and prove my worth?"

"You have succeeded in many of the tasks you have been set and we are pleased. You have already helped many people and will continue to do so. However, you have also presented us with an unexpected dilemma."

His words strike fear into my heart. I've tried to limit the damage I've done, but obviously it wasn't enough.

"I know I've done wrong. I wish I could say I would do it differently if I was given a second chance, but I cannot lie to you. Nothing prepared me for the feelings I have for Alex. I'm ashamed, but all I can say in my defence is that some emotions are so powerful they take over your mind, heart, and soul. My beliefs are still strong, but I was even stronger when I was with him."

"It's all academic now." The words are communicated without emotion.

"What do you mean?"

"You succeeded in changing your fate. What happens next is entirely up to you."

"But what about Alex?"

"His fate, too, lies in your hands. I'm here if you need me."

The silence inside my head is deafening.

***

It was the longest night of my life. I awoke and began pacing the floor. What does this all mean? Is my life now a blank page with regard to Alex? How can I steamroller into his life again after the pain I've caused him?

I sit at the kitchen table, my hands wrapped around a strong cup of coffee, in the early morning gloom. Little thrills of excitement keep coursing through my body and I have to try really hard to remain calm. What is the next step for me now? It's a little after four in the morning and I wander into the study.

I open up the laptop and go straight to the spam folder. It's full of junk and nothing from Alex. I click compose and type "I'm sorry" into the subject line. What should I say? For a long while I sit looking at the blank space in the body of the email. It glares back at me, as if to say there are no words to right this wrong. Is that true? Maybe this is about learning more than one lesson. If fate doesn't lay out the path in front of us, it suddenly becomes rather frightening to take a step into the unknown. My fingers begin typing and I'm eager to see what appears on the screen.

My darling Alex, I'm sorry. I love you,

I love you, I love you, I love you, I love you, I love you, I love you,
I love you, I love you, I love you, I love you, I love you, I love you,
I love you, I love you, I love you, I love you, I love you, I love you,
I love you, I love you, I love you, I love you, I love you, I love you,
I love you, I love you, I love you, I love you, I love you, I love you,
I love you, I love you, I love you…can you forgive me? I will love
you forever. C xxx

I have to lift my fingers away from the keyboard so that they will stop typing and add the word "forever". I press send without a moment's hesitation, knowing full well that it's probably too late. That might be the next lesson I'm being taught…be careful what you wish for, it might just come true. I can only hope my spirit guides continue to look out for me as I fight for Alex's love.

***

I have no choice but to pack my bag and head off to a psychic convention. I'm making a personal appearance and it's a three hour journey by train. It's in totally the opposite direction to where I want to be heading. It's taking me further away from Alex. I keep checking my emails, frantic when I lose the internet connection on my phone. Nothing. Maybe he isn't online today, or is he simply avoiding me? Is he sitting in front of the pc, my email in front of him and the cursor hovering over it, unable to decide whether to press open or delete?

The day passes, the evening passes, and after hours of agonizing I'm back in the hotel room. Still there's nothing from Alex. I pack my bag ready to leave early in the morning. I know he works from home most of the time and that's my next step.

***

There's no reply when I knock on the door. I ring the bell once, twice, three times, and eventually a neighbour comes out onto the landing.

"No one's home. He's been away for a couple of days." The woman eyes me suspiciously. I suppose I was hammering on the door and then pressing the doorbell frantically. It must look very suspicious.

"Oh, thank you. Do you know where Alex went?"

Clearly she has no intention of sharing anything at all with me. She looks me up and down as if she just caught me trying to break in.

"No. I don't know." She shuts the door and I'm left standing, not sure what to do next.

***

Another day passes. No emails and no reply when I call at Alex's apartment. I don't have his mobile number on my new phone, so I ring Sheena and ask if she can text it to me.

"Ceri, why on earth do you want Alex's number after all this time? It's kinder to leave the poor guy alone. I think he's seeing someone now," she says, gently.

"Alicia? No, it's not what you think. Ethan told me, she was just a flat mate. Alex wasn't sleeping with her, only helping out an old friend." I don't like hearing the desperation in my voice.

"This is a new friend. They were together at the fun run the other week. I didn't say hello or anything, but I saw them and they are clearly an item."

It's like the floor has opened up beneath my feet. It's too late and that is the lesson I'm being taught! I was warned a long time ago…don't change anything as the ripples spread out and the only one to blame here is me.

"You're sure about that? There's no mistake about them having a relationship?"

"Her name is Macy and she has a daughter. That's all I know."

I feel guilty for grilling Sheena, as I know she's only doing this out of sisterly love. "Just because they've been out together doesn't mean there's any commitment between them. This is too important for me to take anything at face value, Sheena."

"He told me himself, I'll send you the email. I thought you'd moved on…what about Ethan?"

"There never was anything other than friendship and shared interests between us. I know how it looked when we went out for dinner, but so much has happened since then. I can't explain now, I can't rest until I'm satisfied I've done everything I can. I will have to live with this for the rest of my life—whichever way it goes."

"The email is on the way. Good luck honey."

I disconnect and pick up the text, saving Alex's number to my contact list. After six rings it goes straight to voicemail.

What can I say? I press the end call button, knowing words are going to be inadequate. When I sit down in front of the laptop I have eighteen emails. None are from Alex, but one is from Sheena. I open it with trepidation.

From: Alex385ID71@pcit.com

To: cheerfulchic01@gmail.com

Re: Thanks for your support

Hey lady! Nice to hear from you and sorry I didn't spot you in the crowd of runners. I was with Macy. She's a client and fast becoming my significant other. We really enjoyed our day and the run was exhilarating. You couldn't have picked a better day for it. Unfortunately we can't make the next one, as it's Macy's daughter's birthday and I'll be meeting her for the first time.

Hope things are good with you.

Alex

I scroll down to read Sheena's original email to Alex.

From: cheerfulchic01@gmail.com

To: Alex385ID71@pcit.com

Thanks for your support

Hi Alex, I just wanted to thank you for coming along and supporting the cause. I caught a glimpse of you, but before I could make my way through the crowd, you were off and running again. I hope you can join the next fun run and maybe we can catch up.

Take care,

Sheena

My chin sinks down onto my chest and I gently expel the air from my lungs in one long, agonizing gasp. Alex's dream is about to come true. A woman who can love him without reservation or complication and a daughter to help fill the void he's always felt from the loss of his own biological child. I delete the email, then delete his number from my phone. Within seconds all hope has died, as I know I can't destroy his chance of happiness with someone who is at least normal. The fact that it isn't Alicia is probably my fault too. What other effects have rippled outwards because of my inability to accept my fate? I can't retract the email I sent, I can only hope it goes into spam and will be autodeleted along with all the other trash.

CHAPTER EIGHTEEN

New Friendships & Strong Bonds

The one very positive aspect about the bad things in life is that the more knocks you receive, the easier it is to drag yourself back up from the floor the next time around. Alex doesn't respond to my email and I'm relieved. Why make a nightmarish situation any worse?

However, I have to see for myself that he's happy. I can't totally let go with good grace until I know for sure he's in a stable relationship, especially after the misunderstanding over Alicia moving in with him.

My plan is to hang around close to his apartment and follow him. Only until I can see for myself that he's really picking up his life in a meaningful way. I don't intend to interfere or complicate things, but I have to be one hundred per cent sure this time around.

Two days following, I'm there from seven in the morning, but there's no sign of him. As each day drags on I begin to wonder if he even lives there anymore.

Then, on day three a taxi pulls up at the kerb. A tanned, fit guy steps out and before he even has a chance to turn around, I know its Alex. He leans in to pay the driver and as the taxi pulls away he's left standing with two large suitcases and some hand luggage. He's wearing a white straw panama hat and he looks so good I groan out aloud. Then I have to throw myself across the passenger seat, as his head turns in my direction. After a few minutes I look up, but he's already carrying the luggage inside.

I feel like a private investigator. Okay, he's been on holiday, but he could have gone on his own. He looks good…so good, that a tingly heat sensation begins in the pit of my stomach. Concentrate, Ceri. What do I do now? I sit and wait, watching for any sign of movement at the windows on the second floor. I spot him once or twice as he passes the bedroom window, no doubt unpacking his suitcase.

An hour and a half later and I'm thinking this is stupid. It's stalking. I'm just about to put the key in the ignition and go home to drown my sorrows with a bottle of wine, when he steps out into the street. He saunters down to the corner and heads in the direction of the local shops. I quickly follow him on foot, trying not to run to catch up, because I know he won't be going very far. I can take my time. I don't want to look suspicious, or draw his attention.

He's not in a hurry, but he has long legs and I have to take probably two steps to each one of his strides. It makes me feel very subconscious and I draw a strange look from a young woman walking towards me. He stops a few times, once to take his wallet out of his pocket and he checks to see whether he has some cash. I have to jump behind a tree. If he turns his head slightly he will see me, despite the discreet distance I've been keeping. Where is everyone when you want to disappear into a crowd?

He isn't in the shop for very long and when he comes back out he has a small bag. It looks like milk, bread, and the usual things you need after you've been away from home. But he has one other, unexpected, item: a small white dog on a lead. As Alex walks off, talking to the dog, I recognise Geoff, the owner of the shop as he steps out and shouts after him. He walks briskly up to

301

him and hands him a small bag, which I assume contains doggy things, and they both laugh. Alex juggles the two bags and the leash, shouting a "thanks" over his shoulder.

The dog begins pulling on the leash and Alex walks faster, but after a few moments the dog is really straining to push forward. Even from forty paces away I hear Alex's voice carry on the wind. "Harry, slow down. We're going home, boy."

The walk back is tortuous. How I wish I could sidle up to Alex and pass the time of day. To be able to engage him in conversation as if we were old friends bumping into each other. Instead I have to keep hiding behind things as the dog continues his stop/start journey homewards. He's a cute little dog, I think he's a Westie. He's pure white and has a very male gait to his walk, despite his little legs.

At the front door Alex has to juggle the shopping and the dog. It's all I can do to stop myself leaping out from behind the rubbish bins to open the door for him. Once he's inside that's it for him for the rest of the day. At eight o'clock I head for home, weary in mind and body.

***

I assume the next morning Alex will have a lie in, then take Harry for his morning walk. I arrive around seven-thirty and I'm right. Moments after I pull up he comes jogging around the corner, Harry trotting alongside him. His tee-shirt is sticking to him and his hair is flat to his head, but I can't take my eyes off him. He disappears inside and I see him pass the window maybe five or six times. It's a work day for Alex and I suspect he will be in the study most of the time. A few people come and go during the morning, but it's hard to tell if any of them are visitors. They are all male, so even if they are visiting him it's better than a succession of attractive women calling at the building. This isn't going to work. I could sit here for days and still not know what's happening in his life.

It's too obvious to involve Seb or Sheena. I can't approach Ethan as I don't think the two of them have spoken for quite a while. Think, Ceri, think! Then the answer presents itself. One of Alex's neighbours, a young guy named Pete, steps into the street and he begins walking in the direction of the shops. I quickly start up the engine and park the other side of the small row of shops. I casually saunter inside and walk up and down the aisles several times, as if I'm looking for something. Suddenly I hear my name.

"Ceri! Hey, you're looking good. What are you doing in this part of town? You haven't moved?"

"Pete. Hi! No, I'm passing through."

"Not visiting Alex?" he asks.

"No, no, nothing like that. I'm on my way back from an event and I need a sugar lift. I haven't seen him in ages, I heard he's in a serious relationship these days." I reach for a big bar of chocolate as if I really don't care what the answer is.

"Well, if you count Harry as a relationship, then yes, I suppose his is." He laughs. "Are you, you know, are you seeing someone, because if you aren't…"

I can't believe he's hitting on me! My head is spinning, if anyone knows whether Alex is seeing anybody at the moment it would be Pete. He makes it his business to check out everything that happens in the building. I realise he's looking at me expectantly.

"Um. I'm sort of off men at the moment."

His eyes widen. I don't like the thought that crosses his mind.

"Really…" he replies, then I realise he thinks I've changed sides. I say a quick goodbye and head off to pay for the chocolate.

As I exit the shop I have a big smile plastered over my face. I open the wrapper on the bar of chocolate and pop a large piece into my mouth. I hear my name being called once more. This time its Alex's voice that carries through the air.

"Alex?"

"Ceri? What on earth are you doing here? And why are you watching my apartment?"

Panic sets in. I don't know what to say. Harry leaps forward, knocking the chocolate out of my hands and he's all over it before Alex or I can stop him.

"Don't you know chocolate is poisonous for dogs?" He scoops up Harry before he can finish off the last little pieces. He looks frantic.

"Jump in," I unlock the car and open the rear door. "There's a rug in the back if you want to wrap it around Harry. Where's the nearest vet?"

"Head towards the bridge, then hang left. Second on the right, you can't miss it."

Harry starts growling, and for such a small dog it's quite a vicious sound. A constant low rumbling.

"Is he okay?"

"How do I know? I've never been stupid enough to give him chocolate before. Only a tiny amount can be very dangerous for a dog his size. He's never growled before, so can you please just concentrate on getting us there in one piece as quickly as you can."

It's only a couple of miles, but the journey is agony. Please don't die little dog, or Alex will hate me forever.

I drop Alex at the door and he dashes into the building with Harry in his arms, still growling. I park the car and venture inside, taking a deep breath before I open the door.

The receptionist looks up. "I'm waiting for Harry," I mumble.

"Oh, yes, chocolate OD." It sounds funny and a small smile creeps over my face, but she gives me a withering look. I don't know anything about dogs, but even I know they aren't supposed to have chocolate. I have no idea why, though.

"I'm the driver," I offer, jangling my keys in front of her to prove it and her face relaxes.

"Your friend is very upset," she says.

"How dangerous is it?" I ask.

"It contains theobromine, which can cause cardiac arrhythmias, epileptic seizures, internal bleeding, heart attacks and eventually death. It depends on the quality of the chocolate, only a couple of ounces in a dog that size can be fatal. He's in safe hands, please take a seat."

Just when you think life can't throw anything else at you, there's always a surprise around the corner.

Thirty minutes later the internal door opens and Alex steps through. Harry isn't with him. He shakes the vet's hand and walks over to me. He runs a hand through his hair. "I need a drink. Harry's going to be fine, but they are keeping him overnight."

I hurry out the door after him.

"Alex, I'm so sorry, I don't really understand about the chocolate thing and dogs, but the receptionist said it causes poisoning."

"Yes. They gave Harry an injection and it made him sick. The vet seems to think the residual effects will go in twenty-four hours. Harry's a bit hyper at the moment and they will be watching him around the clock."

I'm mortified.

"Well?" he stands with his hands on his hip, empty leash swinging from his wrist. "Are you going to at least drive me back to my place?"

"Of course." I unlock the car and Alex settles into the passenger seat.

"I think you owe me an explanation." His voice is grim, and the rest of the journey is in total silence.

CHAPTER NINETEEN

Coming Clean

Alex laughs, then he roars, and then tears begin leaking out of his eyes. He rolls around on the sofa as if he's in pain. All I can do is sit, watching him and grasping my car keys so tightly in my hand that little spots of blood begin to break through the pressure points.

He takes a few minutes to calm himself. It's hardly the reaction I expected after he dragged the full, sorry story out of me.

"You're really telling me that you've spend the last few days sitting in your car just watching me?"

"I had to know whether you were happy." I know it sounds pathetic, but there it is.

"Poor Harry has gone through all of this because you couldn't dial my number or send me an email, like anyone else would have done?"

"I rang you and there was no answer. I did send you an email, too."

"Okay, maybe I haven't been picking up my calls. But I've been away on business and the flight home was a long one. Where's the email? It's not in my inbox." He looks at me accusingly.

"Look in spam."

He stands up and walks through into the study. Two minutes later he shouts out "The answer is yes, I can forgive you, and of course I love you, idiot—even if you did try to poison my dog."

He reappears and before I know it we are kissing as if we've never been apart.

"There's no one else?" I ask.

"No, I decided that nothing could top what we had, so what was the point in kidding myself that I could settle for less? The thing about soul mates," he breathes softly into my ear, "is that it's forever."

CHAPTER TWENTY

Is There Such A Thing As Happy Ever After?

Eighteen months later...

As I finish doing my hair, Alex appears in the doorway.

"I want to take you out for breakfast. Throw on something nice, I'm talking about the best joint in town." I have no idea who exactly he's trying to impersonate, but it makes me laugh.

"Is that Irish, Australian—American? Give me a clue."

"It was the Godfather actually, Marlon Brando at his best!" He flashes that cheeky grin at me and my heart melts, as if it's the first time we met all over again.

"Well, I'm thinking French toast, maple syrup and crispy bacon. Can you stretch to a Bloody Mary? I always think it's such a decadent think to have for breakfast! And why exactly are you spoiling me?"

He walks across to me and as I stand up, we hug. He lifts me in his arms and spins me around.

"Because you are you," is all he says.

There's something really wonderful about the crisp, morning

air and a leisurely walk to a gourmet breakfast.

"Where are you taking me?" He tightens his grip on my hand and gives it an extra little squeeze.

"Lanbury's. I booked a table yesterday. I thought it would be a rather nice way to end one amazingly, unbelievable week."

As we wait for the traffic lights to change, Harry strains forward and Alex eases him back. We stand there smiling. Not necessarily at each other, but at life in general.

"Can we take Seb and…" before I can complete my sentence, Harry's collar breaks away from the lead and Alex suddenly lets go of my hand. It's so unexpected that it takes several seconds for it to register and for my gaze to follow them. One moment he's here, next to me and then…

Alex yells at Harry, frantically waving his arms as he careers towards the scared animal, who has stopped in the middle of the intersection. One moment Alex is running and the next he's in the air, hit sideways by a car that didn't see him. A woman scoops Harry up and cradles him in her arms. Everything has come to a halt and my legs automatically begin running, even though my mind cannot accept the scene I'm witnessing.

The driver is in a state of shock and someone is talking to her through the broken side window, urging her not to move. Where's Alex? He must be fine, I can't see him. As I run around to the other side of the car he's there, lying on the floor with his eyes closed. As if he's asleep. There's very little blood, but it's coming from the back of his head. I drape myself lightly around him, letting him feel the warmth of my body, as his soul hovers above him, waiting for his spirit guides to help him find his way back home.

WHAT REALLY HAPPENED AFTER 'THE END'?

FALLING INTO PLACE

CERI

CHAPTER ONE

When The Day Is Finally Done

"…and CUT! That's a wrap folks. Well done guys, that even brought a tear to my eye," the director shouts and then begins clapping. The applause ripples around the vast number of people involved in shooting this grim scene.

"Are you sad they went with such an emotional ending?" Alex turns to look at me, realising that the scene has affected us more than we thought it would. We'd read the script of course and knew well in advance this was how our story was going to end on the silver screen. At the time I had been stunned, it was completely unexpected. Seeing it acted out in front of us felt surreal and I knew it was fake blood on the floor, but the horror of it was still shocking. Even with the cameras and being privy to the unglamorous bit behind the scenes, it didn't take that away.

When the diary I'd written—and upon which the film was based—was sent to a few agents, one of them began talking about possible film rights. I always assumed there had to be a book before that could happen, but in this case it was the other way around. Someone passed it to a contact and he showed it to a producer. Things happened very quickly. It hadn't occurred to me that the film wouldn't necessarily be a faithful representation of the events that happened—how naive am I? It seems the real ending was too ordinary, not enough impact. So it has become a work of fiction, loosely based on fact.

"Yes, and no. Yes, because I think our ending is uplifting and inspiring. On the other hand, I have to stand back and remember that it's just a film and people will know that. Everything happens for a reason and I hope people will walk away wondering, 'what if?'"

I swing myself around and into Alex's arms, desperate to feel him close and wash away the negative thoughts from that last scene. He nestles his face into my neck, his lips warm against my skin. He smells citrusy.

"We're so lucky," he murmurs. "The guy gets his girl!"

"No Alex, it isn't luck. We've been granted this gift because something extraordinary has happened. Something even destiny couldn't foresee. We've been blessed."

"Well, I never thought our story would end up on the big screen. It would have been nice to let the audience know we did it, though. Sometimes love can overcome the seemingly insurmountable. Or maybe, in our case, it's all about knowing the right people," his eyes glance upwards, his face sporting a mischievous grin.

"That's one of the perks of marrying an angel—it's not what you know, it's *who* you know," I wink at him and he tilts his head back, erupting with laughter. Finally accepting that we've crossed a line.

Grabbing my hand, he gives it a loving squeeze, "Come on, let's go home. It's been a long, and emotional, day."

CHAPTER TWO

The True Story Is Revealed

When I flick over to the final page on my Kindle and the words, *The End*, stare back at me, my heart misses a beat. So this is our story, after all of the edits and the proof checking, it's finally ready for publication. Unlike the film version, nothing material has been changed in any way.

In real life this book marks the end of the first part of a journey and the start of a new beginning for Alex and me. I know that even death isn't the end, so why do the words unsettle me?

I remind myself that everything happens for a reason. The initial idea to submit my diary to a few literary agents wasn't mine. It was my brother Seb's suggestion. It came to him as such ideas often do. Not merely plucked out of the air, as most people assume when they get that sudden moment of inspiration, but given to him for a purpose. Since the film, people have been clamouring for the ebook and I've been working with Margaret Haines, an editor with thirty years' experience. She's helping me to prepare my manuscript for self-publication. After the shock of that surreal ending to the film, I've decided I want to be in total control. The film ended up being a romanticised version, with so many deviations from our story that at times even I didn't recognise it. It makes me sound like some temperamental artist, but I simply feel people need to know what really happened.

Margaret is a fervent sceptic, who felt it was important she was very clear about that from the start. Even so, as the weeks have passed she has admitted it's a truly inspiring story that touched her heart. A little spark has ignited, deep inside of her, awakening her curiosity. Over time, I have no doubt that will become a desire to know more. The sub-conscious reaches out and the universe will respond. Gradually, little chinks of light will appear in the wall she has erected to keep those thoughts at bay, until she has her first, personal experience.

For some it's potentially life-changing. The idea that a loved one they thought was lost forever, really is walking alongside them, is powerful. Sometimes it's the first step towards believing; for others it will be something from which they will run and hide.

A sense of unease sends little warning ripples through my body. Akin to when you leave the house and pull the door shut, only to realise you've left the keys inside. The feeling is one of knowing there will be a repercussion for an action taken, even when it's a mistake. Many will dispute the link between our love story and an emotive subject that, to many, will seem little more than science fiction. We live in a world that requires proof, even though we are intelligent enough to understand that's one dimensional and relative. There was a time when people believed the world was flat and many have not moved on beyond the point where seeing is the only form of believing. Even then, it's a case of continually dismissing incidents, as our minds are trained to rationalise that there *must* be some other explanation. Anything at all, that allows us to avoid the leap of faith that is belief.

In my experience it usually takes dozens of isolated incidents and the more meaningful they become, the harder the mind works to find some simple explanation. That's human nature.

Alex has been watching closely for my reaction, checking

nervously throughout the evening to see which chapter I was reading. He wants me to be happy with it and I am, but all of my senses are on edge and the excitement I'd anticipated has evaporated.

"What's wrong?" Alex's eyes seek out the concern I'm trying so hard to mask.

"It's strange reading the story of *us* and trying to see it through the eyes of a stranger. I guess the reality of it all is beginning to kick in. People will get to know the *real* us. Some will be totally unable to relate to our experience, because they need to cling on to their belief that this life is all there is. I regret that the film detracted from the message our story gives out."

"We managed to overcome all of the obstacles and prove that soul mates can survive whatever this life, and fate, throws at them. That's something to celebrate! The film has attracted a lot of attention and I'm not sure you would have gone on to write the book without it. I'm very proud of you, Ceri, for sticking to the truth because you could have chosen to turn it into another work of fiction. In many ways that would have been easier. But you don't do easy. We both know the whole point of this is to make people think about something that is often a taboo subject. The editor and the cover designer have done a great job and it's going to look the business. You haven't spotted something we've all missed?" A moment of concern flashes over his face.

"No, there isn't anything I would change. I'm happy." But for some unexplainable reason, I'm not. Sheena read the penultimate draft and she said it was an emotional roller coaster ride for her, understanding for the first time the enormity of what we'd been through. She didn't hesitate in giving permission for me to include her as a part of the story and hugged me like the sister she has become. The bond between us surpassed mere friendship a very long time ago.

Alex saunters across and sinks down into the sofa next to me, snuggling in. His body presses up against mine and the warmth of him permeates through our clothes. It begins to seep into me, dissolving the inner chill that has begun to spread outwards from my core.

"I'm excited about the way things are moving forward—our future together," Alex whispers, his mouth brushing my cheek. I turn to look at him and his eyes are bright with love and happiness. He takes my hand in his, looking for reassurance, checking that I'm not hiding anything from him. I can't even liken my feelings to a premonition, this is different: maybe something, maybe nothing. Is it merely nerves, in anticipation of how readers will receive a story that wasn't easy to tell and hasn't been given a commercial spin?

"I think it's the right decision to go ahead and publish the book." Hearing that said out loud, I realise my voice doesn't reflect the positivity of the words. I give myself a mental shake, forcing a smile to reassure Alex. "I hope that it encourages people to think about more than just the here and now."

"You've been helping people with your mediumship and this is yet another next step in that direction. Writing this book is a start and now you've written one, you can write another. We both know the power of words. Goodness knows, we read everything we could get our hands on in the early days. You know, when we weren't sure what was happening …"

He's right, of course, and I know that.

"I'm so lucky having you by my side," I murmur, looking up into his eyes. He turns to wrap his arms around me and, once more, I feel safe. You are my world, Alex, you are everything to me.

CHAPTER THREE

A Step Too Far?

Sometimes things happen so quickly that it makes your head spin. The ebook hit number one in the top one hundred best sellers list and suddenly everyone wanted to find out more. Offers came flooding in from publishers, eager to put it into print and commission a sequel. It was overload, but Alex encouraged me to think seriously about another offer that came in rather unexpectedly. The Psychic Channel wanted me to take part in a pilot show for their network.

"I'm nervous," I look up into Alex's eyes for reassurance. Positivity shines back at me, he is my rock and I have no idea what I would do without his guidance.

"You'll be fine. Don't think about what's going on around you, this is just a chat with a client looking for some answers. Forget that it's being taped and try to relax. You've done this hundreds of times before and this is simply one more session. Break a leg." He kisses me gently on the top of my head, wrapping his arms around me for one last, reassuring hug.

I turn and walk across the short expanse of floor between the camera and the set. An assistant attaches the microphone, hiding it beneath my jacket and indicates for me to take a seat. The chair opposite me is empty. I haven't yet met Hilary James and that adds to the pressure. I have no idea if this lady will be receptive, or have expectations that I can't possibly fulfil. This pilot show is a risk and if I totally flop, then it will be a lost opportunity. That thought weighs heavily upon my shoulders.

Without warning the overhead lighting is turned up and the gentle ambience of a soft glow becomes a flood of light. I look back across the floor of the studio, where only a glint from the camera lens is now visible. It's comforting to know that Alex is among the small group of people watching, his positive thoughts acting as the boost I need. An assistant ushers a woman I assume to be in her early thirties, towards the set. As I stand to greet her, my legs buckle slightly beneath me. For one horrible moment I wonder if I'm going to faint. When I was in the dressing room earlier, I knew then that this was going to be a difficult session. As I meditated and opened up my chakras the spirits were there, loved ones eager to come through to help this very unfortunate lady. My mind became over-crowded and I had to ask them to stand back a little, to wait patiently until it was time.

As I shake Hilary's hand she clasps mine in both of hers. The look in her eyes at this moment takes my breath away. The production company chose her from a long list of potential candidates who came forward to appear on the show. This crew work on two other psychic programmes, although both are very different. One is location-based, with live footage of a group of psychics who visit places reported to be haunted. The other is a series of shows with a different guest medium each week. Questions are invited from the audience in an open forum. This is the first recording with a one-to-one interview format and it's going to be called *A Chat with Ceri*. There are no guarantees it will be developed into a series, but hopes are riding high. People's jobs depend upon a good result today and the pressure is intense. What if I fail? My thoughts are interrupted as an attractive young woman with bright red hair, kneels down in the small space between the two armchairs. She has a clipboard in her hand.

"Ladies, my name is Jess. I'll quickly run through what's going to happen. Last week we taped psychic medium, Thomas Cardelle, introducing Ceri and explaining how a medium prepares for a personal sitting—general background stuff. The intro runs for about six minutes in total. Today, Ceri, you simply need to introduce Hilary and begin the session whenever you are ready. If there's a pause, please don't worry about that. If you need a break I will be watching, so raise your hand to catch my attention and we'll turn off the camera. Hilary, how are you doing?"

Hilary is sitting bolt upright in her chair with her arms crossed and looks like she has changed her mind. I can't blame her. It feels like we are on a floodlit island in the middle of an ocean of darkness. It wasn't so bad when people were milling around and there was some background chatter, but when Jess stops talking the silence is heavy.

"I'm rather nervous," Hilary shifts position. Her hands drop down into her lap and she clasps them tightly together, albeit in a tense fashion. I think her moment of indecision is over; she's going to go through with it.

Jess turns her attention to me.

"Are you ready, Ceri?"

I look directly at Hilary, learning forward a little in my chair so I can lower my voice.

"Hilary, if something comes through that you don't want me to expand upon, please stop me. I want to assure you that whatever messages I'm given are not mine. The words won't stay with me because I'm merely the voice. If we meet again in the future, nothing from this session will remain in my head. The information that comes through is for you alone. But that means it might also be very personal and it's impossible for me to filter that. I have no control over what I'm given, so I will have to be guided by you."

Hilary smiles back at me and I can see that her mood has

changed. She's full of hope and I have no idea what her personal situation is, but it's clear she's seeking closure. I've seen it so many times before.

"We'd prefer the session to run until it reaches a natural stopping point," Jess looks at Hilary and then across at me. "It will have to be edited down anyway, so we can address any issues Hilary has after the taping. It's probably best not to interrupt your flow, Ceri. If your mind goes blank don't worry, put up your hand and we'll stop the camera for a short break."

I'm eager to get started now and in my head I begin going over the short introduction, which I've had to change as the first message is already being given to me. Jess leaves the set and walks back, standing to the side of the camera but within our line of vision. She begins counting backwards from five and suddenly the moment is here. I relax my face into a gentle smile and hope that when I open my mouth something will come out.

"Welcome everyone and thank you to Hilary James, my guest for this one-to-one session. I have no idea what Hilary's question is going to be, as we met for the first time only a few minutes ago. However, what I can tell you is that there are a number of loved ones around her who have been with me since earlier this morning. That happens sometimes, although not always, so first I'm going to ask Hilary if she's ever been to see a medium before?"

I turn towards Hilary, who looks startled and panic begins to rise up from my stomach as I wonder if nerves will overcome her. She swallows and nods her head. Thankfully the words follow seconds later.

"No. I've thought about it for a long time, though. I always felt that an opportunity would arise at some point and it did."

We exchange sympathetic smiles and a moment of trust, and relief, passes between us. She realises I'm equally as nervous and that establishes a common bond. I can relax in the knowledge that this isn't going to be all one-sided. She also has a positive attitude and that's always one of my main concerns. I settle back into my chair, my arms relaxed in my lap. This is it. I take a few deep breaths, although that's only to calm my nerves as a voice in my head is becoming very insistent to be heard.

"I have a gentleman who has a message, so do you mind if I ask you for your specific question a little later? I would also prefer not to have any clues in case that influences how I interpret what I'm being given. I will only ask for information from you where it will help me to clarify a message."

"That's fine, thank you."

The silence in the studio seems magnified, even though it's merely a second or two before I begin speaking. My mouth is a little dry, but before I can worry about whether there's any water to hand the words come tumbling out.

"I don't feel this is your father, he's an older gentleman and he might be your grandfather. He's an artist and he's showing me a painting. It's a water colour and it's a summer scene with a river and rolling fields in the background. I don't think it's the painting itself that is important, but he keeps pointing to it. There's something subtle here he's trying to tell me ... was this his secret? He's very positive that this will mean something to you."

Hilary too, has relaxed and her hands lay open in her lap. Her eyes are bright as she replies.

"It's Granddad, my mother's father, and he was a farmer. He loved the land with a passion, but to relax he turned to painting. My grandmother was a very practical woman and never understood the need for anyone to have a hobby. Life was work and sleep, with little spare time for anything else in those days. He worked long hours and I can never recall them ever having a holiday away from the farm. Still, though, he found time to paint, much to her annoyance."

I make no attempt to stop Hilary speaking, although she's giving out information I don't need to know. The man seems happy, though, and he's passing on an overwhelming sense of love and warmth in response to her words.

"Well, he's moving back, but leaving behind a wonderful feeling of his love for you. He also wants you to understand that you are not alone. Whenever you are at your lowest, he's there with you and always will be. Um, as he leaves … he's holding up some wellington boots covered in mud and laughing. Does that mean anything?"

Hilary smiles and nods her head. "Yes, when I was very little and playing on the farm, I waded into a muddy area and became stuck. Fortunately for me it was only about a foot deep, but it spilled over the top of my wellington boots. I cried my eyes out as he rescued me and hosed me down with cold water." A tear glints in her eye, but she's happy. He's given her a memory to make her smile, but more importantly it's a meaningful connection.

Two spirits are trying to step forward in my mind at the same time. Seconds pass as I wait for a clear message and I wonder if I should wave out to Jess for a break. Suddenly one of them steps forward with determination.

"Hilary, I have a middle-aged lady here, with short hair. There is a young boy standing behind her. I feel this lady's message is going to be very personal. Are you OK with that?"

Warning bells are sounding in my head, but Hilary is now hooked, wanting more and no doubt hopeful that whatever her question is, will be answered. As the woman begins, I struggle to pull together the pieces of what appears to be a complicated message.

"Slow down, please, I'm not sure …" As soon as I realise I've spoken out loud, I reign myself in. It's not professional and I know it worries people. They accept words that seem to be plucked out of thin air, but to witness someone speaking to a departed soul in their presence, that's a different matter. Hilary looks thrown and I notice that she has entwined her hands, white knuckles indicating how tense she has become.

"This is to do with the little boy who has stepped back. I have no information about him, but this lady is acting as a shield. She's trying to protect him. I think she wants you to know that she's always there for him. Or, maybe, she's sorry about something. OK, so now I'm confused. He's stepping forward again and now he's older, a teenager I think. Do you know a child who died at the age of six, or seven, maybe?"

I hate asking that question, as Hilary is looking very anxious and tearful. She nods to confirm, making no attempt to speak.

"OK. Hilary, let me explain how this works. In order for me to give you meaningful information, I need to see a physical impression of the person and work on deciphering the message. For example, your granddad appeared as an elderly man showing me a painting. It linked his age, hobby and his working environment. That was meaningful to you—it's called validation. This young man clearly passed over as a child, but the lady seems insistent that I tell you I can see him growing up. That isn't how it works and I'm puzzled. They can present themselves to me however they wish. An old man could choose to conjure up the image of how he looked at a much younger age. Age itself doesn't mean anything in that sense. In the afterlife it's all about the spirit, which is the essence of the person, not the earthly shell. However, I need a representation of their physical appearance at the point at which they died, in order for you to recognise the person coming through."

I look at Hilary to see if she understands. Usually I receive a string of messages and yes, they aren't all easy to interpret, but this is puzzling. I glance towards Jess to gauge her reaction, but she's listening intently and makes no attempt to halt me.

"Give me a moment." Once again, I'm conscious of the seconds as they tick by, but I'm not sure I understand what I'm seeing here. The young man has stepped back again, well, it was more that the lady pushed him back and she's clearly upset about something. It's not to do with his passing. It's to do with the older version of him. She's looking back and I can see the little boy quite clearly and the teenager standing next to him. Wait, there's a difference. The older version of him isn't as clear—it's not a spirit. I'm really trying to focus on the teenager, as I feel that is where I will find the clue to message. Suddenly, the young boy projects an image into my mind that is both terrifying and bleak. A black hole opens up and I'm being swallowed, taken down and down on a journey I don't want to take. I can feel what he felt and a scream rises in my throat, which I struggle to contain. I'm gripping the arms of the chair in an attempt to regain control and push away the haunting images. He releases me, pulling back his energy and I know he meant no harm, he merely wanted me to understand. But I don't understand as I have no reference for this horrific scene. Bringing myself back into the moment I have no idea how long the episode lasted, but I assume it was merely seconds rather than minutes, judging by the look on Hilary's face. She's watching me intently, but doesn't look frightened by whatever I might have given away.

"Hilary, can you help me on this, or should I move on?" A part of me hopes she will let this go.

The message is meaningful, but if it's not the one Hilary came here seeking then maybe now is not the time to dig any deeper.

"I lost a son, many years ago." Her words are stilted as she struggles to hold back tears. "I didn't know he had died until a few years ago. He ... he was adopted."

She mops at her tears, steeling herself to remain composed. I look across at Jess, but there's no response. I want to stop, but Hilary makes no attempt to halt the proceedings and I feel it's not my judgement call. Reluctantly I go on, but it's with great difficulty and a feeling of dread.

"I don't know how to say this, Hilary. I think this lady, and I believe it's your mother, is trying to tell me that the boy who died wasn't your son. Your son is now a teenager and is alive. I could be wrong, but that's how the message is coming across and she's insistent. In fact, she's calmed down now, as if she's satisfied that what I've told you is correct."

Hilary stares at me, her eyes showing total disbelief, her head moving from side to side in an emphatic *no*.

Jess's voice calls out, "We'll stop there, guys."

"He died, she told me he died." Hilary grabs my arm, learning forward as she utters the words. "Why would she lie?"

"I don't know, I'm sorry ..." I pull off the microphone, dropping it together with the power pack on to the chair and run back towards the dressing room. Alex is close behind me, calling my name but I don't stop until I'm safely inside and he closes the door a moment later.

He throws his arms around me as I stand, trembling and breathless.

"You weren't to know, Ceri. It's always a risk. You've given unexpected news before, you know the score."

"Yes," my voice wavers. "But to lose a son and then to be told he isn't lost ... What if I'm wrong? You saw the look on that woman's face. This is about something that's driven her to the edge on many occasions and from which she has no respite." I sob into his shoulder as he holds me tightly, comforting me in the only way he knows how.

The inherent responsibility that comes with giving out messages like that is sometimes too much to bear. Should I have held back and given nothing at all, simply choosing to move on? Even stressing that I might have been wrong, those words will probably have been pushed aside in Hilary's burning desire to know more.

When the tears stop he lowers me into a chair and seconds later there's a knock on the door. Jess appears looking rather flushed.

"I'm sorry ..." Alex shushes me, kneeling down to place his hand over mine.

"Ceri, that was amazing. Hilary is tearful, but fine. We have a counsellor with her now. We're going to stop taping because, clearly, you are both rather upset by what's happened. Alex, the car is waiting to take you home whenever Ceri is ready. That was powerful stuff!"

She sounds remarkably happy given that the session was rather short and ended so abruptly. I feared she'd be annoyed at the waste of everyone's time and worse, the upset I've caused Hilary

James. I'm tortured by the thought that I unravelled that garbled message incorrectly. This isn't simply about me failing, it's about the damage I might have done to someone else's life.

Alex takes charge, draping a coat around my shoulders and shepherding me out through the labyrinth of corridors and into the car. All I can think of is the look in Hilary's eyes. It was a mix of fear, anguish and hope.

CHAPTER FOUR

Running From The Truth?

A month passes and things soon settle back down into a routine. I continue to do my weekly author platforms on the psychic circuit. All of the messages I receive are helpful and meaningful, according to the recipients. Yes, there are surprises and sometimes a warning that needs to be heeded. There's a massive difference, though, between a message that gives direction, hope or closure, and a message that could be misleading.

What I struggle to comprehend, is why that should have happened for Hilary's session? Was it a warning that the TV programme was the wrong step to take and I've veered off course? Adam, too, seemed reluctant to talk about it and we closed the door on it, having no choice but to move forward—until I receive the call.

"Ceri, it's Tom Sheldon from The Psychic Channel." I was expecting a call from Alex, who is already an hour late returning from a meeting with a client.

"Hi, Tom." My stomach churns, fearing the worst. Hilary is going to sue us and I can't blame her.

"Awesome tape so far, unbelievable. We need you back in the

studio to do a follow-up interview with Hilary James. I wanted to check out when you were free."

I've only met him once and he was a nice enough guy, but is this a joke?

"Um ... I'm not sure there's any point. It really didn't go as expected and Hilary might not want to go over what happened. Anyway, I don't have any further information, I'm afraid. There's nothing I can add that would be helpful."

He's distracted, whispers something, then apologies.

"Sorry, Jess was on the other phone talking to Hilary and has just given me a list of dates she's available. How about next Tuesday afternoon?"

"What sort of interview are we talking about?" If Hilary is looking for an apology, I understand that and it's fine, but if she asks for an explanation—what on earth can I tell her?

"Our researchers will brief you on what's happened in the interim. We have the studio tape, plus an additional twelve minutes of tape from another interview with Hilary outlining her story. We thought it would be nice to finish up with one final chat between Hilary and yourself."

I feel I have no choice but to agree to the meeting on Tuesday and put the phone down, unable to piece this all together. What exactly have they been filming? I have no idea why Hilary would agree to have it televised. If I were her I would withdraw permission for it to be used. I don't want to be a part of an act and reality TV has to be well handled, or it quickly turns into a spectacle. This started out as an insight into what happens in a one-to-one session. It was supposed to give comfort. Instead, it turned out to be a great example of what can go wrong. That doesn't happen quite as often as people might think, which is why I can't comprehend the timing of it. I assume Hilary didn't get the opportunity to ask her question for a reason. That reason is known only to a higher power. Acceptance is one of the main attributes of belief; the ability to accept something without proof is, I know, the ultimate test.

But why present the opportunity if it was only to have it fail? It didn't just fail, either, it seriously dented my confidence and might have caused irreparable damage.

I need to talk this through with Alex and get his take on it. Alex, where are you? You were supposed to be back an hour ago and I'm beginning to panic. Everything seems to be closing in on me again.

I look around the room knowing someone is here, but choosing to remain unseen and silent. Why won't they come forward?

"What?" I throw the question out in the hope of receiving a response, anything other than stony silence. As I continue to scan the room, convinced something will present itself, gradually the air changes. Like watching fog rolling in and then, when I think of Alex, there's no comforting vibe of him around me. Come home Alex, my inner voice screams, come home *now*!

ALEX

CHAPTER FIVE

The One Moment That Truly Mattered

The choice was Ceri's, it always was going to be and I think we both knew that. It was simply easier to sweep it out of sight, so we couldn't dwell on it. The change in her began on the day they shot the final scene in the film version of *Ceri – Angels Among Us*.

She became convinced that if we continued to flaunt the rules, then I would be taken away from her. As we stood watching the actor who was playing my part, and Ceri saw the growing pool of fake blood, she paled. Turning to look at me, I could see the realisation in her eyes and knew she thought it was a warning.

We pretended everything was fine, but for a while she had begun to feel that she was on shifting sand. Everything that had previously been a source of energy and encouragement to her in her work, seemed to set her on edge.

With hindsight, I can now look back and see that I missed the one moment that truly mattered. It was lost in a sea of words and out-pouring, that began on the fateful day she found out that the message she had given Hilary James, had been correct.

I'd arrived home late to find Ceri distraught at the prospect of a wrap-up interview for the pilot show. I rang Tom Sheldon immediately to get to the bottom of it and he told me the full story. I sat Ceri down and repeated what he'd told me.

"Hilary's mother believed she had tracked down her grandson, who had been given up for adoption shortly after his birth. Hilary was sixteen years old at the time and her mother was a widow, so it's seemed like the best solution for the child.

"Sadly, her enquiries led to the discovery that the lad had drowned in a swimming pool when he was six-years-old. It was a freak accident, he was one of a large party of school children and by the time it was noticed that he was missing, it was too late. His body was found at the bottom of the pool, but attempts to resuscitate him were unsuccessful. It was shortly before Hilary was due to be married and, unable to escape the feelings of guilt and love she always had for her child, she had hoped to make amends. She began her married life carrying all of the pain and regret associated with her situation and that never left her. She went on to have two children with her husband, and instead of healing that old wound, it made it worse. That's why she was chosen for the programme.

"Her mother died, believing that the information she had obtained was true. However, the research team managed to get to the bottom of what really happened. It seems the family had a biological son and he was the one who died. Hilary's son is alive and well. Hilary was reunited with him after a series of meetings with the family. His name is David and he's fifteen-years-old."

Ceri had cried uncontrollably, and what hit me was how vulnerable she had become. I hadn't noticed the strength seeping out of her, leaving a shell that appeared to be so fragile I began to fear for what might happen next.

That night we lay on the sofa, bodies entwined as the darkness descended.

"If I had to choose your life or mine, you would understand if I chose your life, wouldn't you Alex?"

"Hey, what's all this? Stop worrying, we're going to be fine. It's

336

never that simple, Ceri, and you know that."

We lay there for hours, content to savour every single second we were in each other's arms. I thought it was the beginning of a healing process, as I tried so hard to infuse her with my own energy. I was confident I could build her up and make her strong once more.

I awoke with a start, wondering why my arms were empty and my body felt chilled. She was gone and I realised I'd missed the one moment that truly mattered.

Epilogue

Written by Ceri's childhood friend, Sheena

Seb rang to tell me that Ceri's true story was going to be re-released as a tribute to mark the tenth anniversary of her disappearance. It touched my heart, because I understood the sentiment behind it. Without a funeral how can you really say goodbye to someone and move on? It was going to be combined with some new material celebrating Ceri's psychic work. It came as a total surprise when Seb went on to ask if I would write this epilogue. He told me that it needed an ending and I was puzzled, but honoured.

I wondered, 'Why me?', surely Alex's words would have been far more meaningful and appropriate? But Alex has been to hell and back, we all knew that and maybe it would have been too much to ask of anyone.

As close as Ceri and I were, I was on the side-lines for much of what happened between her and Alex. It was only when Ceri asked me to read the advance review copy of the original book, that I was able to see the whole picture for myself, for the first time.

The question you will be asking is what happened after that fateful night? The answer is simple. Ceri disappeared and ten years later there are still no clues as to what happened. At the time everyone lived with the hope that she simply needed a little peace and quiet to think and that she would return when she was ready. After all, she'd done that once before. Alex was convinced she was having some sort of nervous breakdown. The police, after receiving information about a number of sightings, rejected them all as bogus and were convinced they were dealing with a suicide. A body was never found.

I lost touch with Alex, and sadly, so did Ceri's family. That was rather inevitable, I'm afraid. There were too many raw memories, too much pain and we all had to find a way of dealing with it. I heard that Alex married a few years later, but didn't know any details. Then, one day I bumped into him when I was at the Mall, shopping. He had a baby carrier strapped to his chest, with a very young baby nestled inside. He held hands with a little girl who was probably around three years of age, her other hand was held by an attractive lady with light brown hair. He looked happy, no, more than that—he looked fulfilled.

As recognition set in, I witnessed a whole range of emotions flashing across his face. He disengaged his hand and spoke a few words to his wife, leaving her with a smile and turning to walk towards me. We were out of earshot when he stepped up to me, taking my hands in his, the tiny baby between us making it impossible to hug.

"How are you?" His voice was soft and I could tell he was pleased to see me.

"I'm good. Life is busy. Two children?" I indicated toward the baby, extracting one hand from his to touch the tiny little head. The downy hair was soft, like touching a peach.

"This is Amelia. That's my wife Cheryl and our other daughter, Chloe." He turned towards them, a proud smile on his face.

"You look happy. I'm glad."

As good as it was to see him it was hard to find anything to say. The questions whirling around in my head could never be spoken, of course.

"I'm doing what she wanted," he whispered, turning his head

to look directly at me. There was a gleam in his eye, was it hope?

I looked up at him, unable to understand what he was trying to tell me. As I searched his face for clues, all I noticed were a few extra laughter lines and that same old boyish grin.

"Ceri saved Cheryl."

He let go of my other hand and with an enigmatic smile, he walked back to his wife and daughter. I waved out and they waved back, then I hurried away.

That night I couldn't sleep as his words went round and round in my head. What did he mean? At three in the morning I slid out of bed, made a mug of coffee and began surfing the net. I started with Alex's Facebook page, trawling through the list of friends until I found Cheryl staring back at me. Clicking through to her page very little showed up, the content was restricted to friends only. However, as luck would have it, her Facebook header included her maiden name in brackets. When I typed *Cheryl Johnson* into Google search, a phenomenal amount of pages came up. None of the photos on the first search result page looked anything like her. I kept scanning until suddenly I found a newspaper headline *Young woman survives against all the odds*. There wasn't a photo, but a link to a story which included the name *Cheryl Johnson*. Apparently, Cheryl's appendix had burst and during emergency surgery her heart had stopped beating, not once, but twice, on the operating table. The second time it stopped for three whole minutes and the doctor said it had been a close call. That was about four months after Ceri's disappearance.

It didn't explain anything, other than the fact that Cheryl had been very lucky. Alex wouldn't have known her at that point. He would still have been in the throes of drinking himself into oblivion. He went through six months of hell, living in the hope that Ceri could return at any moment. However, fate brought Cheryl and Alex together at some point and she would obviously have told him her story.

Did Alex really believe that it wasn't merely a coincidence? That

Ceri had the power to save Cheryl somehow? That she had been instrumental in bringing them together and giving him the gift of a happy life? The next thought that crossed my mind was too weird to entertain and I instantly dismissed it.

I climbed back into bed at six o'clock, but my head was still whirling. That one thought wouldn't leave me.

If Cheryl was Ceri reincarnated, Alex would know that and would have shared that fact with me—wouldn't he?

As my eyelids drooped I hoped that the truth would come to me in my dreams. The place where, for me, Ceri would live on forever.